The Night From Whence She Came

Chase Collier

Dedication

I'd like to dedicate this book to my wife Shelby, who has always been my rock and inspiration, as well as the entirety of my world.

Acknowledgement

I am required to acknowledge my dear brother Mike who has kept me out of prison up until this point and my dearest friend Blake who has given me boundless support and encouragement. I would also like to thank Mr. Erik at amazon publishing house who has nearly heard me die twice over the phone as we discussed publishing this book and Miss Emi, whom I told I would have things ready by saturday no more than three times. I would also like to acknowledge Miss Sophie Brown, who's enthusiasm for this book was a great boost and drive to finish this process.

Table of Contents

Chapter 1

The relief of evening had just begun in a small farm some ways south of the Mason Dixon. Two men poured sweat as the heat had finally started to fade. It would glimmer in the light as it flew from their brow with each stab of the posthole digger. The smaller of the two sat upon an upside-down five-gallon bucket, watching the other.

The larger man had given him a break; after all, only a few holes were left, and soon they would carry out the pine four-by-fours and wire. The smaller man watched, the larger, making sure he was on their line or not too far from the mark. He knew Me-Maw would have a stroke if the fence row was not equally spaced or straight. He couldn't help but be impressed by his friend and brother. Digging an eighteen-inch post hole in two strikes would seem inconspicuous to a regular onlooker, but to the callused hands of a working man, the fact that he had kept the same pace the entire day was near inhuman.

The man standing before him, posthole diggers in hand swayed over his shoulder, stood a strong six-foot three. A roughly kept beard hanging from his chin, matching his dark brown hair with streaks of red laces within it. His shoulders were broad, and his back was strong. One gnarled and cut hand gripped both handles of the diggers while the other wiped the sweat from his forehead in a vain attempt to stop it from burning his piercing blue eyes.

"Man fuck, I thought it'd cool off a little bit when the sun when down," he said.

"Well shit, Coal, we been at it all day anyhow; let's finish this up," replied Jim-Bob.

"Let's get the four-bys in the holes, and we'll just fill 'em up tomorrow, I'm so hungry, dude."

"Bro, I'm too hot to get over a fuckin stove, man!" Jim-Bob ached.

"Fuck that noise. Let's just go to the diner."

"Hell yeah, they started serving Texas toast burgers."

"Fucking what?" asked Coal.

"Yeah, man, two pieces of Texas toast with some garlic aioli and Swiss," Jim-Bob answered.

"Hop in the truck. We done for the day."

"Thank God"

Jim-Bob hopped from his bucket, and the two quickly threw the remaining four-by-fours into their newly dug holes. Coal climbed into the driver seat of his new pick-up truck as Jim-Bob took shotgun. Jim-Bob exhaled deeply as he stretched across the new leather seat. His back let loose an agonizing pop as he suddenly froze in pain.

"Was that your back?" Coal asked.

"Yup," Jim-Bob squeaked.

Coal let out a laugh, "Shit, man," As he did so, he cranked the truck and turned up the air conditioning.

"Oh, damn, we got AC now?" Jim-Bob chuckled.

"Yeah, the new trucks got AC,"

"You ever gone fix your old truck's AC?"

"Probly not, had her for years without it."

"I'm only ever riding in the new one, I did my time." Jim-Bob chuckled.

Coal turned up the radio, and the two listened to music for the remainder. Despite a perfectly functioning air conditioner, Coal still had his window rolled down, arm propped against it. The wind blew rapidly through the burnt umber curls of his hair. It was a twenty-minute drive to the diner, but he reckoned he could make it in fifteen. Though darkness had begun to drape across the roads, Coal was all too familiar.

He looked for a moment at his best friend Jim-Bob, who had lasted five whole minutes before passing out and leaning against the window. Though Jim-Bob was the older of the two, by only a year, he was smaller in stature. He was six-foot-one with a much leaner frame. He certainly didn't fear the hard work and toil on Coal's new farm; however, he definitely wasn't built for it. During the long hours of the first few days, one could easily think that it was sweat glimmering from Jim-Bob's body when, in fact, it was ten layers of sunscreen. It was necessary to shield his delicate white skin, for without it, his skin would match the rich hue of a well-steamed lobster.

Coal appreciated the company. Sure, he could have done the work by himself if needed, but Jim-Bob had made a miserable slog into a few fun days of joking and drinking. The diner was a few minutes away. It was an old but well-maintained family-owned restaurant that Coal frequented. Its large red neon sign above the four-way was something to behold. It was a big, old-school pin-up waitress with a moving arm and tray. The tray seemed to wave traffic right in, seeing that the place was always busy. It was right next to a truck stop and weigh station, so the owners had staffed it to be open twenty-four hours a day. If you had been there often, you would have come to learn that the number of guests rarely differed, being five PM or 2 AM. The food was delicious, and Coal was very much looking forward to their new menu items. It had been weeks since he could stop in due to his business, and the staff had started to worry for their favorite customer and his brother.

"Oh, Shit!" Coal exclaimed

"What? What's going on?" Jim-Bob awoke.

"Smoke shop closed?"

"Nah, man, I think you said they closed at nine last time."

"Sweet, you mind if we take a quick detour?" Coal asked.

"Not at all, man. I'd say you earned a smoke or two."

Coal continued to drive past the diner, deeper into the city. He was driving toward a large strip mall that had a modestly sized smoke shop, which contained a well-stocked humidor. Coal may not have been quite particular about the brand of cigar he smoked, but he definitely knew what he liked. He had had a hankering for something creamy with notes of vanilla. This humidor, in particular, had a few brands that matched such a need quite well.

They nearly reached the shop when Coal could see something out of the corner of his eye. Far to the right of them, across the parking lot, was an alleyway carved between two outlet stores. Out of this alleyway came four figures. A young woman was desperately running from three strange men. These men were sickly pale, even by Jim-Bobs standards, and terribly emaciated. Their gaunt figures didn't even seem to run properly. It seemed to be a ferocious but desperate sprint but weighed heavily by malnourishment and delirium.

The fleeing young woman, however, was beautiful. Her flowing licorice black hair caught the wind as she ran, and the lights of the street caught the sparkle of the tears flowing from her orchid eyes. The three gaunt wretches were beginning to gain on her slender figure.

"Ayo, what the fuck?" Coal yelled out.

Jim-Bob quickly snapped back awake and saw what was happening. "Hell's goin on over there?"

"Are those fucking meth heads?"

"I don't know, what would they want with her?" Jim-Bob asked.

"I don't know, but we finna handle that shit!"

Coal quickly swerved his truck over and threw it in park. He threw the door open and began his run, followed closely by Jim-Bob. The sound of their steel toes was like thunder as they charged ahead, a rumble from the ground as each step propelled Coal's large and imposing frame forward. His stride was huge and fast for a man of his size.

The poor girl was running with all her might, but she knew. She knew it wouldn't be long before the depraved husks of men caught up to her. She had been so close to escaping. Everything appeared to slow down around her. Spurred on by their master, the three had reached inhuman speed. The fastest of the three had finally caught up, reaching his hand out to grab her soft wrist. She could feel it, the death of hope, as a cold, wretched hand clenched her wrist from behind. She had been so close to freedom, to a brave new world that didn't know her, but now, the chase was over. Tears streamed down her face as she turned her head. She wanted to cry out, to scream for help, but she didn't know anyone. Everything here was new to her, and she knew nothing of the people residing in this strange new place. She continued to turn her head to see the dead-eyed thing pulling her wrist.

In a moment, her unspoken prayers were answered, and in a moment, the fiend was gone. The sounds of his heavy breathing replaced with a sudden, quick succession of cracks. Coal, at full sprint, had speared the husk from his flank. His spindly silhouette buckled from the force of impact as a wave of energy cascaded through the body, bouncing off of bone and crashing through organs, interrupted only by a second have derived from the wall of the store, stopping his flight. His head cracked against the wall, sending him to a well-earned rest.

In the next moment, the second thrall was on to Coal, leaping at him with both arms stretched out to grab him. His leap would be cut short by Coal's powerful arms, shooting out quickly and grabbing the fiend by his chest, stopping him mid-flight, sending his insides forward and a horrible lurch. The husk hissed at Coal and tried lashing out at him but was stopped as Coal tightened his grip and yanked the wretch toward himself, delivering a face-shattering headbutt to the nose before throwing him to the ground. The thrall tried to quickly scramble to his feet but was stopped by a penalty-styled kick, once again to his face. Coal would look up from this kick just in time to see Jim-Bob delivering a kick of his own. A beautiful flying double-footed drop kick straight to the skull of the last of the three would quickly retire him to unconsciousness. Jim Bob's catlike physique and reflexes would allow him to land on all fours. Jim-Bob hopped to his feet and turned to face Coal. The two delivered an echoing high-five.

The young lady was grateful but still sobbing. "We have to run! There's more of them!"

"Shit, head to the truck!" Coal hollered as he waved the woman towards the truck.

The three of them ran towards the truck as Jim-Bob sprinted ahead and opened the door for their new passenger. She leaped into the backseat, and Jim-Bob closed the door behind her. Coal entered the driver's seat, and Jim-Bob once again claimed shotgun. As Coal cranked the truck, the radio he had forgotten to turn down in haste began to blare. This would terrify their rescue, as Coal stomped the gas, and the three peeled out of the strip mall parking lot. No one was brave enough to speak as Coal screeched through the winding roads, making the twenty-minute drive only half the time.

They arrived at the gate on the outskirts of Coal's property. The gate was closed, right next to the unfinished fence, a steel barrier of entry next to floating four-by-fours not even filled in yet. Jim-Bob exited the truck and began to walk over to the gate.

"Seemed fucking funny when we closed it leaving earlier," he pouted.

Jim-Bob opened the gate, and Coal pulled the truck in. The truck stopped and waited for Jim-Bob to rejoin them. Jim-Bob carefully closed the gate and jogged back to the truck. Coal contemplated pulling the truck up slightly as Jim-Bob reached for the handle but thought it best not to. Jim-Bob climbed back into the seat, and they made their way down the long driveway. The house they were pulling up to seemed welcoming even in the dark. It had a nice A-frame front with a few rooms coming off the side. It even had an upstairs master bed and bath that Coal was quite pleased with. The truck came to a stop.

"You don't think we killed those guys, do you?" Jim-Bob asked, eyes suddenly widening.

"Nah, man, it takes a lot more to drop a druggie,"

"Yeah... Yeah, you're right... you're right."

"We should call someone."

"We should call someone."

They all exited the vehicle and rushed to the house. As they entered, Jim-Bob walked to an old cabinet with the glass missing from the door. He reached in and pulled out a rifle, then grabbed the phone on the counter next to it.

"Man, you check on her, I'ma keep watch while I call the sheriff, we gotta warn him about these packs of meth heads stalking his streets," Jim-Bob explained to Coal as he made his way upstairs.

"Copy that, buddy, I'll be up in a minute." Coal replied, he then looked at the young lady. "You good?"

She had managed to stop sobbing and compose herself on the ride up. "I think I'm fine now."

"That's good to hear... So what'd you do to them meth heads that had them hunting you?"

She suddenly realized the possible repercussions of her actions, but her lips moved before she could stop them. "Those weren't meth heads, whatever those are, they were thralls." she sniffled.

"They were what?"

"I can't tell you anymore. If you get involved, it could be dangerous!"

"Bruh, we just dropped like three'a them dudes, we past that now, baby girl, you need to tell me what's good."

"I'm a vampire, well, half vampire."

"Bitch what?" Coal, confused, lost all composure.

"I'm a half-vampire, my dad runs this region's household."

"Ain't no muhfucking way, prove it!"

"FINE!"

The young lady threw up both her hands pointed at Coal as if she were about to peak-a-boo a small child. In an instant her beautiful orchid eyes flickered as her nails grew rapidly into sharp daggers. She opened her mouth and hissed, as she did so, all of her teeth grew to serrated points. Her canines were the most pronounced of all. They grew an extra inch and seemed to tear out of her jaw as if they were wicked mandibles ready to lunge at prey themselves.

Coal looked up at the ceiling in exacerbation, letting out a deep sigh. "Those were not fucking meth heads." he exhaled. "Welp, let's not keep ole Jim waiting. Follow me."

Coal walked past the stairs into the kitchen. He opened the fridge and pulled out three beers in dark amber bottles. "Can you?"

"I need to."

Coal grabbed an extra and made his way up the stairs. The young vampire followed him up. "The balcony is just past my bedroom." Coal explained. As they walked through, Coal held out his left hand. It was offering a beer whilst pointing at the bed. As she took the beer Coal's fingers curled to more distinctly point at the bed. "Just so you know, if you have a few to many of these, you could wind up there." Coal joked.

"If I get hungry later, I'm sure I'll be there anyway.

Coal suddenly stopped walking and turned around and looked at her, eyes wide but somehow squinting, with his mouth slightly open.

"I'm just joking... REALLY!" She suddenly panicked, realizing such humor may not be so well received by someone below her in the food chain.

Coal could see her panic. "Ah hell, you'd be the prettiest girl to ever hop in. I'd take that trade."

The two smiled at each other and continued on to the balcony. Jim-Bob sat there, staring into the darkness, swallowing the drive up to the house.

"We were supposed to set up the solar torches today." He said, "Fuck,"

"Cheer up, buddy," Coal said, stretching his arm out, beer in hand, "We've got way bigger problems than that to keep you down."

"Nah, the sheriff said he got a call in and sped over quick and picked up them three dudes. We might be in the clear, we just gotta figure out why they were chasing that girl."

"They were hunting her for her vampire dad."

"Her fucking what, bro?" Jim-Bob exclaimed

"Show him."

"Nah, that shit won't be necessary." Jim-Bob stopped them.

They all stopped and looked at each other for a moment. Jim-Bobs stomach rumbled. He looked over at Coal. "You open yours yet?"

Coal tossed him another beer, and then the same for the vampire girl. "Diner?"

"Diner."

Jim-Bob looked over at the vampire girl. "You eat?"

"Yes."

"What's your name?"

"Marcella."

"Well, I'm Jim-Bob, and that's Coal. We're taking you to dinner."

"Pleasure to meet you."

The two opened their second beer, and the group walked downstairs. Jim-Bob carefully placed the rifle back in the cabinet. The two threw their first bottles into the trash while Coal loaded up and started the truck.

"Sheriff, give us the all clear?" Coal asked

"Yeah, he said he's got a couple cars out in the area now."

The group was now enjoying a quiet drive on the way back to the diner. The crisp, cool air felt incredible as it gently caressed Coal from his open window. Jim-Bob was soaking in the new truck AC and was unable to fall asleep for this trip. Marcella stared out as she leaned her forehead against the window.

She was filled with such a wide range of emotions. Surely, she knew that her father would not simply let her run away from home. She was scared to face his wrath, but she couldn't return home knowing what supported it. She felt comforted by the men she very nearly believed to be her new friends. She was worried she had drug mortals into her own realm of darkness, one that she herself was not fairing particularly well. She was granted a moment of respite as red neon struck the dash of Coal's truck, catching the corner of her eye. She gazed upon the giant neon pin-up girl waving her in to join them for dinner.

Coal stepped out of the truck and opened Marcella's door for her. She took his hand as she climbed out while Jim-Bob rushed to get them a table. As they entered the diner, it was as if they had stepped into the roaring twenties themselves. All the tables were solid wood, with deep, rich colors glossed over. The counters and lower half of the walls were all white enamel with bright red trim, while the upper half of the wall was cherry red. The waiters all wore vests and bows with hair slicked back. The group was taken to a table and treated to the new menu, which included many old favorites as well as their daring new items. Coal had come specifically for one of these fun new items.

Marcella reviewed the menu also. It was filled with classic americana, such as burgers, shakes, and po'boys, but also contained a few Italian items. It had a strange spread from fast food to Michelin stars. There was a roast duck on the menu that caught her eye, but it seemed too expensive, so she had elected, in her mind, to go with a nice full Ceasar salad. The waiter had yet to arrive when Coal looked up from his menu.

"You ain't gotta look at them numbers next to everything, honey, this one's on me. I owed dingus here for helping dig my fence posts." Coal let her know.

"But I haven't helped with anything, I've really only caused trouble," Marcella responded.

"Who you been troubling, baby girl? We whooped some ass, then we brought you here. I'm not finna bring a young lady like you to a diner then sweat a ticket get what you want, cause I'm bout to. Coal chuckled.

"Ok, if it's fine with you.

The waiter approached them. "And what can I get for you all this fine evening?"

"I'll take two double Texas toast burgers and a large fry, with a Dr. Pepper and a large chocolate milkshake. Please, Sir." Coal requested.

"I need the spaghetti and meatballs with double meat, and if you could just leave the parm grater, that'd be awesome," Jim-Bob ordered.

"And what to drink?"

"Sprite, Please, sir."

"And what about you miss?"

"The roast duck and a coke, please," Marcella asked. "Thank you."

"Excellent orders all around, I'll be back with bread shortly."

"I'm bout ready to kill for that bread." Coal Joked.

"You ain't lying." Jim-Bob laughed. "I figured you were doing the heart attack speed run when you ordered two toast burgers."

"It ain't been a good one, so it may as well be a short one."

Both men laughed while Marcella looked about the diner. It was moderately busy. She had found something she was fixated on, though. In a glass display was a large red velvet cake with a slice cut out of it. Coal had noticed her staring into it.

"I got a good-sized fridge; we'll grab one on the way out."

"No! You've already done too much, really." She replied.

"Nonsense, we all eat the red cake, plus we got working to do tomorrow, and I doubt I'll feel like cooking again."

"Thank you."

The waiter had finally brought the bread. It was a beautiful brunette loaf with whole grains stuck to the side of it. Its freshly baked smell was mesmerizing. Jim-Bob waited for Coal to take the knife. Coal sliced a piece and handed it to Marcella, then Jim-Bob, then himself. They each had a butter knife and took small pads for themselves. With each bite, light, buttery sweetness filled their mouths. Before they knew it, they had finished the loaf. They sat for a moment, looking at each other, waiting for their entrées.

"So what's the next part of your plan?" Coal asked.

Marcella looked down at the napkin on her lap. She simply found a chance to slip away and started running. She didn't have a plan, much less a clue of what was going on or a penny to her name.

"I... I don't know." She said as the severity of the situation had finally settled in.

"Welp, reckon you can stay at my place if you need to." Coal offered.

"No, no, you've already done so much for me! Too much even!"

"Relax, it's just a room, it's not like I ain't hid stowaways before."

"There's no way I could even pay you back!"

"Someone needs help, you help them."

This simple statement struck a chord in Marcella. She had never heard something so honest and basic, with real intent behind it. No underhanded deal waiting to be sprung up later, no backstab waiting in the woodwork, just an honest man offering help. Tears began to well in her eyes.

Coal saw these tears begin, and his eyes immediately widened. "I'm not tryna be rude but could the petite young lady sitting at the table with two grown men who look like they just buried some fucker not start crying."

The tears stopped, and Marcella began to giggle. She could hardly believe she had let her guard down long enough to have been laughing with these strangers for as long as she had.

"So, is your dad some kind of vampire lord?" Jim-Bob abruptly asked.

"No, there haven't been any vampire lords for a while, well, any real ones. He's just the head of a household."

"So, a house full of vampires?"

"No, there may typically be more than one house, think like noble households with like, retainers and vassals."

"So like a LORD?"

"No, see, the title lord is really reserved for vampires of a certain pedigree or level. Papa's got a very nice pedigree and leads a house, but he's not on the same level as the vampires that were known as lords."

"Oh, aight then, but he still has goons and cronies?"

"Almost definitely, oh, and rivals too."

"So, like vampire dudes who would want to take you for leverage?" Jim-Bob was becoming quite overwhelmed with worry.

"Yeah, they'd kill for an opportunity like this." Marcella politely explained.

Jim-Bob was now staring at Coal, unable to hide the insurmountable level of concern that he had built up. Two hours ago, they were blissfully ignorant of the creatures of the night, and now, one would be living with his best friend for a time. One who was being hunted by the rest.

"You gotta relax, man, they lost her in a city nestled on one of the biggest highways in the states. And hell, we live 20 miles into the middle of nowhere." Coal assured him.

"What the hell you gone do if they find you?"

"How the hell they gone find me? Look at her, she ain't from around here. They sure as shit can't ask around, most of these folk don't fuck with outsiders."

"I reckon you're right."

"Course I'm right, you can't name a time I was goddamn wrong."

Jim-Bob stared at Coal a moment. "You really ain't gotta bring one up right now." Coal joked.

"I can think of a few."

"I can think of a few more."

"Suppose that's why you do the thinking."

"Suppose"

Both men laughed as Marcella looked with disbelief. She began to worry that below the imposing figures, there were two idiots that didn't take the severity of the situation seriously enough. She was, however, incredibly grateful that they were so willing to help her, even if it was because they were dumb. An incredible guilt loomed over her. She had accepted the aid of two mortals who could scarcely conceptualize the world that they had not only entered but now stood in front of. So many thoughts were racing about beyond that of the two beings of her subconscious sitting atop each shoulder. It was more akin to a cacophony of voices, both harsh and soft, confused and happy, and yet, most of them all, fearful and hopeful. They argued in her mind as the entrees were brought out. She had no other options but to accept the help of these two good men, men who, without even knowing her name, had charged to her rescue and, in doing so, damned themselves. She didn't want to let that happen, but they were the first nice people she had met since she had fled, but she couldn't bear the responsibility for their fate. She had resolved that she would accept their help and flee as soon as she was able.

The entrees had arrived, and by judging the look on Coal's face he surely didn't expect his Texas toast burger to be so large, and he had ordered two of them. The same could be said of Jim-Bob's double-meat spaghetti. Marcella looked down at her flawless roast duck. It was beautifully sat atop a mound of homemade mashed potatoes, with a sauce cup of spiced blueberry sauce to the side. The duck itself had been carefully scored with precise diamonds, the cracks filled with a dry rub, of course, sea salt, pepper, and paprika, before being glazed over with honey. Marcella had never experienced such an inviting meal before. The aroma gently caressed her nose, inviting her to take a bite out of such a delicate bird. For a moment, she could feel her teeth serrating, and her fangs begin to pulsate as if to lunge. She composed herself silently while neatly grabbing her fork and knife and carving a small slice. Once again, she was forced to restrain her voracious appetite as the slice revealed the luxurious juice still hidden within the waterfowl, but the final blow was the pristine, ever so slightly pink flesh hiding below the surface. She was a properly raised young lady, which made this task no easier, but she did not want to embarrass herself in front of her friends. The thought quickly perished as she looked next to her as Coal had already obliterated half of his Texas toast burger. Jim-Bob had also finished the majority of his plate, and the two had noticed her looking at them.

"We skipped lunch." Jim-Bob insisted.

"You've been staring at your duck for like five minutes. Don't judge me." Coal joked. "You can take a bite now."

"Oh." Marcella realized.

She finally took her first bite. It was a burst of sweet and salty with a hint of mild spice. These were not so pronounced that the duck itself could not subtly push through and reveal its cooked perfection. Her eyes glazed over for a moment, and her mouth began to water until a small line leaked from one side of her grin. It had been quite some time since she had eaten, and for the first meal since her escape to be so incredible was more than her senses could handle.

Coal slowly leaned in toward Jim-Bob "Nobody say shit when she come to."

"Bro, I shoulda got the fucking duck," Jim-Bob whispered. "How's the toast?"

"It's the shit, but it's so heavy I'm finna die."

As they were finishing, the waiter approached and asked if they had left room for dessert. They all looked around at each other and realized they, in fact, did not. Coal asked for the check and some to-go milkshakes for everyone. A chocolate shake for coal, vanilla for Jim-Bob, and a strawberry for Marcella. Coal tipped well, and they made their way back to the truck and climbed in.

"So, what are we doing now?" Marcella asked.

"We can all crash at my place, I got one guest room and a badass futon in the game room." Coal answered.

"That is a sweet ass futon," said Jim-Bob. "Plus, it's close to the cabinet."

"Yeah, and I'll suit the dogs up and turn'em out for the night. I got that underground wire thing for their collars, so they can't leave." Coal added.

"You got the motion lights up over the chicken yard yet?"

"Nah, it's on the list, I might need a few more now, all things considered."

"Yeah, that way, Briggs and Straton can see who they maul." Jim-Bob joked.

"Who?" asked Marcella.

"My two pits. They solid black and built like tanks and make real good hog and guard dogs." Coal Answered

"Yeah, and when they're up in their Kevlar, they have to be the scariest pair of anything any robber ever saw," Jim-Bob added.

"They watch my chickens." Coal continued.

"You have chickens?" Marcella asked.

"Yeah, I'll introduce you to everyone when we wake up tomorrow before I get to chorin."

"Ok, sounds fun."

Coal nodded and turned the radio back up. It was a calm ride back to Coal's house. They once again pulled up to the gate, and Jim-Bob hopped out and opened it. Coal pulled the truck in, and Jim-Bob closed the gate and jumped back into the truck. Coal then drove down the long driveway and parked right by the deck. They entered the house, and Jim-Bob went to the game room and started unfolding the futon while Coal went out the backdoor. Marcella followed Coal.

As she stepped onto the back patio, she could notice that it had been made into a very nice outdoor kitchen. There was a smoker, grill, and even a homemade brick oven, all covered by the extended roof of the A-frame. Coal made his way down the steps and began to follow a brick path to two large kennels. Each kennel is a two-stage entryway, where the first door led to what appeared to be a prepping station, and the second door led directly into the kennel. Observing the whole kennel, Marcella became confused as to why regular cage doors were on the opposite side of the kennels. Coal entered the first door to the staging area and opened a door that lead to a small closet. Inside the closet was a large spiked collar with a small box with prongs pointing to the interior and a Kevlar vest. Coal then opened the second door and began whistling.

"Straton, come on, boy." He whistled as he patted a platform in the staging area. "Hop on up, little buddy, come on."

The creature that emerged from the dark was certainly not a little buddy. The dog was huge, with paws that tore the ground as it ran. The ground itself seemed to buckle as the beast propelled itself onto the platform. Its coat was sleek and shining, while its eyes were dark and intimidating. Marcella was unnerved for a moment as the dog's gaze seemed to pierce right through her. Its ears shot to the back of its head as its form lowered, muscles tensing in preparation. Coal noticed this and scratched behind Straton's ears.

"I don't think he know you well enough yet, do me a solid and wait in the house, would you, hun?" Coal asked.

"Oh, yeah, sorry."

"No problem."

Marcella went back into the house. She could hear a shower running and assumed that Jim-Bob was there, so she began wondering about the house. The first room she entered by chance was the guest room. It was quaint but welcoming. A nice double bed with a TV in front of it. The TV was on top of a solid wood dresser. Off the side of the bed, there was a small but adequately sized desk. The covers of the bed were a dark cream color with light grey pillows, they were all incredibly soft. She then noticed a small nightstand with a fan facing the bed on it. While not luxurious, it certainly seemed comfortable.

Marcella left the guest room and made her way to the kitchen, and as she did, she saw that the game room Coal spoke of was actually the living room. She knew this because it was an open concept to the kitchen. The game room contained a couch with a large TV in front of it, two desks with laptops on them, and a futon next to the TV. There was a large window facing the front of the house, with the blinds closed.

She then moved on to the kitchen, which was clearly the main focus of the house. It had a large bar attached to the stove. The gas stove had 4 eyes and a large flat iron, with gas ovens below it. Behind the stove there was a double doored fridge. The right door being the fridge, the left the freezer. There two large counters, one had two instapots and a fryer, the other had a small dry-aging box and a miniature barista. There were also many cabinets, but Marcella didn't feel quite right opening them all. She did, however, remember what was in the fridge. She opened it to see two separate boxes filled with beer, one labeled tripel one labeled extra. The one that she had enjoyed earlier was the extra, so she opened the box and helped herself to one.

"Mind tossing me a tripel, please, ma'am?"

The sudden voice behind her sent a chill down Marcella's spine as she shot straight upright and grabbed her beer with both hands as she tensed up. She inhaled deeply through her nose and began to register that it was just Coal's voice behind her. For those brief moments, her heart was racing.

"My bad didn't mean to scare you." Coal said.

As he spoke, he leaned from behind her and stretched his arm out to grab the handle to the beer box. The box was slightly stuck, so as he pulled it, he pulled himself forward. He was already leaning and felt himself begin to fall forward. Without thinking, he grabbed Marcella's side to catch himself. It was the soft spot above her hip, and she couldn't help but let out a startled "eep." Coal had caught himself and stepped in as he opened the box and grabbed his precious tripel. However, he had not been paying attention and was now pressing slightly against Marcella from behind, just right of center, with his hand still on her waist, but she was still to startled from earlier to move. No thought ever occurred as he stepped back and turned to look for his bottle opener.

"Scuse me." He said as he stepped back.

Marcella's's chest had stopped beating against itself, but now, for just a brief moment, there was a slight and unfamiliar tickle in her stomach. She was taken aback by how firm but gentle Coal's grip was. She could help but think of how solid and warm his form was. She took a fast, deep breath in from her nose and exhaled through her mouth. She turned to Coal, who had leaned against the counter and was opening his bottle.

"So what do you do?" Marcella asked.

"A little bit of everything." Coal chuckled. He popped the top of his beer and, flipped the bottle opener in his hand, and reached out, offering it to Marcella.

"But, like, humans have jobs, so like, what's yours?" She said, taking the bottle.

"Welp, before I got this house and property, I was a maintenance man at the factory just down yunder way. Before that, I was a mechanic.' Coal replied before taking a sip.

"So what do they do?"

"Maintenance men or mechanics?"

"Maintenance men."

Coal thought for a moment. "Well, I kept the lines running and productive and worked on the robots when they'd crash."

"Ok, and that's how you got all this?"

"Nah, I got a good chunk'a change from a lawsuit when the factory bout killed me." Coal answered.

"How the hell?"

"Engineering, in their genius, bypassed a key switch and the E-stop on one of the heavier arm cages, so when it got triggered and started running, none of my buds could stop it. Broke three of my ribs when it crushed me up against the cage swinging around, so I hopped that som'bitch before it started the next process."

"That's horrible!"

"Shit it was worth it with the change I made! And it got them audited by OSHA, and the boys found plenty of shit not right, so I probly saved some boys down the track that weren't as fast as me. Soon as they ran out of appeals, I bought this place, and my buddy Diego and his cousin Carlos helped me build this house, my shop, and my chicken pens, a barn too, I think." Coal explained. "Now I can just find me a decent part timer, side hustle with my chickens and shop, and live a pretty good life."

"That does sound pretty nice."

"For three ribs, it's fucking sweet." Coal laughed.

Marcella took a sip of her freshly opened beer and smiled at Coal. She wanted to continue talking, but she was getting tired and didn't really know what to talk about. She was excited to see the farm in the morning, though. She felt a shiver when she heard the dogs begin to bark outside. Coal saw her shudder for just a moment.

"You ain't gotta worry bout that. If they were really barking, you'd know. Plus, you'd prolly hear some screaming shortly thereafter." Coal assured her.

"Why do they have those big spikey collars and vests on?" Marcella asked.

"They're my little buddies, and we got hogs and coyotes out here. They watch the chickens while I ain't around. Keep the property safe."

"Oh, OK, can I make friends with them?"

"If you stay awhile, it's bound to happen."

"I'd really not want to inconvenience you."

"It really ain't one. Jim-Bob lives for that futon when he's over, and we're pretty much chilling when we aren't busy. Just don't bring any drugs or other types of illegal shit on the property, so we don't give unwanted visitors probable cause."

"What?" asked Marcella.

"My fault. You're probly a good girl and don't even know what I'm talking about."

Marcella quivered for a moment, being called a girl, and she didn't know why. She hadn't really heard it before in her stern household and the sound of it made her want to smile. "I really don't know, but I don't do drugs or illegal shit." She smiled.

Jim-Bob had finally finished his shower and was walking into the kitchen to join them. He was wearing a grey T-shirt and green shorts. His pasty shins practically illuminated his path as he walked.

"Your turn, amigo." He said.

"You leave me any hot water in there?"

"Hell no." Jim-Bob snickered.

"You bitch."

"Bro, just wait like fifteen minutes. It'll warm back up."

"Fair enough."

"Um, do you think I could hop in the shower, and you use the one upstairs?" Marcella nervously asked.

Jim-Bob and Coal stared at each other for a moment. They couldn't believe their own stupidity. Perhaps they had just forgotten, after all it was a new house. Maybe they weren't complete imbeciles.

"Yeah, actually, that is a great idea. I'll use the second bathroom." Coal muttered.

"Ok, Thanks!" Marcella said.

"I'd still wait for the water to warm up." Coal suggested.

"Bruh, didn't Carlos hook you up with one of those new water heaters, though? Like the water honestly wasn't even cooling off when I got out." Jim-Bob explained.

"Bro we're so fucking stupid, he did, he did dude." Coal lamented.

"WE? Cuh, you helped build this fucking house," Jim-Bob stated in disbelief.

Marcella couldn't help but start laughing at the two men arguing. Anyone looking in would almost believe that they hated each other, but she could tell they had known each other for quite some time. They argued like children, so surely, they were childhood friends.

"Anyways I'm pulling a futon dive, so if you need me holler." Jim-Bob saluted as he turned and leapt over the back of the couch onto the futon section. He then produced a remote from the side of the couch and used it to turn the lights in the game room off. "That shit's still fucking sweet."

Coal waved to Marcella as he began to make his way upstairs. He was halfway up when he stopped. "Towels and rags are folded up in that cabinet to the left when you get in the bathroom." He then stepped up the rest of the way.

Marcella had nodded and waved back before Coal had gone up the stairs. She then made her way to the bathroom. There were still droplets on the shower door and fog on the mirror, but the floor looked like it had been wiped after Jim-Bob had finished toweling off. Marcella looked for a while in the mirror. Her purple eyes off set by hints of reddish pink from holding back her tears. She could smile and wave all she wanted, but she still felt alone. She had fled the only place she ever knew, and everyone she ever cared for. Tears slowly began to stream down her face. It was the first time she could stop to process everything. She turned the water on, then sat and reflected as she waited for it to warm up. She opened the cabinet and grabbed a towel and wash rag, she thought it strange that they were all teal, but it was just a strange observation. She began looking into the mirror again to see the buttons on her cropped grey jacket. As she pulled it off she noticed a few light reddish pink droplets on her cream-colored shirt.

"Oh my god I squirted duck juice all over me." She spoke aloud

She was in disbelief that no one had told her, but she remembered that her new friends were most assuredly not the types to judge. They probably hadn't even noticed, and if they had, they knew she had much deeper concerns to fret over. She removed her shirt to reveal a black bra with light lace work on it. Marcella checked herself for any scratches or bites. She had run through the woods before making it into the town so she was quite concerned with the prospect of any insect that could be crawling on her. Next was to drop her grey, neatly pleated skirt. The young vampire quickly realized that in her self reflection she had forgotten to take her shoes off. They were very nice black flats, shiny and polished with small buckles toward the in-step. Once the shoes and skirt were off Marcella was back to checking herself. There were no ticks but was a small set of scratches on her ankle where one of the thralls had lunged and grabbed it in an attempt to catch or slow her down. Her arms were stiff and sore from the running and climbing during her escape so unhooking her bra seemed nearly impossible. Her chest was a respectable size, but these tiny five hooks were soon to be the death of her. Finally, the greatest sigh of relief escaped Marcella in days. Her breasts were no longer pressed up and against her and were free, and the horrible strap gripping her back was gone. She raised both of her arms up, interlocking her fingers and pressed her palms upward, she leaned back while doing so, and experienced the best stretch of her life. She then reached her hands downward just below her belly button as she slipped her thumbs behind a little pink bow. She let her hands slide to her sides as she pushed downward and removed her silk panties. Steam had filled the room and what was once fog on the mirror was now entirely condensation. Drops of sweat were forming on Marcella's body from the heat and were now beginning to bead down from her defined collar bones down to her chest. The water was finally hot enough to cleanse all of the grime and worry away. She opened the door and stepped in. She looked around for the shampoo and soap. They were both painfully generic, but they would get the job done with generous use. After quite the over lathering and rinse she was now faced with a new problem.

Coal had finished his shower quickly and had gone straight to bed. After all, he had quite the list of chores that needed to be done. He had been enjoying the restful sleep that his new house had brought him. He was safe and secure in his own little castle.

"Hey, hey, wake up!"

Coal shot straight out bed. His eyes were sharp and alert, and his hands were just out slightly past his face. His hands were slightly open but tensed up and ready. Coal's shoulders had naturally rolled forward and pressed against his neck and jaw. His head had stooped low. All this had happened in an instant and he was now staring into the eyes of Marcella. Marcella jerked slightly from Coal's startling reaction as Coal looked into Marcella's eyes, his softened. He relaxed his arms and shoulders and arms as he smiled at Marcella.

Coal let out a yawn, "Everything alright? You ok?"

"Yeah, everything's fine, but there's just one problem."

"Shit is Jim-Bob naked sleepwalking again?" asked Coal.

"Again?! What? No, it's nothing that serious it's just that..." Marcella's hand finally found the light switch and she flicked them on.

Coal could scarcely believe his eyes before him stood what he may very well have thought to be the most beautiful woman he had ever seen. She stood there at the foot of his bed, wearing nothing but a tightly wrapped towel that barely covered her chest. Her long flowing black hair was wet and shimmering. Her eyes looked like rare and beautiful purple flowers hidden away in some dense forest, and they were looking right at him.

"I only had my dress and jacket, I don't have anything to sleep in." Marcella nervously said.

"Oh my bad, yeah there's plenty of T-shirts on that bottom drawer to your right, right yunder." Coal answered and pointed at a solid pine wood drawer.

Marcella walked over and looked at the drawer. It looked far older than any of the furniture. It was full of dents and dings, and she could see a name carved on the corner "Coal." She then bent over to open the drawer. Much to the shock of Coal, Marcella hadn't yet put her underwear back on, and before he realized it was too late. Marcella had porcelain skin through and through. She had an impressive and well-toned behind. It was one of a runner, or soccer player, or a predator. Coal worried about the latter for only a moment, for as Marcella shifted weight from one leg to the other, as she searched for a T-shirt she liked, Coal, for just a second, could the slightest bit of fairytale pink press past two perfectly shaven lips. Coal caught himself and began to stare at the ceiling. Marcella found a red T-shirt that she thought looked nice, grabbed it, and stood up, clutching it against her stomach. She turned to thank Coal and saw him staring at the ceiling. She reached under her towel and soon recalled what she had forgotten. Her face turned red as she bit both of her lips, absolutely mortified. Coal could sense tension and looked down to see Marcella on the brink.

"Whoa now, everything's fine." Coal said.

"I can't believe I just did that."

"Did what? Babygirl I seen that coming from a mile away and turned my head."

"You promise!"

"Of course!" he lied.

"Thank you for the shirt!" Marcella squeaked before scurrying out of the room to hers.

"Lord forgive me for that little white lie, but I don't reckon she needs all that right now, Lord I'll go get her some clothes tomorrow after the morning chores when the suns out and it's hot. See me and Jim-Bob through all this if you got the time, and if you don't just toss me some strength and I'll do my best till you do." Coal prayed. He closed his eyes and began to drift off. His dogs were out on patrol and Jim-Bob was right downstairs so he could rest easy and work hard in the morning. He didn't know why, but he was very excited to introduce Marcella to his dogs and chickens.

CHAPTER 2

Marcella awoke to a chorus of roosters. She stretched and looked over at the clock; it was six AM when the sun had broken and triggered the crowing. She had never been up so early, but while she was up, she needed to ask Coal for a toothbrush. Marcella began searching around the house but couldn't find Coal or Jim-Bob. She looked out the back door and saw that Briggs and Straton were back in their cages, eating away at their breakfast. She double-checked herself before stepping out and remembered she was only in her new T-shirt and panties. Marcella didn't think she would survive any further embarrassment, so she returned to her room to put on her skirt. Once she was dressed, she headed out the back door. She stood on the back deck and looked around for a while. Down the hill were two large barns and at least Forty tiny little A-frames that she thought looked cute. They had two cream-colored walls with a bright red ridge cap. Next to each tiny little frame, or on top of them, stood a black rooster. She thought they looked pretty as she walked down the hill for a closer view of everything and to look for Coal and Jim-Bob. She could hear a ruckus coming from one of the barns. As Marcella stepped to it, the noise only grew louder. It was filled with angry squawks and loud peeps. She rounded the corner to see two large doors mounted on black metal rails slid open. Within the barn were Coal and Jim-Bob. Coal was in a pen that was built into the lean-to portion of the barn. He was on all fours, catching new chicks from under their furious mother. Jim-Bob stood just outside the pen. Coal would hand Jim-Bob a freshly caught chick, and he would then take it over to a table in the middle of the barn. There, he would wingband it, record the number in a ledger, and place the bird in a box with his siblings. Marcella watched them repeat this process until all the chicks were caught, banded, and recorded. Then, one at a time, Coal would take them out of the box, examine them, record his thoughts, and place them back into the pen with their mother. As he was writing, Marcella stepped up to him.

"Mornin' sleepyhead!" he chuckled.

"Good morning, I was trying to see if you had a spare toothbrush."

Coal reached into his pocket and tossed Marcella a pack of spearmint gum. "Sorry, that's gon have to hold you till we can get you some shopping done. We'll head to town when the morning work's done." Coal explained.

"No really, that's not necessary at all!" She blurted out.

"Hush with all that bullshit. Besides, Jim-Bob would love to skip all the mid-day work if he can help it," said Cole.

"I ain't say that."

"You ain't have to!" the two bickered.

"Thanks again, can you tell me what you're doing with the bird?" Marcella inquired.

"Wing banding them."

"Which is?"

Coal began to explain the process, "This here's a near fresh hatch, they're getting old enough to let them out on one the runs, but before that we have to put these little bands on their wings so we can keep track of them."

"Oh that's neat, does it hurt?"

"Bout like getting a shot." Coal replied.

"Alright, is there anything I can help with?"

"Nah, I figured once we finished this we'd throw feed out to the Teepees and head to town. Jim-Bob If you don't mind running down the measuring cups, I gotta mix the feed today." Coal requested.

"Yeah man, no problem at all," Jim-Bob answered as he went to a small set of cabinets. They were just over some large plastic trash cans. "You got the vitamins and supplements?'

"Yeah bro, should be in the cabinet right next to it."

Marcella began to examine the barn around her. She could see that one side of the walls was composed of several pens, each with a pair of chickens, one rooster, and one hen. Some of the pens did not have roosters, but just hens and their chicks. Across from the pens were more pens of the same size, with slide doors that lead to the outside in each. These were where the hens with much older chicks were.

"So what is all this?" Marcella asked.

"It's the game farm I been trying to start for a while, we finished moving all the birds over not to long ago." Coal answered.

"What's a game farm?"

"Where we raise game chickens to breed and sell."

"Ooohhhh… What's a game chicken?"

Coal stared in disbelief. Before he could say anything, the sound of skidding tires could be heard in the distance, followed by the rumbling of gravel brought on by a truck who had taken the turn too rapidly. Marcella shrank back.

"There's no way! How could they find us?" she began to shake.

Coal lifted up his finger as if to ask for a moment. As the sound drew nearer the roar of gravel could be heard the sound of acoustic guitars and maracas. "That ain't them, that's our beer money for the day." He smiled.

The group stepped out to see outside. The truck had pulled around to the barn before they knew it. It was pristinely white and freshly waxed with a large inclosed trailer hanging from the back. Looking at the trailer, Marcella could see an AC window unit installed. Out of the truck stepped two small Hispanic men. The one who stepped out of the driver seat wore a white button-down with bright silver paisley trim and a pair of deep blue starched and pressed jeans. He also wore a baseball cap. Out of the passenger, a much redder in complexion, man. He wore a gray T-shirt and a black cowboy hat. From his hat stemmed a large pair of sickle feathers from a black game chicken. His jeans were also starched but not as cleanly pressed. The one in white approached arms wide, speaking in Spanish.

"Eres la mujer más hermosa que he visto en mi vida, ¡deja a este hombre y ven a casa conmigo!" He yelled as he looked at Marcella.

"I'm sorry, I don't understand what he's saying, is he talking to me?" Marcella asked.

"¡Ella te va a patear el trasero!" the man in gray said to the other.

"¡Tonterías, ella me ama y le mostraré la noche de su vida y haremos hermosos niños juntos!" the other replied.

"Diego, you son of a bitch, how have you been?" asked Coal.

"Bueno mi amigo!" Diego laughed as the two hugged.

"I'm sorry I don't know if he was talking to me. I can't speak that language." Marcella tried to explain.

"Don't you let that man fuck with you like that! He speaks perfect English." Coal chuckled.

"No, not only a bit, a little," Diego replied.

"He went to state."

"I was only in the top ten of my class really!" Diego began to laugh. "Carlos barely speaks English though."

Carlos waved and smiled.

"Then what did he say? Is he messing with me?" Marcella asked.

"It's better you don't know." Coal smirked.

"That's not very nice," Marcella added.

"Apologies, little miss. Anyway, can you show us the birds please Mr. Coal?" asked Diego

"Sure thing."

Coal took them out to the yards outside the barns, to where the teepees with the roosters were. He took them to a yard further away than the rest where the old were. They were tall, high-stationed birds. Their combs and wattles had been trimmed, and their spurs were cleaned and cut to an inch and a half from their heels. Their red eyes were alert as many hopped to the top of their houses to greet the visitors. All the birds were black, and some had red streamers laced in their plumage, while some others had red saddle feathers.

"These might be some of the best birds you've ever produced," Diego said.

Carlos had stepped up to the closest bird and picked it up. He examined its eyes, tail feathers, legs, and body conformation. He was very pleased. He quickly paced about the yard and then stepped back to Diego. "All. All Good."

"Still two-fifty a bird?" Diego asked.

"Yessir."

"We'll take twenty."

The three men shook hands, and Diego handed Coal several neatly banded stacks of cash. Coal didn't even bother to count it and began helping them choose and catch their chickens. They then went and opened the trailer. Within the trailer, there were two walls of cedar boxes with holes in them. They were just large enough to comfortably transport a rooster. Cool air bellowed of the trailer as it was opened. The men placed all twenty chickens in their boxes and closed the trailer, now standing just outside of it.

"So how long ya'll in town for?" asked Coal.

"Another night," Diego answered.

"Hell, we oughta hit the town then, don't know when I'll see you again." Coal suggested.

"Soon as we check the ranches and drop off the birds, we're actually heading back up to house hunt," Diego explained.

"Well, hell yeah, that calls for celebration."

"It does. Call us amigo, I'm off to take a siesta."

"Sure thing, man, talk to you later."

Coal exchanged hugs with the two men, who then drove off in their truck.

"Welp, I reckon we can button up chorin here in a bit. When the sun comes up, we'll head to town." Coal told Marcella and Jim-Bob.

"Thank God!" Jim-Bob exclaimed.

"What're you bitching about? The chicken barns got AC!"

"Yeah, but concrete work is next on the list!"

"Well, shit." Coal chuckled.

"What are we going to town for today?" asked Marcella.

"To buy you some more clothes." Coal answered.

"You really don't have to…" Marcella was interrupted by Coal.

"I ain't running the washer and dryer every day for 1 set of clothes! Relax, it's just an excuse to get Jim-Bob out of the holler." Coal joked.

"Ok, ok."

"Aight, if we all settled then, let's load up." Coal spoke as he waved and walked toward his truck.

The gang all piled into the truck, Jim-Bob once again taking shotgun. They pulled up to the gate, and Jim-Bob hopped out and opened it. Coal glanced over to his unburied fence posts as he pulled past and stopped.

Jim-Bob closed the gate and hopped back into the truck. Coal then began the drive to town.

"So, what stores are we going to?" Marcella was curious.

"Supposedly, there's this fancy new outlet center that's supposed to be real nice. They got a couple'a boutiques that oughta have clothing for you. They should have some stuff for me and Jim-Bob to check out too, and some cool eateries." Coal explained.

It was about a thirty-five-minute drive to the outlet center. It was in the middle of everything, not too far from the courthouse or the town hall. Several real-estate companies had joined forces to make this center and, in an effort to outdo each other, had created an immaculate stretch of town. It was a well-composed mix of Renaissance and antebellum architecture. The planning was also thought out well enough that everything was reachable on foot, and that the shopping centers were easy to get lost in. There were roads, but they cut through in a nearly seamless way, with lights and raised crosswalks to prevent accidents. It was filled with an incredibly diverse selection of stores, from designer boutiques to pro shops, down to an Amish general store. This selection was only matched by their restaurants, which included the down-south buffets, Greek, Mexican, Italian, real Italian, and other interesting choices. Marcella was mesmerized.

"They got enough people to shop here?" Coal asked as the view of the center was made clear from the overpass.

"That parking lot is full, my guy," Jim-Bob replied.

"Well, shit."

They had finally reached the parking lot, and searched for a good place to park, rejoicing once one was found. They weren't parked too far away from a nice-looking Greek restaurant, and they decided they would meet there later and eat. They climbed out of the truck and gathered around.

"Alright, the first place we need to go to is a place that sells purses." Coal said.

"Coal, all of these places sell designers. That'll be way too expensive!" Marcella pointed out.

"It be aight."

"It most certainly won't be!"

"Marcella, you need a purse, you need clothes, you need a lot right now, and I'm not going all the way to damn wall-e' world to get it. Just relax, we got you covered." Coal explained.

"No! It's all too much! I don't even know why you're doing all this!"

"Because I don't know what's gonna happen to you!" Coal yelled. Marcella shrunk back in shock. Coal calmed himself. "I done been in a place where someone next to me spent the last few they had fucking miserable. I didn't even realize they'd be gone soon as they were, and we were miserable." For the smallest moment, tears welled in Coal's eyes, but they vanished as soon as he blinked.

"Why don't you get you a smoke break, Coal, I'll take Mars to go get a purse," Jim-Bob said as he pulled a cigar tube from his pocket. It was a vanilla cream cigar in a perfecto shape, one of Coal's favorites. Coal took the tube and handed Jim-Bob a band of cash. Coal then walked back to his truck to get a lighter. "Come on, girly, let's get to shopping!" Jim-Bob said in his most effeminate voice. The two began heading into the outlet.

"Jim, I'm really sorry."

"Jim-Bob, and relax. Ya'll both right, just neither know why."

"Please explain."

"A designer purse is hella expensive for a lot of people, especially for someone you just met."

"See, I knew it!"

"Hush up, now understand. Coal wants to make sure that if, and I mean if, you ain't long for this world, you'll be smiling for days before you do. If you didn't know him you'd think you were taking advantage of him, but it'll fuck with'im if you're not all set. Now we ain't broke by no means, so we're all gone have us a great day or so. Help me I will throw the bitchiest hissy fit you have ever fucken seen."

"What happened?" asked Marcella.

"That ain't my place to discuss, girl. Can we please, PLEASE get this purse?

"Yeah."

"Thank god!" Jim-Bob could have nearly leaped with joy.

The two finally stepped into a clothing outlet that had purses. There was a wide variety of items, but Marcella immediately fixated on a lambskin pochon, It was a washed black, with a gunmetal chain to throw over her shoulder. She was in love with the color scheme and it was much less than what Coal had given Jim-Bob.

"I love this one!" Marcella spoke up.

"Yeah it looks pretty nice! I bet this'd be the place to buy some clothes that went with it too." Jim-Bob remarked.

"Yeah definitely!"

Marcella continued to shop until she came upon a gray sundress, its skirt came just above the knee and it was ruffled, it had what almost looked like a turtle neck for a color and it was sleeveless. There was a black bunny mesh, wide brimmed sun hat atop the mannequin that Marcella also adored. She didn't want to cause Coal or Jim-Bob anymore worry, but the sun was beginning to burn her. It was like Jim-Bob turning red, it was as if very prolonged exposure to full sun made her feel as if she had third degree burns, but she would only lightly pinken. She knew her new hat and some sunscreen would solve the problem.

Marcella and Jim-Bob finished shopping and stepped out. As they did they could see Coal sitting on the bench finishing off his cigar. He looked happy to see Marcella with her new purse and shopping bag. Jim-Bob, just behind Marcella, gave Coal a thumbs up.

"That looks great Marcella, here's something to put in it, have fun shopping, me and Jim-Bob will catch back up holler if you need us." as Coal rushed through his sentence he tossed two more bands into Marcella's purse. Before she could protest he had turned and began to walk off. Jim-Bob rushed to catch up.

"Man that kinda money makes her super uncomfortable. Coal that shit ain't cool." Jim-Bob protested.

"I know, you're right, but right now I need her distracted. We gotta go see T. Rell, he waiting at one of these fountains."

"Waiting for us? Why?" Jim-Bob asked.

"We finished his roster with some of our secret sauce for that big ass main down in louisiana." Coal explained.

"Yeah, and?"

"And ours fucking swept, he took second and he's got a nice chunk of change for us. I'll have to drive out to his place later this week to get the birds back." Coal continued.

"Fuck yeah, bro, I knew they'd do it. But on the real man, you gotta chill."

Coal wiped his face and shook his head. "I know I do really, but I'm just… I don't know how to deal with that shit man. We're just humans dude, you shoulda seen her vamp out. She's our buddy sure, but shit like that, that's full blooded is hunting her man. Just what I know of."

"Coal," Jim suddenly said in a serious tone. "You better get your head right boy, and you better find a way to handle it."

Coal suddenly snapped back into himself. "You fuckin right. Hell, we can ask her when we get home. She'll know how to pop them bastards. And if I get a real idea of what's coming, it won't be shit to worry about."

"Fuckin A, now let's go get this bread and go shop with our half vampire soon-to-be goth girly."

They had started walking toward one of the fountains and could begin to see T. Rell. He was a medium built black man. He had clean rows on his head, with a well kept beard and mustache. He wore a black graphic T, with deep blue blue jeans with tears at the knees. On his blue jeans was a large belt buckle with two crossed feathers with a bird skull above them with the words "Bird Up" written below.

"T. Rell man how you doin? Coal asked greeting his friend.

"Man cuh, I'm doin great man, I'm blessed to be here you know." T. Rell answered.

"Hell yeah we all been blessed this week." Coal laughed.

"Shiet you ain't lyin, this be yours right here." T. Rell produced a small humidor and handed it to Coal. "I ain't want yo bread to go stale you feel?"

"Yeah I do."

"There coulda been more, but them sweater crosses wasn't feelin it like you said yuh hear?" T. Rell explained.

"Yeah, man it happens like that sometimes."

"Yeah, man, but holler at me when you come down to pick up your babies, I'm finna finish up here, go home, and dive in some liquor."

"Hell yeah man, hey take it easy though, we all going out with Diego and Carlos tonight before they go back to Mexico for a little while." said Coal.

"Oh word? yeah I be there, drop a line when you head out, I need to holler at my little homies it been a minute."

"Yeah man, sure thing. Well it was great seeing you man, glad everything turned out good!" Coal waved as he began to walk away.

"Ay cuh that's on you, I'll see you tonight. Stay Blessed!" T. Rell yelled as he began to walk to an urban clothes store.

"Bro he is so refreshing." Coal told Jim-Bob.

"Man he's always blessed, I need that positivity."

"You hear me?" Coal and Jim-Bob laughed.

"Let's go find our vampire," said Jim-Bob

"Yeah. Honestly we shoulda went to wall-e' world cause I really don't think them two bands gon last long with all this designer shit." Coal replied.

"Shit you done overdid it and made her super uncomfortable," Jim-Bob added.

"Yeah, but shit man that all fucks with me. Like what do I do in all this bro? Just distract her from it all, you know?"

"I really don't know Coal, shit. I'm just hoping they lost track of her."

"Yeah, and that day walking shit sure helps, like she out shopping right now."

"Yeah, I think we lost track of her too." Jim-Bob joked.

Marcella had resolved to enjoy her day, and allow herself to shop. She wasn't sure what would cause someone to be so flippant with money like Coal, but she supposed he had his own reasons. She quickly learned that the money she received from Coal would only go so far with designers, but she could get far enough with nice brand clothing, of course if there were a designer item she felt as though she couldn't live without, she could be tempted. She had also decided that she would surprise Coal, so she purchased a few other articles of clothing.

She had looked at the clock and realized it was almost time for her and her friends to meet at the Greek place in the middle of everything. As she was walking toward the restaurant she suddenly felt a lurch in her stomach. Her eyes began to dart about the streets and sidewalks around the stores. She could see a man sitting begging for money, men with hoodies up walking past, and men with caps and shades. There were large crowds in every direction. The rapid beating in Marcella's chest was undeniable. She had been made, and she had no idea who had, or what she could do. She quickly paced to the Greek place and the safety of her friends. They were sitting at a table outside waiting for her.

"Coal, Jim-Bob, I think I…" Her heart felt as if it would explode. Everything around her seemed to suddenly shift causing her to lose her balance. Her head was spinning in and her knees suddenly buckled. She was fortunate enough to have made it to the chair. She was breathing rapidly, and her eyes shook, rapidly looking in every direction. She could feel the sudden onset of cottonmouth and powerful nausea.

"Marcella, what's wrong?" Coal leapt up from his seat and rushed to her side.

"I… I don't know, I think someone saw me, and now I, I can't breathe." Marcella panted.

"What can I do?" Coal asked.

"I don't know. I'm so dizzy and my head hurts so bad." Tears began streaming down her face.

"Don't you worry Marcy, we'll take care of you." Coal smiled trying to reassure Marcella. In his left arm he scooped up all of her shopping bags and lifted her legs. In his right he grabbed her waist and picked her up from her chair. "Jim-Bob, get us some to-go homie, lamb it up for me, I'll meet you at the truck."

"I got you big homie!" Jim-Bob spoke as he hopped from his chair, and ran to the line.

Coal began carrying Marcella to the truck, he looked down and tried to reassure her again. "Don't you worry, you just put your arms around my shoulders and squeeze just as tight as you need to. I got you Marcy."

"I'm so sorry, I don't know what happened." Marcella sobbed.

"Shhh, it's ok. Everythings gonna be fine. We're gon get you home and snuggled in a blanket and I'll turn the dogs out." Coal told her.

She continued to cry, "It's not going to be fine Coal, I never should have come here, they saw me. They probably saw you. You and Jim-Bob are such nice people and it's gonna be all my fault! I'm so sorry!" Marcy squalled.

Coal gripped her tightly and held her close and spoke softly in her ear as he walked. "I'm not good at this sort of thing, and I'm not good at dealing with emotions, but Marcy I'll promise you this: As long as you need help and you're under my roof, I'll take care of you. Ain't anything your fault and I'd help anyone just the same."

Marcella held Coal's shoulders and pressed her head up against him, "Thank you." Her grip began to loosen. Coal's strong arms brought her such a sense of safety, and as all the stress and panic melted away, she could feel just how tired she had become. She dozed of In Coal's arms before they reached the truck.

Coal had eventually reached the truck. He very carefully opened the doors and gently placed Marcella in the back seat, and her shopping bags on the floorboards. He patted Marcy's head and stroked her hair. "Don't nobody have to be scared when I'm around, you just rest easy ok?"

There was no answer from Marcella. She was sleeping rather heavily. Jim-Bob had finally caught up, with arms full of gyros and chip bags. Coal opened the door for him and placed all the food on top of the center console.

"She ok?" Jim-Bob asked.

"I think she had a full on panic attack buddy." Coal shut the doors so they wouldn't disturb her.

"Who did she see?" asked Jim-Bob

"I ain't got a clue, for all I know it could be paranoia, or some supernatural instinct." Coal answered.

"Well at least we got her some clothes and such."

"Yeah, and we got to see T. Rell, so not a bad day so far. Let's hit the road and get her easy'n come up with a plan."

Coal and Jim-Bob began to climb into the truck, when they, in unison, stopped. They both felt uneasy. The two men made eye contact and realized it had hit them both and began looking about the parking lot.

They could see nice families heading toward the shopping center, and some people selling paintings and crosses outside the grocery. They watched as crowds simply walked around, going about their business. Still, the unease persisted.

"You reckon all them thralls look sick as shit?" asked Jim-Bob.

"I don't know, honestly, I was so worried about vampires I forgot those gangly bastards."

"We can whoop any human ass, but them things can be out in daylight, I don't do great thinking they can blend in."

"No shit."

Coal and Jim-Bob stepped into the truck as quietly as they could, and began the drive back to their house. They ate their extra large gyros on the way to the house. Coal took care not to hit the curves as hard as he normally would, to avoid throwing Marcella from her makeshift bed.

"We gotta check the mail when we get home, a buddy of mine dropped off a box of smokes I had ordered." Coal spoke up.

"Yeah I got you, you get'em from the smoke shop we tried to visit?" asked Jim-Bob.

"Yeah, I know Jerry, he works there, so I texted him to see if I could beg him to drop off a box or two and I'd paypal him or the owner. He just texted me to let me know."

"Sweet, a box or two oughta put a dent in that edge you on." Jim-Bob chuckled.

"Hell yeah, they some kind of Cafe' Tobac type shit. Coffee and creme inspired."

"Sweet. Hey we still hittin up the bar with the boys or do we need to call them?" ask Jim-Bob.

"Nah we should be good, Diego and Carlos' hotel is south of us instead of north of us, so we heading the opposite way." Coal explained.

"Thank God, 'cause I need a drink." The two men laughed.

They had returned to the house. Coal pulled up to the mailbox, grabbed his box, then pulled up to the gate. Jim-Bob hopped out of the truck and went and opened the gate. Coal pulled in and stopped the truck. Jim-Bob hopped back in and the two men looked at their posts, before driving up to the house.

Coal stepped out, and carefully opened Marcella's door and slowly picked her up. Now that things were calm, he couldn't help but notice how soft she was. Her fair skin, however, hid a solid structure behind it. Coal could feel her heft, and could think of only one reason such a small and thin beauty would be so heavy, muscle. She certainly seemed human, but as she shifted from being carried, Coal's fingertips could feel the coils and fibers writhing. The girl was a beautiful and sweet fearful thing, but her body was predatory. She was built like a tiger, ready to pounce, fast as a coiled viper with her fangs. None of this mattered to Coal. As far as he was concerned she was a nice lady who had nowhere else to go, and needed help, however, he couldn't shake the thought of her kin, after all she was a half breed. Her predatory features and instinct were seemingly washed away by the soft and supple traits of a woman.

Jim-Bob opened the front door for Coal. "Get her settled in, I'll start suiting up the dogs." He said as Coal walked past.

"Yeah, man, I appreciate it." Coal replied.

Coal began to carry Marcella to her room. As he did, she shifted in his arms. She grabbed his collar and pulled herself in. She nestled her head between his jaw and shoulder, she nudged her nose against his neck. He could feel a sudden sensation shiver through him as she took her soft and nearly pointed tongue and began to lick his neck. The tip of her tongue was coarse and felt as if it was barbed, the rest was perfectly soft and moved about him gently, almost pleasantly. He was far more concerned with the barbed tip however, for it didn't feel as though it was sensually gliding across him. It was searching. Coal suddenly froze, the barbs had found their mark, and Marcella had begun to gently nibble the skin above his carotid. There were thankfully no fangs, and the sensation sent a different feeling to Coal, however, Marcella was still asleep.

"I sure as shit won't ever let her skip breakfast again." Coal thought to himself. He gently opened the door to her room and tried to place her in her bed, as he sat her bags down. She still clung to him. He tried to stand from where he had knelt down to place her, but still she held him. Her gentle nibbles were starting to escalate to chewing and he could feel her grip tighten. He could see her skin begin to turn a gray shade, as the muscles in her arms revealed themselves as she pulled him back down to her bed. It had never occurred to Coal that he would need to keep his guard up, but she was half vampire, and she was scared. He could remember times in his life where raw instinct had dragged him forward. He could neither judge nor blame her, but he sure as hell wasn't letting her eat him, not before he had his shop built, not before he bought the big fancy lawn mower he dreamed of.

"I'm real sorry if this wakes you." Coal said as he gently placed his hands under her arms and began to push. Marcella began to struggle against him, both of her arms were now a light gray and grabbed him back. He could hear her gums begin to squelch as her teeth began to shift and her fangs slowly protruded. "Yup, super sorry." He shifted his right arm as she began to push her head forward and caught her by the throat just in time. She hadn't quite given up, but her original color was returning. Coal tightened his grip as he began to push harder. Both of Marcella's hands clapped around Coal's wrist with powerful force. Coal was almost alarmed but the grip suddenly loosened, as her color completely returned. Her right hand began to caress Coal's arm as he pushed Marcella into her bed. As her head sunk into the pillow her back bounced on the mattress sending her spine into an arch and pressing her neck further into Coal's grip. She quickly grabbed Coal's arm and began pressing against her neck further as she let out a moan. Coal jerked back in shock and woke Marcella up as he pulled his arm from her grip, leaving soft scratches in his skin.

"Coal? Is everything ok?" she asked. As she spoke, she could see her drool and teeth marks on Coal's skin and neck. "Oh my God!"

"Now, let's not panic or jump to no conclusions!" Coal insisted.

"What did I do? Are you ok?"

"Hell, best time I had in a hot minute before you actually started chewing."

"What?!" she exclaimed.

"What?" Coal jested. "Look, ya just skipped breakfast and slept through lunch, and apparently, you're a bit of a sleep eater."

"A bit of a sleep eater? Coal, are you ok?"

"Marcy, I'm fine, really." He once again insisted.

Marcella had noticed the scratch marks on Coal's arm. "And what are those?"

"Well, you are a bit clingy."

"Excuse me!"

"Damn, girl, I ain't think I'd hit a nerve on that one, look, "Coal said as he lifted arms, "I'm all good here, nothing to worry about."

"Then explain that," Marcella smirked as she noticed something pressing from within Coal's jeans.

Coal looked down for a moment, then dropped his jaw in shock. "Well... like I said, it was great till you started actually eating me.:

"Oh my god." Marcella dropped her face into her hands. "I'm so sorry, I've never been so embarrassed in my life."

"Oh, I ain't complaining by no means," Coal laughed. "Lil more warning next time, though. I sure would appreciate it."

"Please, please go somewhere, I can't right now."

"Fair enough." Coal began to laugh as he exited Marcella's room, closing the door behind him.

As soon as he was clear, Marcella buried her face in her pillow and cried out in embarrassment. She had just nibbled a man's neck. She hardly knew him, but she could still taste him. The moment she realized she could still taste him she buried her face back in her pillow. She had almost eaten him. In her hunger and sleep, she could have very well ended Coal. She had tried. But he was so strong he could hold her off. She rolled over on her back and lightly pressed against the red marks on her neck. She could still feel Coal's strong grip on her throat, but she couldn't feel any more guilt. She moved her hand to match where Coal's had been. Just thinking of his strong grip dominating her sent such a tingle. She had to wait until the marks had faded. She walked to the mirror and looked for a while. She certainly couldn't let Jim-Bob see. How would she explain it? It was nearly worse than any hickey could be. Did Coal leave hickeys? She wondered if he was into something like that, but she didn't really know how she, as a vampire, felt about letting someone so close to her neck, but she couldn't help but think of exposing herself to Coal.

Coal had stepped into the kitchen and grabbed some paper towels. He wiped Marcella's drool from his neck and washed his hands. He then went outside to suit up Straton. Briggs had opted not to listen to Jim-Bob and had run through both doors and was now refusing to come to Jim-Bob, barking occasionally to taunt him. Jim-Bob stood there, one hand on his hip, the other holding Briggs' vest.

"Come on, you big black bastard! You know you can't pull security without your vest!" Jim-Bob hollered.

"Bark"

"I know you're so big and strong, boy, but the vest is for your own good."

"Bark"

"Fuck you say about my momma?"

"Woof"

"Aight, you sum'bitch," Jim-Bob said as he began to chase Briggs across the property.

Coal had finished gearing up Straton up by the time Jim-Bob had caught up to Briggs. Jim-Bob wrestled the dog to the ground and began putting the vest on him. Briggs flailed about in order to be the biggest nuisance possible. Jim-Bob, after much effort, buckled Briggs in.

"What are those vests for?" Marcella asked as she stepped out the back door.

"They keep the dogs safe." Coal answered.

"From what exactly?"

"Hogs and Coyotes."

"Where do you get them?"

"They're called catch vests. You can get'em online." Coal answered, "They're not ballistic vests or anything fancy like that."

"Oh, Ok, so what's the plan for the rest of the day?"

"We finna go inside and game til we all hit the bar with Carlos and Diego." Coal explained.

Marcella winced a bit. "Would that be safe?"

Jim-Bob interjected, "We're heading south instead of north this time, plus you'll be surrounded by some of the baddest folks around. I couldn't think of anywhere safer, honestly. For you, that is. Diego's bound to stir some shit up." He began to laugh.

"I guess you're right," Marcella replied.

"Of course I am. Now let's go inside so you can eat your gyro, and tell us how to kill vampires," said Coal.

"What?"

"You need something to eat, and I need to know how to kill these things."

"You know I'm half of one of those things, right?"

"That's crazy. Are you the one hunting you?"

"What? No!"

"So half of you ain't got shit to do with this?"

"Listen, you sarcastic son of a…" Marcella let out a deep sigh, "No, you're right."

"Hell yeah, I'm right. I can't remember a time I was wrong." Coal noticed Jim-Bob begin to open his mouth. "Nope, not on this one" Jim-Bob closed his mouth and nodded in agreement.

"Fine, but this gyro better be good."

"I'm just glad it's something else's meat in your mouth."

"It could be your meat in my mouth if you keep that up!"

Coal tripped up the stairs as he and Jim-Bob burst out laughing. They could barely breathe as Coal began rolling downstairs. Tears filled Jim-Bob's eyes as Marcella stood confused. Suddenly, it clicked what she had just said. Her face grew a deep red as she stomped her feet and yelled, "You guys are such idiots! Little children!"

Coal and Jim-Bob could only look at each other and laugh louder. Coal stood up and, dusted himself off, and attempted his way back up the stairs. "Holy shit, she bout killed me."

Jim-Bob had regained his ability breathe, "Me too, bro her face when she realized."

"Fucken priceless."

They made their way into the house and went and sat in the kitchen. Coal waved over Marcella. She pulled her gyro bag out of the fridge and sat with them.

"Aight, spill it. What kills ya'll?" Coal bluntly asked.

"It's not really that complicated. Garlic burns and weakens, ash stakes through the heart, total incineration, and decapitation. Oh, and if you can tear their heart out with your bare hands." Marcella explained. "Oh, blessed weapons stop them from healing super fast. I think the church has their own ways though."

"Oh cool, seems easy enough." Coal said, and as he did Jim-Bob stared into his very soul, briefly before detecting the sarcasm.

"Actually, a lot of ash wood stuff really hurts them." Marcella continued.

"Y'all don't eat each other?" Jim-Bob asked.

"No, only those in the Cannibal's house that bear his mark can eat other vampires, but no one has seen one of his marks in ages, at least, that's what my dad says."

"I'm sorry, the Cannibal?" Coal asked.

"He's the oldest living and unbound vampire lord," Marcella answered.

"I thought you said there were no real vampire lords left?" Jim-Bob piped up.

"We don't really count him because he retains no noble stature. He is a lord through power alone." Marcella explained.

"So he's not much of a ballroom dancer, but he's scary as shit?" Coal questioned.

"Yeah, basically."

"Cool so any other tips and tricks?" Coal inquired.

"Yeah, a lot of vampire households hold themselves with great esteem, so, like, fight dirty."

"Stake the vampire in the balls, gotcha." Jim-Bob chuckled.

"If it works, it works." Marcella giggled. "Any other questions?"

"No, I think that bout covers it." Coal said.

"Awesome, glad I could help." as Marcella finished her sentence, she tore the wrapper of her gyro so quick and cleanly that the gyro simply fell onto her plate. She crumpled up the wrapper and tossed it into the trash can. She then picked her gyro back up and made eye contact with Coal. Marcella proceeded to lick her lips and stick out her tongue as she opened her mouth wide and slowly slid the gyro down her throat. Coal and Jim-Bob's eyes grew wide. As the gyro reached halfway down Marcella's tight throat, she quickly bit it clean in half, and in only three chews and a swallow it was gone. Coal and Jim-Bob both winced in pain of the thought. "Still wish that was your meat Mr. Coal?" she asked in her most sultry voice.

"No ma'am." Coal politely declined.

"Awww, but Coaly I'm still hungry."

"There's still half of your gyro." Coal squeaked.

Jim-Bob quickly stood up from the table, "Welp, I could use a smoke break," he said as he began to walk outside.

"You don't smoke, get back here!"

"I do now."

Marcella began to giggle. "You should see your face Coal. See I can joke too! Don't you like being teased?" She continued to giggle, until she stopped and made eye contact again. Her voice became low and smooth as she cracked a half smile, "Oh don't you like being teased Coal." She returned to normal and continued to giggle. When she managed to stop she then finished her gyro. "Lamb is so good." She patted her lips clean with her napkin. "Come on, show me how to play some of these games."

"Yeah, here in a second, let me finish my drink." Coal said.

"Come on, you can drink it over here. Sit next to me on the couch. I don't know the controls." Marcella demanded.

"Yeah, in just a second."

"Come on, Coal, is everything ok?" Marcella was becoming paranoid. She knew she had nibbled his neck, that she had almost bitten him. She was starting to panic that her new friend suddenly thought she was a monster and had grown fearful of her. "Coal, please, I'm so sorry. Please come sit with me. Please don't be scared of me! Please! I know we just met, but you and Jim-Bob are all I have left."

It became clear to Coal that Marcella wasn't teasing or playing anymore, however, the reason he couldn't stand had nothing to do with fear or disdain, it was far more embarrassing to him. "Marcy, relax. Here I come." He was beyond hopeful she wouldn't notice.

Coal stood and began to walk toward the couch, but his hopes were in vain. Marcella had indeed noticed. How could she not? Her guard was down, and she simply gazed into the large bulge in Coal's jeans. Marcella blushed, and Coal's face grew red from embarrassment. Marcella could feel more fluttering within her stomach, but she suppressed her thoughts and feelings of that nature for as long as she could. Coal sat next to her on the couch and picked up his controller. Both sat in silence as they waited for the TV to cut on and the game system to load up. Despite her best efforts, the red blush on Marcella's face was there to stay. The gaming console took its time to load up, and the branding and logos lingered on the screen for what seemed like a lifetime. Coal sorted through the menu and found a game that Marcella thought was interesting. She had seen a new co-op RPG that looked cool. They created their characters, and Coal enjoyed watching Marcella struggle through the tutorial. They were killing time before they needed to get ready to go out and meet the boys. T. Rell had texted Coal to ask if it would be OK if he brought his fiance' and Coal said everyone would love to finally meet her. Coal and Marcella had made it to the first town. Jim-Bob had leaned back in the recliner next to them and had started a nap. Without noticing, Marcella curled up and leaned into Coal, who wrapped his left arm around her so he could hold his controller more comfortably. Their characters were exploring the forest outside of town when the alarm Coal had set went off.

Jim-Bob awoke from his nap and went straight to the bathroom. Coal and Marcella got up from the couch and went to their rooms. Marcella remembered that she hadn't gotten a toothbrush yet, so she walked upstairs to find Coal. She barged in without knocking. Coal had already put a fresh pair of jeans on and was unfolding his shirt. Marcella could see his back. His shoulders were large and toned, but the muscles on his back couldn't seem to distract her from all the little burn scars on it. Tiny little dots speckled the top half of Coal's back, but small scars from cuts were also noticeable throughout his body. Coal turned to greet Marcella, and she could see that his chest was just as impressive as his back, but his abs were carefully hidden beneath his minor beer gut.

"What can I get you, Marcy?" He asked.

"I forgot to get a toothbrush!"

"Think I might have a stash. Hang on." Coal answered as he put on his nice polo and walked into his bathroom. He could be heard rustling through his cabinets. "Hot damn, got one!" He returned with an unopened box of three toothbrushes. He tossed them to Marcella.

She caught them and smiled, "Thanks!"

Marcella went back downstairs and noticed Jim-Bob was out of the restroom. She went in and quickly brushed her teeth, and went to her room. She picked out her new gray sundress and a pair of black leather-heeled sandals. She had also gotten a new lustreglass princess pink lipstick that went well with her skin tone. She finished her look with white feathered thigh highs held up by a white lace garter belt. Marcella stepped out to meet up with Jim-Bob and Coal. She caught Coal's eye first. Coal couldn't help but step back and admire her beauty. Her incredible orchid eyes, framed perfectly by her raven hair and gray sundress, were seemingly highlighted by the sheen from her lipstick. She couldn't help but smile when their eyes met, and when she did, she sent Coal's stomach into knots. His heart raced for a few moments before he brought it under control. It felt as if air tickled the inside of his chest. He had to remind himself to breathe.

"How do I look?" she asked.

As Marcella asked she brought one knee close to her waist and gave a twirl. Her thigh highs were unable to hide her well toned calves, the featherwork drew Coal's eyes to her quads and their incredible definition.

He was entranced, such a quick and well poised twirl in a sundress filled his eyes. He thought everything about the woman before him was nothing less than stunning.

"I'll have to hide you from the moon so it don't get jealous, but for you, I think I could take it." Coal answered.

Jim-Bob's eyes widened as he cocked his head and looked at Coal, but Coal was far too distracted to notice.

Marcella lightly blushed and moved her right hand over her mouth in an attempt to hide her smile, but it was too wide; she couldn't help herself. She hadn't ever been spoken to in such a manner. Not with such sincerity and admiration. She had never been in someone's eyes as a beauty to behold and not some abomination or object of jealousy. She could feel a hint of something just beneath the stress and worry; there was a spark of happiness. She was almost scared to pursue it. Marcella was dumbstruck, looking into the gray storm of Coal's eyes. She wanted more time. She needed to be sure. Her body moved faster than her worries though as she rubbed her hand against Coal's chest, maintaining eye contact.

"I like your odds, bring me a rock back would you?" she said, naturally without thinking. Of course it was without her thoughts, after all, her mind was still in shock as she processed what she had just said. Marcella did not speak in such a way her brain told the rest of herself. She didn't know if she would listen though.

"Sure thing." Coal chuckled. "We should probably get going."

"Yeah! This is gonna be so fun! Right Jim-Bob?" Marcella asked.

As they looked around they noticed that the front door was wide open, and Jim-Bob was halfway down the drive. Marcella and Coal loaded up and began to drive. They caught up to Jim-Bob as he was opening the gate. Coal pulled the truck through, and Jim-Bob closed the gate behind him. Jim-Bob climbed into the truck, and the two men looked at the posts that were supposed to be a fence before the weekend was over, and here they were, going out drinking on a sunday. They looked at each other, smirked and shrugged. Coal began the drive south to the bar where they would all meet.

They could now see the bar in the distance. It stood out on the mainstreet of the small town they found themselves in. It had a neon sign of a cowboy pig dumping a mug into his mouth. El Cerdo Feliz was the name of the bar. As they pulled into the parking lot they could see Diego's large white truck. It was clear that he and Carlos had gone in ahead. Marcella stepped out of Coal's truck and inhaled deeply from her nose. She exhaled through her mouth. Everything was calm, save for the bass coming from within the bar. Marcella was looking forward to a chance to relax and dance, where Coal and Jim-Bob were quite excited to drink and smoke with their friends.

When they entered the bar, Carlos checked the door to see them. He lifted up his drink and shouted to them. He and Diego seemed to be in an intense game of pool against two large hillbillies. Carlos ordered the group drinks as Diego took his shot, glancing off his target and scratching. The hillbillies let out a loud and abrasive laugh. This seemed to offend Diego.

"You're so cocky amigos, what say we uh, how say? Make this more interesting?" Diego asked.

"Partner we got two balls till the eight and we're pretty well set up." The shorter hillbilly spoke.

"No no no, you can't laugh and eh, chicken out on me like that now can you?" Diego taunted.

"Fine, we'll take your money, name the bet." the larger spoke up.

"One hundred dollars, my cousin wants to buy drinks for the senorita that just came in."

"Two." the larger replied.

"Two?" Diego's eyes widened.

"You get cottonmouth from running it?"

"Three it is." Diego smiled.

"I like how you think boy." As the larger hick spoke he placed the ball on the table, "Eleven on this here corner." he said as he tapped the corner to his right. He let loose his cue and struck the eleven, it sailed halfway across the table, struck the edge and glided into the corner pocket.

"You boys ain't got english like'at where y'all from do ya?" The large man joked. The cue ball bounced and rolled, setting the large man up for an easy corner on the fifteen. In one loud clack it sunk. Diego's eyes stared blankly at the eight-ball then at Carlos, who was rolling his eyes. By sheer luck as the eight bounced into another corner pocket, it tapped the four, knocking it of course and leaving it just outside its hole.

"Well damn." the large man chuckled. "Welp, if you can knock the five balls you got left and the eight, you've got this."

Diego laughed sarcastically. He abruptly stopped and looked deeply into Carlos' eyes as if to beg."Corre la mesa primo."

"Supongo que puedo." Carlos nodded. He tapped the middle pocket with his cue. "Cinco." Carlos bounced the five off the wall into the side pocket. He then pointed to the corner where the eight and four were nestled. "Quatro." He didn't even line it up before shooting. The four was sent straight into the corner, and the cue had nudged the eight from any pockets while setting up the six for a ninety-degree into the side. Carlos tapped the side. "Seis." He bounced it effortlessly again, and the spin he had put onto the cue ball had made it roll in a near perfect arc. "Uno," He said as he pointed to another corner. After the arc had stopped it left him with a straight shot. He put a great deal of backspin on the cue causing it to just barely stop itself from scratching after dropping the one ball. He found himself at a nice thirty-degree angle to throw the seven into a side. He tapped the pocket with his cue. "Siete." His shot was a work of art, but it left his cue ball touching the eight, facing from three-quarters of the table. Carlos walked to the opposite side and touched the corner to his right with his hand. "Ocho." He shot at point black, putting an incredible back spin on the eight itself. Once it bounced the back wall, it all came to fruition as the eight ran straight into the corner pocket to Carlos' right. All of Carlos' friends cheered. The large Hillbilly couldn't help but smile.

"That's bullshit they hustled us!" the shorter hollered.

"Quiet boy, I was raised in the bar. I knew what that man was." He turned and reached his hand out to Carlos. "It just looked too sweet to try and hustle the hustler but I got too excited."

Carlos shook the man's hand. "Good Game Amigo."

"Good game." The man reached into his pocket and pulled out his wallet. He then counted out two one-hundred dollar bills and five twenties, and handed them to Carlos.

Carlos signaled the bartender to buy another round for his friends, and two for his opponents.

The Large Hillbilly saw Coal. "These friends of yours?"

"Yessir." Coal answered.

"And here I thought they had class." He chuckled as he walked to Coal and shook his hand.

Marcella had thought that Coal was a large man but the hillbilly standing in front of him was a Colossus. His skin was very tan, cut up and rough. His beard was long and wild, but his hair was cut short. He had a blue collar man's form. He was replete with muscle from his hard labor, but certainly didn't skip any meals, and thoroughly enjoyed the ones he had. Despite his extra layer the man didn't appear to be out of shape.

"How you been, Obadiah?" Coal asked.

"Can't complain, how you holding up?"

"Just barely." Coal chuckled.

"I hear that. Well let me go teach this dickhead how to play pool, ya'll enjoy your evening."

"You do the same, Sir."

Obadiah took his little hillbilly friend to a pool table in the corner and they continued to drink and play, until more of their friends arrived.

The bar had a sizable dance floor and Marcella dragged Coal onto it and forced him to dance. Coal was many things, dancer, not among them. He simply waved and shifted his hips side to side as Marcella grinded against him. He was unsure how to proceed so he continued shuffling, and drinking. Overall he was having a fairly nice time. Carlos was dancing on his own, Jim-Bob just waved his bottle in the air, and Diego had found a very attractive woman to dance with. Coal had just run out of his beer when he saw T. Rell come in with his fiance'

His fiance' was jaw dropping, she had incredibly dark skin which she highlighted with red lipstick and a cream colored dress and tan heeled boots. Her eyes looked like pools of honey when they caught the light.

"T. Rell, you made it!" Coal yelled as he walked over with drinks in hand.

"Man you knew I wasn't finna miss this, had to get my baby out the house you know what I'm saying?" T. Rell asked.

"Man yeah." Coal replied as he passed them two bottles.

"This right here, Latisha, and Latisha, this my boy, ole King Coal."

"It's a pleasure to meet you ma'am." Coal said as he reached out to shake her hand.

"It's a pleasure to meet ya too Mr. Coal, T. Rell speaks very highly of you." Latisha said.

"All lies I'm sure." Coal laughed.

Latisha met Coal's hand with a surprisingly strong grip and shook it. "Nah, you've got a good man's eyes Mr. Coal."

"Woah now where'd you get a grip like that?" Coal asked as he smiled.

"Cleaning and fixing horseshoes in my Deddy's stables." She answered proudly.

"T. I ain't gone lie she might be too good for you." Coal joked.

"She is too good for me brotha, that's why I had to lock her down. I ain't never had no woman bless my household like she does, you know how it is." T. Rell explained.

"I wish man." Coal laughed.

"He talkin' me up like I'm some angel when really I just be cookin' and cleanin' round the house for him," Latisha said.

"Brotha you can't understand till you've had this woman's crumbles, I'm talkin blueberries, apples, all of'em." T. Rell claimed.

"Boy stop, you gonna make me blush."

"I can't help babygirl, everybody gotta know how blessed I am." T. Rell proclaimed. The two began laughing together as they began walking to the dance floor.

Everything was going quite well. Coal was finishing his third beer, Marcella and Carlos were dancing together, T. Rell and Latisha were enjoying themselves, and Jim-Bob was leaning against a vacant pool table next to some seats. Diego however, had found a way to stir some shit. A man in a snapback and Polo had begun yelling in his face about dancing with his girl, and his friends had begun crowding Diego.

"Senor, please. We were just dancing. I didn't know." Diego explained.

"Nah bro, you grinding up on my girl like that." the Polo man yelled.

"No senor she was grinding up on me!"

"The fuck you say?"

"That's not what I meant, senor, I am simply saying that I had no idea!"

"And I'm simply saying I'm gonna whip your ass!"

"Please, sir don't get yourself hurt like this!"

"Then you don't run your mouth you fucking beaner!" As the man yelled this he began to rear his arm back, but before he could throw a punch a bottle flew from across the bar and smote his head. Before the man's friends could respond, Diego had front kicked him to the ground. Coal and T.Rell had jumped the two men behind the polo before they could move up to Diego. Several others from outside the dance floor began to approach. Jim-Bob was the only one to notice the greek letters on some of their hats. Coal and T. Rell had quickly been cornered by five of them with a few more on the way.

Jim-Bob acted quickly by attacking two of the fraternity members shamelessly from behind, performing a double-legged take down on the first and opening with a crisp backhand to the second man. The man tried to reply with a haymaker, but Jim-Bob ducked it and landed a huge uppercut, knocking him out.

Coal and T. Rell had found themselves in quite the predicament with their backs against the corner rails of the dance floor.

"Well, hell, this don't seem quite fair." Coal nudged T. Rell.

Coal quickly stepped into a left handed jab into the face of frat boy number one, followed by a violent right cross to the jaw. The second frat boy threw a punch, which Coal quickly rolled under and responded with a right hook, followed by a left hook. T. Rell grabbed the third frat boy by the shoulders, stepped forward, and wrapped the back of his head, and sent a knee to his chest, causing him to fold over, using his momentum, T. Rell stepped back, pulling his victim further forward, before delivering a right knee to his face. T. Rell then shuffle stepped to the fourth and gave him a right legged cut kick to his quads just above his left knee, throwing the man's leg out from under him causing him to fall.

Two men began to approach Marcella and Carlos as they danced. Carlos had noticed them as they approached from the corner of his eye. He turned his head to make eye contact. Without skipping a beat, Carlos reached into his pocket and pulled out a small handle, revealing its blade with a quick click. Carlos then smiled at the men and shook his head. The two men quickly turned around, and Carlos folded his switch, returning it to his pocket. Marcella, facing the opposite direction, didn't even have the opportunity to worry.

The fraternity brothers picked up their unconscious friends and left to lick their wounds. Coal could see the looks of disapproval on the face of the bartenders and staff. T. Rell and Diego were laughing with Jim-Bob as Latisha filled Marcella in on what she had missed. Once the floor was cleaned, everyone returned and started dancing again. Coal had stopped at three beers, and Latisha did not really drink. The rest of the group, however, were enjoying themselves a great deal.

"So you still in the horse business?" Coal asked.

"Nah, my Deddy is though, I moved up here to manage a little HR team over at a temp company in the city." answered Latisha.

"Wait, how's an HR manager meet T. Rell?"

"Church."

"Lord, you know his Memaw, and you still said yes." Coal joked.

"His Memaw ain't a problem if you don't stir nothing Mr. Coal," Latisha said as she popped Coal's shoulder.

"What you mean?" Coal asked.

"Boy, I seen where that bottle came from."

"Yes, ma'am, I'm sorry." Both started laughing. Latisha picked up a bottle and brought it over to T. Rell. The two started dancing with each other. While everyone else was enjoying themselves, Coal had walked over to Obadiah and his friends.

"Hey, Obadiah, you still running a logging crew down here?" he asked.

"Yeah, I'm still cock of the walk round these parts, ain't no way them ribs ready for work though," Obadiah replied.

"Just about, but I had wanted to ask if you'll had any ash trees ya'll'd be willing to part with."

"How many you need?" Obadiah asked.

"Just one if it's not to much trouble."

"No trouble at all. I could get you a good saw log for about a hundred dollars."

"Sold, y'all deliver?"

"Nother fifty"

"I appreciate Mr. Obadiah, thank you for your time." Coal said as he shook Obadiah's hand. He then pulled one-hundred and fifty dollars from his wallet and paid the man. Coal then returned to the bar area to order some debris fries and wait for his friends. It was a great night.

"So, have you ever played pool, Mr. Coal," asked Marcella as she stumbled off the dance floor.

"I've pocketed an eight or two," he replied.

"Can you play like Carlos?"

"Nah, not quite like Carlos can."

"What do you even do Coal?" Marcella hickupped, "I live with you now, but you're still such a mystery."

"Naw, I'm pretty much an open book." he laughed.

"You know I can be pretty mysterious too, Mr. Coal."

"I'm sure you can, Marcy."

"Marcy? I like your little pet names, Coal, but you know what I'd rather you call me?" Marcella asked as she fumbled over her words.

"What might that be, Marcella?"

"Mommy."

Coal exhaled deeply as he stared up at the ceiling. He blinked long and hard, but when he looked back down, there was a very drunk Marcella hunched over, with both hands in fists closed together in front of her mouth as she maintained eye contact and giggled.

"I think you might have had a few too many."

"Who might have had too many?"

"Marcella, you're a bit too drunk."

"Who's too drunk?"

"For fucks sake," Coal thought to himself, then he grinned. He took his right-handed index finger and lifted Marcella's chin, then took his thumb and lightly gripped the tip of her jaw as he leaned into her left ear, "Mommy, I think it's time we went back to my place."

Marcella let out a happy sigh as she smiled with her mouth half open and eyes glassed over. Coal could see that his friends were winding down, so he waved them over. Latisha was going to drive T. Rell home, and Coal insisted that Diego and Carlos could come home with him in his truck.

"Gracias, amigo," Diego said as he began stumbling to Coal's truck. Carlos helped him climb into the back seat.

"Jim-Bob, You gotta ride in the back this time," said Coal.

"Why do you hate me?"

"Marcella's too much of a lightweight. She's gotta sit up front."

"Fine, but I'm opening the fucking gate!" Jim-Bob tried to shout as he raised up his finger to point at Coal.

"All yours, bud."

"You're goddamn right."

Coal helped Jim-Bob and Marcella into his truck and began the drive home. In minutes, everyone but Carlos and Coal were asleep. They drove quietly and were twenty minutes down the road when Carlos spoke up.

"Hermano, left ahead."

Coal took the next left and drove for a minute before Carlos waved to go left again. Coal nodded. They took two more lefts and were back on the main road on the way to Coal's house. Carlos lifted his thumb and pointed back to a car that had just pulled off the road they had just exited.

"Cuatro, hermano."

"Yup, Good eye, amigo." Coal replied. "Let's stop for diesel." Coal drove for five more minutes before a station was in sight. As he slowed to turn, he opened his glove box open and pulled out a model 3 top-break revolver. Carlos reached up and grabbed it. They pulled into the service station. Carlos unlocked his door and undid his seatbelt. He then began peering out the window. Coal hopped out and thanked God that the pump took his card.

The car that had been following them slowed as it came to the station. Before it reached the turn, it regained its speed and continued driving. Carlos and Coal both breathed a sigh of relief. Coal filled his truck up and then hopped back in. He made eye contact with Carlos, who had been staring out the window.

"Tres." He said. "Uno olsqueó por la ventana."

"Why the hell'd he sniff out the window?" asked Coal.

"Ninguna pista," Carlos replied. "Hunting dog?" He chuckled.

It had occurred to Coal that no one but he and Jim-Bob knew about Marcella. They just thought she was a friend that was staying over. He honestly hadn't properly introduced her because he really didn't know how. They were still miles away from the house. There was no way whoever was sniffing them out the window had that kind of smell. Bloodhounds couldn't even pull off such a feat. Coal was starting to get tired, though. They had had a great night, but a long one. Carlos seemed perfectly fine, but he was used to long, grueling hours followed by looking after his crew while they went on a bender, only to show up on time for another shift. Coal was grateful to have his steely Mexican compadre with him. Carlos may not have spoken often, but he also rarely asked questions, simply responding to his situations with speed and competence.

After another ten minutes of driving, they returned home. As if a strange sixth sense had taken him, Jim-Bob awoke, climbed out of the truck, and went and opened the gate. Coal pulled the truck in, and Jim-

Bob closed the gate and crawled back into the truck. The three men that were awake gazed at the unburied posts resting in the holes as they passed through.

Once they had reached the house, Coal carefully opened Marcella's door and carried to her room. Jim-Bob opened the futon, and Carlos tossed Diego onto it. Jim-Bob collapsed next to Diego. Coal grabbed two of his cigars and went to the front porch. Carlos went to the fridge and pulled out a tripel, and then, hidden further in the beer fridge, he pulled out an import. Carlos then sat next to Coal and traded the tripel for a cigar. Carlos stared at the crown on his import while he waited for his turn with the lighter. Coal successfully lit his cigar and passed his lighter to Carlos. As Carlos held the flame to the tip of his cigar, he took a hard drag. As the cigar lit, the notes of vanilla, cream, and coffee filled his mouth. He exhaled deeply, and smoke billowed out of his mouth as if he had just fired a musket. The aroma of coffee, vanilla, and tobacco filled the air. Coal used a bottle opener, which he kept on his keychain, to open his tripel, and Carlos used his belt buckle. It wasn't a quiet night as the two friends drank. The sounds of frogs and crickets filled the air, with the occasional hefty steps as Briggs and Stratton patrolled the property. Carlos stretched and leaned back in his chair, taking a heavy hit from his cigar.

"You good hermano?" He asked as he looked over to Coal.

"Yeah, man, I'm making it." Coal replied.

"Level with me, hermano."

"It's a long and unbelievable story."

"Diego conduce mañana, all night bro." Carlos responded.

"Few days ago, we saved Marcella from some dudes we thought were methheads. Turns out she's half vampire, and those methheads were actually thralls sent by her father to bring her home. Now, we might be hunted by a vampire household trying to bring back their runaway." Coal explained. "See? Unbelievable."

"Window sniffer was sniffing Marcella?" Carlos asked.

"Shit, maybe, I ain't know how many dudes they might have out hunting her."

"I stay here?" Carlos asked.

"Naw, man, I'll keep things handled here. You and Diego have business."

"I make business quick then," said Carlos.

"Ya'll ain't gotta rush on my account, man. We'll be fine, promise." Coal assured him.

"Okay, Hermano, but I come back."

"I appreciate it, man. Ya'll have fun with your family in Mexico first, then you can worry about me, you hear?"

"I hear you Hermano, just no listen." Carlos began to laugh.

Coal joined him in laughing, both men then took a swig from their bottles and a puff from their smokes. They sat in silence a while longer as they finished their drinks and cigars.

"I gotta crash, goodnight hermano, I'll see ya'll off in the morning." Coal spoke up.

"Buenos noches hermano." Carlos replied.

Coal went up stairs to his bed, and Carlos stepped into the living room. He then carefully wrapped Jim-Bobs arm and leg around Diego before taking up the recliner and leaning back. He closed his eyes and slowly began to drift off, his drink with Coal had taken the edge off and Carlos faded into sleep.

Coal continued to lie in his bed, awake and staring at his ceiling, his box fan doing everything in its power to lull him to sleep, to no avail. Coal's mind was racing and planning. He had a bit of a rough work day ahead. He and Jim-Bob had spent the weekend with Marcella, and now he would have to haul concrete bags on his own. He could procrastinate no longer, after all, it was only a matter of time before the sun and humidity warped his posts. Memaw would surely raise hell if the fences were all warped and uneven. She had raised Coal better than to have him accept such shoddy work. He then began lamenting all the two-by-sixes he would have to nail and then paint. Under normal circumstances, he wouldn't be so troubled; it was just working to him, but he knew himself well enough to know that those worries were just a cover for the reality he now found himself in. He had an entire ash log on the way, and then that work would begin. He had enough cash to call some of his carpenter buddies.

The more he planned the less he worried. As he thought of what he could do he soon realized that this was no different to him than any other task, the sudden surprise had gotten the better of him. Now though, alone with his thoughts Coal could make himself more comfortable, and then more prepared. With his thoughts and plans at the end of their respective ropes he could now rest easy.

Chapter 3

The loud crows of chickens, summoned by the first rays of dawn, awoke the group. Coal rose from his bed and stretched. He dressed himself in the day's work clothes and went downstairs. Jim-Bob had popped up and waved his goodbyes. He needed to go to his house to get ready for work. Carlos was laughing at Diego's shock and horror from waking in the strong and handsome embrace of Jim-Bob. Coal walked down the stairs and crept to Marcella's room to check on her. There she lay, sleeping through loud cries of the roosters. Coal smiled to himself and returned to the living area. When he entered, he could see that Carlos and Diego were already pulling eggs and bacon for breakfast. Biscuits were already in the oven.

"Scrambled hermano?" asked Carlos.

"Yessir, thank you," replied Coal.

"I got patty sausage and bacon for our biscuits, is there jam in the fridge?" asked Diego.

"Yeah, grape and blueberry jellies. There's homemade strawberry jam in there, too." Coal answered.

"Memaw's? A gift from God himself!" Diego exclaimed.

Coal and Carlos began laughing. In no time there were plates filled with eggs, sausage, bacon, and biscuits. Carlos and Coal sat at the table as Diego said grace.

"Dear Father, please bless this food, we also ask that you bless our journey, and be with our dearest brother Coal as he continues his and embarks on shaping his new land into something that may please you dear Lord, please keep of safe and give us strength to move forward to the next chapter of lives. In your name, we pray, Amen."

"Amen."

The men immediately dug into their plates. The food from the bar, while tasty, did nothing for their hunger, and they had all woken starving. Diego had taken a large helping of the homemade strawberry jam, and Carlos was eating small portions of everything to offer. Coal had taken two biscuits and patties, painting the interior of the biscuits lightly with the strawberry jam. Once they had finished eating, Coal wrote a note to Marcella in case she woke up before he got back. The group split up and quickly fed the chickens before piling into the truck. Coal pulled up to the gate, Carlos jumped out and opened it. Coal pulled through, and Carlos closed the gate and hopped back in. They began driving back to the bar, where they had left Diego's truck.

Once they had arrived, Everyone exited the truck and exchanged hugs.

"You guys, be safe now and have fun with the family!" Caol said.

"We will Hermano, and we'll be back in two weeks. Make sure you get a good look at the neighborhoods, you'll have to give us the tour when we get back, find us some good property for sale." Diego requested.

"I will, man, it'll be great to have you guys around more often!"

"Likewise, man. Well, we should head out, we don't want to worry, abuela."

"Sure thing, brother, I'll see ya'll in a couple weeks." Coal responded.

"See you then!" Diego said as he climbed in the truck.

"Call if you need me hermano, I'll get in my car and be here before you know it ok?" Carlos said as he hugged Coal goodbye.

"I will, brother. Don't you worry bout me, man. I got it under control."

"See you in two then."

"See you in two." Carlos got into the passenger side.

The truck and trailer pulled off, leaving Coal waving goodbye. He went into the bar and bought a bottle of cola before hopping in his truck and heading home. He drove for thirty minutes before coming up to his gate. He hopped out and opened it. Pulled his truck through, hopped back out, closed the gate and then hopped back in.

"This fucking blows without someone riding shotgun," said Coal before he began laughing to himself. "Think I'll be looking for an automatic gate here soon."

Coal pulled up to his house and hopped out of his truck. The sun was out, but it wasn't quite hot yet. He expected to hear from Obadiah at some point about his log. Until then he finally had to force himself to load up concrete bags onto his old truck and get to filling. He would check on Marcella first, then get busy. He walked up the stairs and opened the front door.

"Coal! Are you home?" Marcella asked from her room.

"Yeah, I'm home, was gone check on you and then get to choring," he replied.

"Wait, here I come!" she yelled.

Coal could hear the sudden scrambling from her room. He waited for a minute until she made it out of her room. He stood in disbelief. Marcella walked out of her room wearing a plaid button up crop top, just barely tied around her breasts, and cutoff jeans that stopped a little way above her knees, showing off her thick thighs and sculpted quads. She had steel toes and a big straw hat. The way she glimmered in the lights of the house, he could tell that she had either stolen all of Jim-Bob's sunscreen or had bought some while they were with T. Rell. She looked incredible to Coal.

"So what do you think?" She smiled and asked.

"You look like a dream."

Marcella was taken back for a moment. She knew how blushed her face was, but she couldn't help herself. She wanted to look nice, but really, she wanted to help Coal with his chores and be a part of the team. Her chest was starting to flutter, and now she didn't know how she could spend the day with him. She also couldn't just sit in the house knowing he was hard at work by himself, either. Marcella didn't know what she was thinking when she bought her clothes, were they nice and cool to work in the heat? Maybe she did want some attention from the guy who had saved her, but she didn't expect him to speak like such a thrown brick. She quickly began to realize that they were going to be alone together for the whole day. She then thought about the rest of the week and panic was quickly setting in.

"Welp, let's get you breakfast." Coal said as he began digging through the fridge. "How you like your eggs?"

"Scrambled, please," she answered.

Coal pulled out the eggs, bacon, sausage and biscuits all from the fridge. He preheated the oven and turned the stove on. He beat the eggs in a bowl, with salt, pepper and cream. He had two skillets. He started the bacon and sausage in one, threw the biscuits in the oven, and then started scrambling. The smell of the skillets and oven crept its way into Marcella's nose. It was a simple breakfast, but it smelled wonderful. She watched Coal as he cooked for her, there was something about it that she couldn't put her finger on. There was a chance she had always fantasized about someone who would just care for her, and maybe even take care of her. It was the first time she had been in a room with a man that saw only Marcella. Not the half breed, not the heiress of her household, not a monster or waif, just Marcella. She gazed at his blue gray eyes as they focused on the skillets. She had rarely taken time to look at Coal. Marcella watched him cook. She knew how strong he was, but she was finally observing the enormity of him. He had well kept dark brown hair lightly faded at the sides framing his bangs. His beard was shaven to a curved point, highlighted by the red within it. His head rested atop incredible shoulders. They were covered by a healthy layer, but she had noticed his muscles ripple as Coal would move or work.

Once everything had finished cooking Coal loaded up her plate and passed it over. He then dug some strawberry jam out of the fridge. He had made a biscuit for himself so Marcella wouldn't have to eat alone. He spread her biscuit then his, the two then ate together. Marcella had almost finished when Coal stood.

"I'ma go see if the old truck'll run." he said as he grabbed an old pair of keys off a hook next to the front door.

"Wait, where's it at?" Marcella asked.

"Don't worry, you'll hear it."

Coal had gone down the hill to the lean-to on his second chicken barn. Once there he walked up to a silver tarp, and uncovered his old truck. It was large, black, and filled with dents. In the back were already bags upon bags of concrete. He climbed into the driver's seat and plunged his key in. He turned it one click, waited for it to heat up, and turned the ignition. In mere seconds all six pistons began pumping as the cylinders roared as they awoke. The loud rumble of the five-nine could be heard from the house as Coal pulled out of the lean-to. Marcella could see the large black truck pulling out and rushed down to hop in.

"So what are we doing?" she asked.

"I'm finna park this concrete by our gate, then go run and hop in the side by side, grab some water and start filling holes." Coal answered.

"I thought concrete was supposed to be mixed in those big spinny thingies," said Marcella.

"If this were a construction site maybe, but I'm just filling the postholes to keep my posts straight. Which reminds me, I forgot my level too." Coal explained.

"You know I've never done anything like this. I'm kind of excited, I really don't know anything about concrete."

"You gone learn today."

Coal parked the truck by the gate and the two began walking back towards the house to get the side by side and water. There was a nice breeze out. It helped keep the day cool for the time being. Coal only noticed how Marcella's hair blew in the breeze. She looked back at him and smiled, excited to help. Coal thought that Marcella had the most beautiful smile he had ever seen. He also knew it was because she had never worked with concrete, and he was going to hate to wipe that smile off of her shining face. Once they had made it to the side by side, Coal filled the tanks in its bed with water. He and Marcella hopped in and drove back down the hill. Coal double checked the truck, where he found his level.

He began prepping the worksite. He first double checked their tie lines, and then explained to Marcella that the bubble had to be in the center in order for it to be considered level. He then explained that they would line up the post along the tie, fill it half full of dirt, and then top it off with concrete mix. After the concrete mix was poured in the hole they hit it with the water off the side by side.

Marcella held the posts and made sure they were level and on the ties, while Coal filled the holes. They had been working for nearly three hours straight. It had grown hot, and Coal was starting to slow.

"Here I'll fill this one, you just hold the post," Marcella told Coal.

"Honeychild, that is a fresh unopened bag of concrete, let me get that." Coal protested.

"Nonsense I got this." Marcella heaved the bag of concrete onto her shoulder. The sudden weight took her by surprise as she fumbled three steps back and dropped the bag.

"Don't worry bout it, Marcy, I got it."

"No you've been at this for hours take a break! I can help!" Marcella ordered. As she did so she bent down to pick up the bag. Coal was treated to an excellent view of Marcella's behind. It was round and well toned, barely being contained by her jeans. Suddenly she squatted deeply and flexed her legs as she lifted the bag up.

"God damn." Coal spoke to himself.

"What?"

"Oh, nothing, let me get this post checked out."

Coal let Marcella handle the bags for thirty minutes until he couldn't stand to let such a beautiful woman do any more hard work. He took his bag position back, and in another hour, the fence posts were done. The fence could now be easily completed with just the boards and nail gun, but that was not on the list for today. Marcella could hardly believe the durability of this human. Her father had always tried to teach her that, despite their sentient lives, they were weak and existed outside of vampire existence to be consumed. She had always felt sorry for the thralls, but she could never truly believe that they were all there was to humanity. They were vicious cretins; they only cared for the chance to ascend to the ranks of lower vampires. Their morals and sense of self had vanished the moment they took on their marks.

Coal, Jim-Bob, and all of their friends were so different from the thralls and so unique from each other. They served as golden examples of her father's lies. Even so, she couldn't help but worry about him and how he was handling her running away. As much as she worried, she had no desire to return. The farms, cities, and people would now always beckon her away from the manor. She could never be locked back within it, knowing the world outside of it.

"Welp, this looks like a good time to take a lunch break."Coal said, snapping Marcella from her thoughts.

"Oh cool, what are we having?"

"Bouta fire up that there grill out the house, throw some steaks on."

"That sounds great. Can I help?" Marcella asked.

"If you want to peel potatoes while I get the pellets loaded up."

"Sure! Are we cooking out on the back patio?" she asked.

"Yeah, it's got a nice breeze out today." Coal said. They were riding the side by side back to the house. Marcella had pulled herself up to the rails and stood as he drove. The wind blew her sparkling black hair as she giggled. Coal had caught himself smiling. Once they had finally reached the house, Coal hopped out of the cart and began searching for his bag of pellets. Marcella looked for the potato peelers. They met on the back patio, and Coal loaded the grill while Marcella started to peel. Once the grill had begun the startup, Coal pulled his pocket knife from his pocket and started to help Marcy. Once the potatoes were almost all peeled, Coal went inside, grabbed a large pot, and filled it with water. He brought it out and sat it on a propane stove. Marcella and Coal then sat on the patio chairs while the waited for the grill to heat up and the water to boil.

"So what are we doing with the potatoes?" Marcella asked.

"You don't know how to make mashed potatoes?"

"I know how to peel them."

"Who doesn't know how to make mashed potatoes?"

"I grew up in a vampire household!"

"Girl, you grew up in a damn southern vampire home, didn't you!"

"Yeah, that's why you're lucky I'm not eating you now!" Marcella jokingly yelled.

"Hell, Marcy, I'd be a lot luckier if you would." Coal laughed.

"What?" Marcella chortled as she began to blush.

"Nothing."

"Sounded a lot like something to me." Marcella began smiling devilishly.

"Just words, honey, I'ont even think they were in the right order."

"Am I your honey Mr. Coal?" Marcella was smiling so widely her teeth were showing, not a nice smile though, hers was far more fiendish.

"Now, Miss Marcy, you can't be talking like that while you're sober, I don't know how to act around pretty and forward women." Coal spoke as he realized he bit off more than he could chew.

"Maybe I'll just get drunk and beg you to call me mommy again."

"Plan b it is."

"What?"

Coal stood from his patio chair, and grabbed the rail of the deck as he jumped over it. It wasn't a long fall, so it was easy for him to catch himself, and after doing so, he began to walk around the house.

"Coal? Coal, where are you going?"

"To the church where the women don't scare me!"

"Coal, you can't call me scary, you'll make me cry!"

Coal continued walking as Marcella laughed harder and harder. She had leaned back in her chair and closed her eyes from the force of it. She let out a long sigh and looked up as the grill started beeping. Marcella leaned over the rail where Coal had walked off.

"Coal, I don't know how to work the grill, and it's yelling at me!"

"It's all good, that just means it warmed up and started." Coal said as he walked out the back door with a bag of marinated steaks and two beers. He took the two steaks out of the bag and placed them on the grill. He then came and sat back on his chair. He opened his beer and took a swig. Marcella held out her hand for the other beer. "Oh no, hun, both of these are mine, you can hit up the fridge, though." Coal chuckled.

"I don't wanna."

"I don't see any other option."

"I do." Marcella stood from her chair and walked over to Coal. She then straddled him in his seat and took the open beer from his hand. She took a large sip and then used her left hand to caress Coal's chin and tilt his head up. His jaw was already dropped, so she poured a decent swallow of beer into his mouth. He swallowed, but his eyes were wide, and she could feel his legs begin to tremble. She immediately jumped off. "Coal, I'm so sorry; I didn't mean to make you uncomfortable."

Coal snapped out of it, smiled, and shook his head. "No, no, you're fine, you just caught me off guard. No worries."

"Are you sure? I was just playing honest!"

"Seems like a fun game. I just don't quite know the rules yet, that's all."

Marcella turned red from embarrassment. "Do… Do you have plans for Friday Coal?"

"Not to my knowledge, why?"

"Do you think we could go out?" Marcella meekly asked.

"Yeah, I could see what Jim-Bob's up to."

"No I meant like, like…" Marcy's voice began to shake as she began to lose her nerve.

"You mean just us?" Coal asked.

"Yeah."

"Well sure, let me flip these steaks real quick." Coal said he grabbed his tongs and began flipping. "What'd you have in mind?"

"I don't know, it seems silly."

"Whatchu mean?"

"I guess I always wanted to go on like, a regular person date. If that makes since." Marcella explained.

"Oh, you meant a date," said Coal, taken by surprise.

"Yeah a date, wait, did you not want to?" Marcella asked as a sudden fear began to grow in her chest.

"Yeah, of course."

"You don't seem sure, Coal," Marcella exclaimed.

Coal took a deep breath, then went and sat down next to Marcella. He placed his hand on her shoulder, and tears began to well in her eyes. She didn't know how she would handle rejection from someone who saved her. She didn't know if she could live in a man's house, being provided for while keeping things platonic. Marcella didn't see Coal as someone she could just be friends with. She didn't understand the whirlwind of the weekend that made her so interested so quickly. He was strong and kind, and held in high regard by all of his friends. Was something wrong with her? Did he think she was a monster? What would cause him to want so little to do with her? So many thoughts crashed like waves in her head, like shores during a hurricane.

"Look now Marcy, you been through a lot." Coal raised his finger to her lip as she attempted to interrupt him, tears streaming down her eyes. "You have got to be the most beautiful woman I have ever seen, you're strong willed, and with a bit of an attitude. Near perfect if such a thing existed. But if I took you out so soon after helping you, I'd just feel like I was taking advantage of your whole situation, and that ain't me."

"It's not taking advantage Coal! I just want to know you better!"

"Marcy please."

"No, if you don't want anything to do with me you can't call me Marcy! You can call me Marcella."

Coal shot up from his chair. "Damn it Marcella, that ain't what I said. It takes two folks to build a damn relationship, and I don't risk shit like that! I just fuckin saved your ass! I bet right now I look like a knight in shining armor but I ain't. So what happens to me when you realize I'm just some hick?"

Marcella took a moment to think. "Coal, you're not just some hick. You're a good man with a temper, and a rough moral compass. And maybe you do excite me in a way, but I want to know you. And even if I find out you're not some knight in shining armor, I'll know you're Coal, the man who saw someone in trouble and rushed in to help. I know Coal has good friends, and I know Coal is almost fearless, almost."

"Marcella, please." Coal spoke.

"Please call me Marcy, Coal, please don't call me Marcella."

Coal began to chuckle "Confusing woman more like."

"I was wrong, and I don't like how it sounds when you say Marcella." Marcella placed her hand on Coal's shoulder. "Now Coal, you and I might just have something here, and I am strong willed, so why don't you take those steaks off the grill before they burn and we can figure this out."

"Yes ma'am." Coal said as he stepped over to the grill and pulled the steaks off, and placed them on a plate to rest. He sat back down next to Marcella. "You know I should probably mash those potatoes while the steaks rest."

"Why don't we talk for a minute, then I'll help you out ok?"

"Ok."

"So I would very much like to go out with you this friday night. Now I know you might think you would be taking advantage of me, I would like to point out that I have always wanted to go on a real date and you are the only man I know who could provide such a service. I also want to add that there are four days for me to cool off and change my mind, and if I do, I will cancel, so there is no real obligation." Marcella carefully explained.

"Marcy, if that's how you really feel, I'd be happy to."

"Mr. Coal to be honest with you I'm not sure how I really feel, so I have devised a test, therefore I am going to have to ask you to relax and not react too quickly."

"Wha.."

Before Coal had a chance to stop her Marcella had straddled him in his chair. She grabbed the collar of his shirt with her right hand, and caressed his cheek with her left before grabbing the back of his head gently and leaning in for a kiss.

Coal's eyes grew wide as Marcella straddled him and he tensed up as she leaned. Coal could think rather quickly, but he had a voice in the back of his head telling him he needed to embrace this. Before their lips touched, Coal relaxed. As her lips touched his, he could feel his chest burn. He grabbed her hips, and she exhaled softly, Coal then pulled Marcella closely to him. Marcella took her hands and ran them through Coal's hair as she tilted his head back while her chest pressed against him. She continued to kiss him as he ran his hands up her sides, giving her goosebumps, until he reached just below her breasts. He quickly gave her a gentle push breaking the contact between their lips. Marcella's heart sank for a moment as she began to worry that Coal didn't feel the same fire that she had, but before she could speak he grabbed her back and pulled her in. Ice coarse through Marcella's body as she felt Coal's teeth gently sink into her neck, and with a surge of excitement clawed his back as he began to suck. It had started as gentle suction but quickly escalated to a pinching, burning sensation as Marcella began to lightly moan. Without thinking, she began to untie her plaid button up. It effortlessly fell off the back of her alabaster shoulders, revealing a black bra that was laced from the front. Marcella broke from Coal's grip just long enough to pull the strings at the front loose. She then quickly slipped her arms through the straps of her bra and pushed it down. She had exposed her incredible breasts to Coal. They were soft and porcelain in appearance in feel. Using her right arm she pressed them up while her left pulled Coal into her chest.

"Come on, baby, don't let up. Show this half-breed how a man bites!" She hollered as she pushed her left nipple into Coal's mouth.

Coal began sucking, and as he did so he slowly closed his mouth as he pulled away, scraping Marcella's teat. Marcella bit her lip and hissed, the sharp pain was exactly what she was looking for. She was quickly realizing that the animal beneath her could make her feel more human. She liked the pain of her mortal side. Coal had pulled away for just a moment before biting the side of her breast, sucking with all his might. It was another sharp pinching sensation that slowly began to burn. Marcella began grinding herself against Coal's jeans. She could feel her instincts begin to take over, only it wasn't the desperate need to feed. It was another feeling that she had suppressed for quite some time.

"Claw my back, please!" She exclaimed.

Coal took his hands and began to light scratch against her back.

"No!" Marcella yelled. She grabbed Coal's head and slung it back. Her barbed tongue fell from her mouth and she slid it up Coal's neck while leaning in to whisper in his ear. "I'm not some half-breed princess you make it fucking hurt!" she snarled.

Chills ran through Coal and grabbed Marcella's back, digging his nails in and raked down her back. She looked up as she squealed and hissed, when she looked down, back at Coal, she was smiling. He could see rows of serrated teeth in her smile that had made their way out as she was overstimulated. She grabbed his shirt as her grinding intensified.

The sound of the potatoes boiling over snapped them back to their senses.

"Oh no!" Marcy yelped as she quickly hopped up to turn the stove off.

As she jogged over Coal could see the claw marks on her back, speckled with sparse streams of red. Marcella turned the eye off then began walking back to get her shirt. When she turned Coal had a clear view of the two massive hickeys he had left on Marcella. One on her neck, and one on her left breast. She knelt down to pick up her shirt, and as she stood she stepped forward and ran her finger up from the start of Coal's thigh all the way to the tip of his shaft, before grabbing it through his jeans and smiling.

"Everything alright, Mr. Coal?"

"You're not the only one who gives in to instincts on occasion."

"Oh?" Marcella questioned as she reached her hand down his jeans, catching her thumb on his button. "And what are those instincts telling you Mr. Coal?"

"That our mashed potatoes and steak are getting cold." He smiled.

"Yeah, honestly I'm starving." Marcy giggled. "Come one I'll help mash them up."

Marcella grabbed the potato masher and Coal grabbed a large wooden spoon. They put the pot between them and started mashing. As Marcella continued Coal left and grabbed salt, pepper, sour cream and mayonnaise. They incorporated their ingredients and once it was done they made themselves a plate. They sat back on the patio chairs. Coal looked over at Marcella. She had yet to tie her shirt back on, so her breasts pushed up from her bra uncovered. The hickey on her breast was covered but the one on her neck was there for all to see.

"You might want some concealer if we have to go to town." Coal joked.

"Why?"

Coal pointed at his neck, where her hickey would be.

"Oh this?" Marcella said as she let out a sly smile. "One of my dad's hunting hounds always said you should mark what's yours."

"Aww, are you saying you're mine, Miss Marcy?" Coal chuckled.

"I think we belong to each other." Marcy's smile widened as she pointed at her neck where Coal's jugular would be.

Coal felt his neck, and as he did so, his fingers came across a bumpy line. Coal pulled out his cell phone and looked. He could see a near-clean cut where Marcella had run her tongue up him. "I reckon you might be right."

"I am. Now eat up before it gets cold."

"Yes, ma'am."

The two sat quietly as they finished their meal. Marcella was impressed with Coal's ability to grill, but what did she expect from a southern man. Her only real gripe was that he preferred his steak medium to medium rare, but no man was perfect so she opted not to hold it against him. She enjoyed her creamy mashed potatoes as well, and the two were nearly finished when a call came to Coal's cell.

"Howdy sheriff, how're things?" He answered.

"Coal, I'm gone need you to head down the station."

"Am I under arrest?" Coal asked.

"Boy, don't play with me, I'd get you my damn self if that were the case, but me and you gotta talk, to-now."

"Aight, let me check my chicken's water and I'll head that way." Coal said.

"Yeah it's getting pretty hot out there, you take care and get here."

"Yes, sir."

Marcella looked at Coal with a puzzled look, "What did the sheriff want?"

"He said he needs to talk downtown."

"And you're just going?"

"Sheriff Lance has always been good to me Marcy, if he needs to talk, then I need to talk." Coal explained.

"I can go with you."

"Nah, that's where they were holding them three methheads and I don't want you anywhere near them or whatever runs them."

"I'm a big girl Coal, I can handle myself," Marcella said.

"And I'm a grown ass man, and I'm not about to put you in a situation where you'd have to." Coal spoke sternly.

"You're going into the same situation Coal!" Marcella began to raise her voice.

"Yeah but this ain't my first rodeo Marcy. Now I got to go refresh these waters and get going."

"I'll help water."

"Thank you baby." Coal spoke he could see Marcella begin to blush.

Marcella's chest fluttered a bit when Coal called her baby, and his genuine concern gave her butterflies. They went down the hill and began refreshing all the cups in the chicken yards. Once all the water was replenished they went back up the hill. Coal opened the door for Marcella as they went into the house.

"So is there anything I can do while I wait for you to get back?"

"Nothing I can think of, evening choring ain't a whole lot, but I'll be back before then. Tomorrow you gotta help me shop for a lawnmower," said Coal.

"Alright, I guess I'll just wait here all by myself." She softly said as she pulled the strings on her bra, allowing her porcelain breasts to pop out. "I just don't know how I'll pass the time." she continued, grabbing the button of her tight jeans.

"Try practicing your game babygirl, my back already hurts."

"You son of a bitch!" She began laughing, and as they laughed together Coal left out the front door.

Coal hopped into his truck and drove down to his gate. He hopped out and opened the gate, pulled the truck through, and then closed the gate. He looked out at the fence posts that he and Marcy had buried together. They were all equal height and straight on the lines. He thought they had made a great team. He turned his music up and began barreling down the back roads on the way to town. After thirty minutes he arrived at the station.

Coal stepped out of his truck and made his way into the station. He waved to the officers as he entered and began walking towards the sheriff's office. He knocked on the sheriff's door a few times.

"Come on in." the sheriff said as he opened the door. As Coal entered Lance pointed to the seat at his desk, and Coal sat.

As Coal sat he looked at all of the knick-knacks on the shelves and the sheriffs desk. He could see many pictures of the sheriffs hunting and fishing trips. He also noticed a quarter full spit bottle, next to the sheriff's three fast draw trophies, two gold and one silver.

"Hitting the dip a lil hard there sheriff, everything alright." Coal asked.

"Fucking peachy before you jumped them goddamn methheads we picked up."

"Woah now partner, calm it down and explain if you don't mind."

"After we locked them up saturday, they got a visitor sunday. This morning we came in and the one that had the visitor, had chewed the carotids out of the other two, and was just sitting there waiting on us." Sheriff Lance explained.

"The one that got visited, did he change any?" Coal asked.

"He's still human and you need to explain to me why you think he wouldn't be."

"What do you mean?"

"Don't bullshit me Coal, I ain't never met a druggy that could keep their mouth shut like them. Fuck is going on? And don't you give me no you won't believe me shit either, cause I just spent an hour on a mop and bleach."

"The girl we saved from those three was a half vampire daughter to some household head, and they're trying to get her back."

"That explains it." said the sheriff.

"It does?"

"You ain't never seen a man eat two other men without them putting up a fight have you?" the sheriff questioned.

"Have you?"

"Not until I looked at my security footage this morning. They trying to take this woman against her will?" Lance asked.

"Yes, sir."

"You got her hidden away?"

"Yes, sir."

"Alright, you keep her safe and hidden, but if this shit gets all up in my city, I'll have to lay down the law." The sheriff narrowed his eyes and leaned towards Coal. "What's she look like?"

"Everything about her is incredible, Sir."

"If that's the case, you get in a bind. You call me right after Jim-Bob, you hear?"

"Yes, sir."

"You done good boy, you done stepped in it too, but I reckon you got choring to do and business to handle so I won't keep you no longer." The sheriff said as he waved Coal out the door. "And Coal!"

"Yes, sir?"

"You be safe, call me if you need me, and we proud of you, all of us."

"I appreciate it, sir, I really do."

Coal stepped out of the station and hopped in his truck. He turned on his radio and drove off. As the sheriff watched him, one of his deputies stepped up to him.

"Was that Lisbeth's son that jumped them weirdos and saved some lady?"

"That'd be him."

"He ain't come up like them, did he?"

"Not at all, so if you hear me running code toward his new house, ya'll be a little late responding to it, alright?"

"Yes, sir." The deputy and all the sheriff's men agreed.

While Coal was gone, Marcella kept herself entertained playing the RPG he had shown her how to play. She had put on more comfy clothes and was curled up on the couch when she heard a horn honking from the gate. She peered outside to see an eighteen-wheeler with a crane arm and large saw log on its trailer. Marcella could hear a large man bellowing out for Coal. She leapt from the couch and ran outside. She went to the side by side and sat in the driver's seat.

"I can't drive."

She then began running to the gate. As she neared the truck she could see the colossus she had come to know as Obadiah and the younger man he played pool with sunday. The third man was tall and gangly, smoking a cigarette. They all had reflector vests and hard hats.

"Scuse, ma'am, is this Coal's residence?" Obadiah asked, he didn't recognize her.

"Yes, sir, let me get the gate for you."

"Thank you, ma'am. Would you happen to know where Coal wanted this log?"

"No sir, I'm sorry."

"It's no problem miss, just direct us way the hell away from his birds."

"Yes, sir," Marcella said as she opened the gate. Obadiah pulled the eighteen-wheeler through and stopped. The man riding a shotgun hopped out as Marcella closed the gate. He jogged up to the end of the trailer, climbed up, and took a seat.

"Catch side saddle with Big O so you can point him to a good spot, if you don't mind." the man said.

"Sure thing!" Marcella said as she climbed into the big rig.

"Howdy, ma'am, where to?" Obadiah asked.

"If you head up the drive and get on the side road by the house, it'll take you behind Coal's chicken barn."

"That up or downhill of his birds?"

"It's downhill, but it's got a flat clearing," Marcella explained.

"Sounds like a plan," Obadiah said as he began to pull off. "So you're Coal's old lady?"

"I think that's about right."

"Damn and he got you visiting while he's off rat killing somewhere?"

"No sir, I live here."

Obadiah appeared puzzled as he looked at Marcella. "I ain't think Coal was the shackin' up type."

"It's complicated."

"Ain't no way y'all told his memaw."

"No sir."

"Boy, you must be special for him to step on that land mine." Obadiah began laughing. They pulled off the side road into the clearing, and Obadiah hopped out of the truck and walked around to the flatbed. When he reached the trailer, he grabbed the edge with his massive arms and, threw himself up, and then made his way to the end of the log. His smaller friend was at the other end, and the smoker was already in the crane. Obadiah and his friend secured the log, and the smoker carefully lifted it up and set it on the ground next to the trailer. Obadiah took some wooden wedges from the trailer and choked the log. After making sure it was safe and secure, Obadiah waved to his men, and they loaded up into the truck.

"You can tell Coal the chocks are on the house. Reckon, we'll head on out."

"Nonsense, Coal will be right back, and we have plenty of mashed potatoes if you boys are hungry." Marcella told Obadiah.

Obadiah held up his radio. "You boys hungry?"

"Man shit, I'm libel to catch the next possum we see on the side of that there road and slap that fucker with some mayonnaise, I tell you what." the smoker rattled off.

Obadiah sighed, "Well, I reckon we can stay for a bit."

"Awesome! I'll see if we have anything we can grill."

"Well we sure do appreciate your hospitality."

Obadiah climbed back into his big rig and drove back up to Coal's house. The three men got out of the truck and walked around to the back patio. They made sure to knock the mud off of their boots before stepping up the stairs. Once there they all took a seat and politely waited. While Marcella was pulling the pot of mashed potatoes Coal had pulled in and was walking in through the front door.

"Welcome back!" Marcella yelled as she dropped the potato pot on the counter, ran over and kissed Coal's cheek. Coal couldn't help but smile and when he did Marcella began to giggle. "Oh I almost forgot, Obadiah's here, they just dropped off a log."

"Yeah, I had seen where he tried to call, so I grabbed some ground beef and buns if they still here."

"Yeah they're sitting out back."

Coal took his bags out back and greeted the three men. He shook hands with Obadiah, then the smaller friend then the smoker. "Sorry bout that man, I had some business uptown and my phone was on silent."

"Weren't no problem, made me uncomfortable to take your cash up front so i had to go ahead and get you handled. Your old lady let us in." Obadiah's face shifted from a pleasant greeting to abject horror. "Brother I didn't even introduce myself or my crew."

"I don't think she minds. Obadiah, this here's Marcella, and Marcella, this mountain of a man is Obadiah, or Big O to some."

Obadiah shook her hand. "Pleasure to meet you, Miss Marcella, this is my crew here. The little one's Dick, and the smoker's Squirrel."

The two men shook her hand.

"It's nice to meet you, Miss Marcella," said Dick.

"Man I tell you what a joy it is to make your acquaintance ma'am," Squirrel added.

"Nice to meet y'all too! Oo I forgot the mashed potatoes!" Marcella exclaimed.

"Yeah, and I gotta go get my mixing bowl for these burgers." Coal explained.

They both went back inside to grab their food and kitchenware. Marcella put the mashed potatoes over the stove and Coal plopped the ground meat into his mixing bowl. He then added salt, pepper, cajun seasoning, garlic, onion powder, hot pepper sauce, and then a few shots of whiskey. He then began mixing the ingredients.

"I can pre-heat that grill for you, boss," Squirrel said as he manned the grill.

"Preciate it man, I shoulda got that before I got my hands dirty." Coal chuckled. "Y'all need a beer?"

"Naw, we got a few more logs when we get back, can't be drinking." Obadiah answered.

"Hell O, I didn't mean for you to take time off for a log. I appreciate it, though."

"Shit, we're the number one crew in the company right now, we didn't clock out," Obadiah said as he began to laugh. "We'll call this a lunch break."

"Aight," Coal laughed, as he started throwing fresh patties on the grill.

Everyone sat down as they waited for the patties to cook, Squirrel leaned next to the grill and kept watch, spatula in hand. As they waited Coal mixed up some strawberry lemonade and passed glasses out.

"So why do they call you big O?" Marcella asked as she sipped her lemonade.

"Tiny weiner." Squirrel snorted.

"Ha ha, but naw, that ain't it," Obadiah responded.

"Tell me the story, I have to know." Marcella pleaded.

"Well, we were about eleven logs away from hitting this fatass bonus, and we had been running behind for a while cause of some heavy equipment failures, and we were this close to pulling it off on the last day when some of our rookies fucked up and sent raw gas through our saws, locked every one of them fuckers up. Our crew lead at the time lost his shit and stormed off. Course, we were cutting big timber to land our bonus, so I could understand his frustration, but we were too close. So I rustle around and find me an ax and walk up to the crew while they're trying to figure shit out, and I tell'em 'any'a y'all pussy out leave your bonus in my lunch box I'm goin down the hill.' I felled seven of the twenty-three trees we finished off by myself and landed me a sweet new crew lead gig." Obadiah finished his story.

"That's awesome," said Marcella.

"Hell yeah it is." Coal added.

"Preciate it," Obadiah responded.

The burgers were finally done and Squirrel had scooped them onto a tin tray. Marcella gave the mashed potatoes a final stir, and Coal went in to grab the buns and condiments. Everyone made themselves a plate and sat back down.

"So what you plan on doing with that log down there?" asked Obadiah.

"Man, I got all sorts of little woodworking projects I got planned." Coal answered.

"Cool, well I'm pretty sure you'll be happy with log down there." Obadiah said before finishing his burger.

"Yes, sir, and I appreciate y'all coming all the way out here for me."

"No problem man, welp we better get going though, we pretty close to finishing this place out and might get some more down time." Obadiah explained. "Thank y'all for the meal."

"Yeah man, good burgers, I'm telling you," Squirrel added.

"Thank y'all very much," Dick continued.

The three men loaded up in their truck and pulled off. Squirrel opened the gate, and Obadiah pulled through. Squirrel closed the gate, then jogged to the truck, and they drove off.

"Why do you think they call him Squirrel?" asked Coal.

"He prolley eats them little fuckers with some mayonnaise," Marcella answered.

"What?" Coal asked just before Marcella burst into laughter.

"So what else is left for today?" she asked.

"I'll probably just check the chickens one last time, then be lazy the rest of the day."

"Sounds good to me."

Coal walked down the hill and chicken his teepees and barn. Took a good long look at how his chicks were coming up. Once he had made sure everyone's water was clean, he went back up the hill. As he came up from the hill, he could see Marcella standing at the top of the steps. She was barefoot in short shorts and a tank top. In her hands, there was a beer for her, and an opened beer, and freshly clipped cigar for Coal. Coal quickly combed his mind to see if he had ever seen a more beautiful sight.

"You must be trying to get married after the first date." Coal chuckled.

Marcella blushed, "Well you might just be the only man who'd ever take me, so I might just need to make a good impression."

"Hell, I can think of ten men off the top of my head that would kill for a woman like you."

"You're too much. You've only known me for 3 days."

"And we have lived together for three days." Coal began to laugh.

"Fair enough."

"Welp," Coal began. "I gotta go make some calls for a little bit, I'll be back in a few."

"You haven't even finished your beer or started your cigar."

"Yeah, but I don't need to put this off for too long."

"You can put it off long enough to curl up and watch the birds with me for a little while." Marcella insisted as she held up Coal's cigar.

"I reckon you're right." Coal smiled.

"Damn right, I'm right."

"Can't think of a time you were wrong." Coal sat down next to Marcella,, who leaned on him and kissed his cheek. She then curled her feet up on the patio couch and started staring out. Coal wrapped his arm around her. He then leaned back and lit his cigar.

"How do they make it smell like vanilla and not just tobacco?" Marcella asked.

"I think these are infused. They're pretty nice."

"My dad always hated flavored tobacco. He always said that it was no substitute for good aging." Marcella began to giggle.

"Think I'll take my roasted vanilla over his burnt leather any day."

"I take it you prefer grape juice to vintage, too, then?" Marcella grinned.

"I'm not a fan of either. I'm a lemonade and apple juice enjoyer."

"Oh, I love strawberry lemonade."

"You a sweet tea type of girl?" Coal asked.

"I've never had any."

Coal began coughing violently and shook his head. "The hell you mean you never had sweet tea?"

"Coal, we've been through this already."

"Nah, naw, I'm taking that shit personally! How you gone raise someone down here with no sweet tea? What'd y'all eat and drink? Don't answer that."

Marcella laughed at the flustered Coal. He was cute in his own way. She also wondered what she had missed growing up in her father's manor.

Coal seemed as though he had lived quite the life compared to her. She worried that she was the odd duck. Of course, she was a half-breed, but they had had so many stories and adventures when compared to her very sheltered life. The two sat quietly and watched the land as they finished their beers and Coal's cigar.

Once they were finished, Coal got up from the patio couch and left to make his calls. Marcella decided to get up as well, to explore the property. She didn't feel like playing video games at the moment and couldn't bother Coal, assuming the calls were important or private. She went down to the chicken yards first. She looked at all the roosters. They were all uniform. They stood tall, with mostly black feathers with red feathers in their saddles. A select few oinanother separate yard looked nearly identical, with the exception of their fiery red and orange hackle feathers.

Marcella stepped into the barn to look at the mother hens and their chicks. The chicks were still young enough that they were still cute balls of fluff. As she continued walking through, she came upon the teenage chickens, who were just now getting old enough to spar. Marcella couldn't help but giggle as the gangly young cockerels tried to square off with bodies they weren't quite accustomed to. She continued up through the barn and started back up the hill. When she got back up, she went to the cages where Briggs and Straton were kept. They didn't bark as viciously when they had first met and were slowly getting used to her. She observed their homes and bowls. Their bowls were pristinely clean, and their home seemed to be custom-made. They were little insulated houses on stilts, with a unit between the cages and houses piping AC to them.

The sun was slowly starting to set, but it was still hot out. Marcella decided she would go inside and cool off. When she entered the house, she could see Coal still on the phone. He was in the kitchen standing over a pot of water that he was waiting to boil. Next to the stove was a large pitcher with an unknown, but generous amount of sugar in it. Close to the pitcher were seven tea bags with the tabs pulled out. Marcella continued to pass and lay on the couch in front of the fan. She could hear Coal's conversation coming to an end.

"Yeah, man, everything's still quiet here on my end, I'm off to buy that new fancy mower tomorrow. Yeah, that real big orange one with the bulldog logo. Yeah, it got a sixty-one inch cut, and it looks fucking sweet. Anyhow, keep me posted if any weird type of newcomers show up. Im'a hit'em with that," and Coal lowered his voice and imitated the deepest southern accent that Marcella had ever heard. "You boys ain't from round here, are ya?" Coal and the other voice laughed. "Aight man, you take care, aye. If you got lunch tomorrow, I'll introduce you. Hell yeah, sounds great." Coal hung up the phone as the water came to a boil. He put the seven tea bags in and looked over at Marcella. "Don't you worry, baby girl, I'm gone cure what ails you."

"What on earth do you mean? What ails me?"

Coal lifted the pitcher with sugar in it and shook it. "I got sweet tea right here, honey child, we gotta expel that vampire Yankee bullshit out of you."

"Oh my god you're so dramatic." Marcella chuckled.

"How you know drama but not sweet tea?"

"What's next, you want me to smoke a cigarette indoors and talk about how my old man is always running the roads and ain't never home?" Marcella said in a horrible accent.

"Damn right, and I'll buy you some big ole shades so people won't know you don't listen fer shiet." Coal added.

"Don't you yell at me infront of our three kids that you hope you're the father of at least one of them!"

"See how you gone know and talk like that and ain't never had any sweet fucking tea?"

"Hell Coal, maybe I just didn't want any fucking leaf juice!"

"You take that shit back!"

The two began laughing uncontrollably. Once they had finished laughing Coal adjusted the heat on his stove so the tea bags would be on a low boil for a time. After a few minutes he dumped some ice from the freezer into his pitcher. He then turned the heat off the tea. Once the boiling had stopped he slowly poured it into the pitcher and stirred it all together. He grabbed some glasses and ice. Coal poured Marcella a glass and offered it to her. She took a sip and smiled. It had a mild tang of the tea followed by the perfect sweetness.

"Where has this been all my life?" She asked.

"Every southern grocery ever." Coal said as he laughed. He looked at the time. "I reckon we can watch TV or play games for awhile, then Im'a grab a shower and head to bed."

"Sounds like a plan." Marcella smiled.

CHAPTER 4

It had just gotten dark outside of the hotel where they were staying. The Kings Suit had a large balcony where the tenants could smoke at their leisure. Two pale figures emerged from the room and sat on two chairs placed at the sides of a large ornate hookah. Each Creature held a glass of single malt scotch. One looked to the other.

"Seems a bit excessive don't you think Eric?" the thinner of the two said. He looked into the sharp and furious eyes that had now trained onto him. They had silently sat in the hotel waiting for news for quite some time, and Mark was now realizing that now was most definitely not the time to break it.

"Well, Mark, given my assignment to retrieve your now ex, and the heir apparent to the House, that you let run off, I believe the level of nicotine and stress relief that I may garner from this device to be most apropo."

"She's a young woman running away from home, I'm sure she'll come crawling back to daddy when things get a little more difficult," Mark explained.

"Yes, because the coddled child being suddenly exposed to the horrors that we perceive to be a necessity will most assuredly return in a most expedited fashion."

"You know Eric, they say sarcasm is the lowest form of wit."

"Yes Mark, but I believe proper communication is one of many keys to success therefore I have elected to utilize language at a level I believe you can comprehend."

"Someone's feeling zesty I see."

"Like a lemon, Mark, like a lemon." As he finished speaking Eric took a massive drag from the hookah and bellowed out a column of smoke. "What have you found gentlemen?"

"What?" Asked Mark in confusion.

"We've searched a few towns, possibly set up a perimeter so we should be able to narrow it down to the rural area between the city and two, towns. I'm taking the pup out tomorrow." Said a large man who stepped out onto the balcony. He was grotesquely muscular. His head was cleanly shaved, and he was covered from head to toe in nordic runes and tattoos. A long, braided blonde beard flowed below his mirrored round shades. Mark was noticeably startled by his sudden appearance.

"Excellent work Hrólfr, this is the same pup you spoke so highly of?" Eric asked.

"Yes Mister Eric, he has the finest nose of the pack. I was briefed on the importance of this hunt, so I could bring only the finest."

"Hrólfr, I believe you simply are the best," Eric said.

"Thank you for your kind words. We will begin once we are properly rested."

"But of course." Eric turned his gaze back to Mark. "Could you at least endeavor to embarrass me as little as possible?"

"He got the drop on me, what do you want from me Eric?" Mark angrily asked.

Eric stood slowly from his chair and walked over to the rail of the balcony and began rubbing it with his hand. He stopped and looked over. "My sincerest apologies for ruining what seems to be a pleasant evening."

Mark shot from his chair and stepped up to Eric. "What are you even talking about? Who are you talking to? Other people I haven't seen yet?"

Eric continued to stare at the lights of the streets and stores illuminating the pitch black night. "Mr. Mark I believe I must remind you that you are here only at the behest of the Father. This circumstance was hoisted upon me despite my most eloquent protest. And I must also remind you that I am very much your senior, and I will tolerate no such disrespect, especially in front of such auspicious guests."

"And how won't you tolerate me?"

"I can see why someone as kind as Marcella would flee. You are too dense to comprehend the situation around you as it evolves and you are certainly too short of temper to maintain even the slightest bit of composure at the mildest of insults. Take some time to reflect upon the repercussions of your incompetence and ill manners as you recover."

"Recover?" Mark asked.

Without warning or hesitation Eric swiftly looked up from the streets, making eye contact with Mark as he grabbed the collar of his shirt and effortlessly threw him over the rails. "Hrólfr, fancy a drag?"

"Of course sir." He replied as he took a seat with Eric.

Mark continued to plunge toward the ground in utter disbelief. His partner had thrown him off the top of a hotel over something so miniscule, with audacity to comment on his temper. He didn't care, he needed to find Marcella. He was only given the chance because Marcella's father hoped that he would be able to convince her to return without the need for force or violence. It occurred to him that Eric was indeed very much his senior, and one of the most trusted vampires within the household. The situation appeared to be so serious that a pack leader was summoned, and he had brought his prodigy to ensure their success. Mark knew that the head wanted his daughter back, but to expend this many resources seemed so far past overkill. He began to worry that there was far more at play than he had been briefed on. Everything seemed so need to know, and no one thought he needed to know.

His thought process was interrupted by his sudden impact upon the concrete of the street. His bones shattered upon the impact and the horrid crackling resonated in his ears. His head began to spin and ache as his brain wrapped around his fracturing skull. In an absolute daze his eyes couldn't help but fixate on his fangs and teeth as they exploded out of his mouth as the force reverberated back through his body. He laid there for at least five minutes before his body had reconstituted enough that he could drag himself into an alley to hide. It was almost fortunate how dead the street was, Eric would be most displeased if Mark had caused a fuss. Mark could only grit his teeth as he continued to crawl. The jagged edges of his broken bones caught what seemed to be every bump and crack in the street, pulling at his already torn flesh. He had certainly learned to hold his tongue when speaking with Eric.

After another hour of hiding Mark could finally walk. He pulled himself up and began to casually stroll back to his room. He entered the lobby of the hotel and politely waved to the horrified front desk clerk.

"I'm sorry miss I seem to have lost my room key, do you think I could get a new copy?"

"Oh my lord! Sir, are you ok?" She asked as she continued to tremble.

"Nothing a good shower won't fix."

"What room?"

"The king's suit."

"Here you are!"

Mark took the new copy then went to the elevator, where a cute couple were distracted with themselves. "Hold the door please!" Mark called out as he began to speed up, but he was ignored. "Hold the door please!" He yelled louder.

He was ignored again, and was infuriated. He broke out into a sprint and caught the door as it was mere inches from closing, and wrenched it open. The couple looked at his blood covered, torn clothes and leapt back into the wall of the elevator.

"Are you really going to ignore me twice while I'm saying please so politely?" Mark asked.

"I'm sorry sir, we were just distracted! I promise!" the boyfriend answered.

Mark let out a deep exhale, and quietly counted to ten. The couple stared at him as the doors closed and the elevator began to move. He shook his head and pressed the button for the top floor and stepped away from the door and stood next to them. The couple sank back into a corner trying to get as much distance as possible from Mark. The elevator door opened.

"I think this is you," Mark said. The couple stood frozen. Mark responded with a puzzled look and began waving them out. They broke from their shock just long enough to run away onto their floor. "It's rude to stare, you know!" Mark called out as they ran. He began chuckling to himself as the doors closed.

Mark quietly let himself back into their suite. He then walked over to Eric who was still sitting on the balcony. Eric was sifting through pamphlets of the local sights and eateries. He was also checking the movies that were playing while referencing their trends online.

"Planning our date Mr. Eric." Mark joked.

"Tell me Mark, when Marcella escaped you, how much money did she make off with?" Eric asked.

"None I think, but why does that matter?" Mark asked.

"Once again, you have underwhelmed me."

"Then would you please explain instead of insulting me Mr. Eric?"

Eric couldn't help but grin. "You see Miss Marcella has been running for quite some time. She has the rare ability to sustain herself off of human food, but do you know what human food is not Mark?"

"Inedible to us?"

"While technically correct you have missed the direction of which we will derive our conclusion."

"What do you mean?"

"We do not hunt ourselves, dear Mark. We hunt Marcella. So what is a key feature of human food?" Eric asked without hinting too much.

"Its flavor?"

"Its cost Mark, food is not free. Now can you think of why I would be researching where in these population centers the density of human activity would be highest?"

"If she can't eat human food, her vampiric instincts will take over her." Mark suddenly realized.

"Bravo Mark, and with her powerful, mortal metabolism it should only be a matter of time before we catch her in a feast. Therefore I am compiling lists and areas within the perimeter that the hunting dogs have established. Lists for day and lists for night."

"I see."

"Excellent, I was beginning to worry what good a blind vampire would be to me."

"So what are we doing tonight?" asked Mark.

"We need to reach out to my contacts in the area and gather intel on the factions that retain power in this region. If we are to hunt in their territory proper introductions and requests must be made."

"What about them?" Mark questioned as he gestured to the sleeping hounds.

"Let my puppers sleep, I need them well rested so they can cover greater distances during the day. They will also start splitting up tomorrow and I need the new hound sharp."

"So where to?"

"A quaint little club I'm quite unfamiliar with, but I am led to believe it may be a small front for one of the local covens," Eric explained. "Our ride will be arriving a short while from now, you have time to shower and put on some clean clothes."

"Alrighty then."

Mark took his shower, then dressed himself in a suit. He took the elevator to the lobby and stepped out to see Eric waiting by the entrance, smoking a cigarette As Eric smoked a black sedan pulled up. Eric waved over to Mark and stepped into the vehicle. Mark entered and found the interior quite surprising. It was rather spacious and the cab was completely separated from the back of the car. Eric had already sent the driver the address, and as Mark buckled his seatbelt the car pulled off.

"So what do we know about this club, Mr. Eric?"

"I know the password to get into the basement VIP section. The main floor will be lousy with humans. We had no real interest in this region so my network is rather weak here and my intelligence is beyond lackluster. It's probably one of the reasons I was assigned to the task."

"Do we know what factions are in the area?"

"No, Mark, I'm afraid we have no choice but to walk in blind," Eric explained.

"Let me guess, I should let you do all the talking?"

"No Mark, If I keep you on such a short leash you won't be able to grow, you have been given a great opportunity to work with me, and I shan't squander it by micromanaging you and stunting your progress."

Mark could scarcely believe his ears. Never had he encountered such arrogance, and yet, he had never been so unsure. He knew Eric had been considered to be the Father's right hand despite being many years younger than many ranking vampires. He was right in all honesty, this was a great opportunity to see what it was that made Eric so special.

They arrived at their destination and stepped out. The bass from the club rattled the signs and businesses outside of it. The two approached the doorman.

"Apologies sir, I'm quite thirsty and seeking a most rare vintage, will you show me to your cellar?" Eric inquired.

"Right this way sir."

The doorman took them through the club. They caught the eyes of many through the strobes. It occurred to Mark that they were quite overdressed. He could see the movements of scantily clad women dancing in time with the strobes. The fog machines added much to the mesmerizing atmosphere. They moved around the dance floor however, never entering it. The neon lipsticks and eyeliners seemed to beckon Eric and Mark. Men of their stature, posture, and level of dress were a rare sight at this scene and the young ladies longed to tempt and experience such rarity. Eric paid them no mind as he scanned the club, assessing everything he laid eyes on. They were finally brought to a large red door. The man opened it, revealing a long flight of stairs descending into an unknown depth.

They two started their descent, and as they did so, the door was shut behind them. The bass still managed to permeate the thick layers of earth even as they descended.

"I can understand the human fascination with loud and explosive drum beats and hard bass, but I find the lack of composition inexcusable." said Eric as they descended.

"You think the strobes and hard bass serve any type of purpose? Like, are they meant to disorient the guests so they're easier to pick off?" asked Mark.

"Mark, I believe you may be correct, while many of the human variants of such noise are wretched, they have yet to create bass and beats that entrance and baffle in such a manner."

After some time the two had arrived at the base of the stairs, in front of another large red door. This large red door had a circle painted on it, and within the circle was a cartoon cat with little bat wings. Eric let out an aggravated sigh as he pushed the door open. The lobby they could now see was filled with a number of vampires sitting at separate tables. A few tables were adorned with the unconscious bodies of club members that had been picked off. At the center of the lobby was an incredibly gorgeous blonde woman in a red cocktail dress. She sat at a large round table and smoked a cigarette from a long ivory holder. She smoked with her left hand, and slowly lifted her right and waved them over with her index finger.

Mark was anxious. He didn't recognize anyone in this lobby. Surely they would have known about a coven this large. Sure, it was some distance from their own household but it should not have been able to fly under anyone's radar for as long as it had. Smoke and sage wafted in the air throwing off his senses, so he couldn't get a real read on any of the unknown vampires. Eric boldly walked straight to the woman's table while Mark took a few moments to gather himself. As Eric reached her table he reached out his hand. She offered hers in return and he took it and kissed it. He then waved Mark over to his seat. Mark sat down first. Eric stood there for a moment, and reached his left arm out, plucking a glass from a passing waiter's tray. He then sat down, leaning back in his seat and crossing his right leg over his left. He placed his left elbow as a brace in the arm of the chair. He stared into the glass as he swirled it.

"Thin, and filled with adrenaline. Your collector must be off his game." Eric said, placing the glass on the table. He slid it to the woman.

"Excuse me?" she gasped.

"You're excused, I had taken the seat for the view but I find your lack of introduction to be repulsive to say the least." Eric stated as he stretched his hands out on the table and brought them together, intertwining his fingers.

"My name is Aria, care to explain why you have so boldly barged into my lounge?"

"Well Aria, I happened to be in the area, and thought introductions were necessary. You may call me Eric, and this is my protege Mark. We are looking for a runaway and were hoping you would be able to help us. Is your head here?"

"We don't use those old titles, and you may speak with me on the matter."

"I may speak with anyone, but I would prefer your leadership were it possible." Eric grinned.

"I am the leadership in this lounge, now tell me about your little runaway."

"They are the heir apparent of our house, but seem to have flown the nest in search of their own glory and riches, but you see his father has fallen under a curse and we must make preparations for a smooth transition of power."

As Eric spoke he searched his peripheral vision. A man with gray eyes with blackening veins creeping on his fate seemed confused. He shook his head and pulled his white hoodie over his head and continued to nurse his drink.

"I'm sorry, but I don't think we can really help," Aria explained.

"That's quite all right, I understand. Do you think it would be possible to arrange a meeting with the leader of this coven?"

"I already told you I'm the leader here, and I'm afraid you have overstayed your welcome and need to leave."

"Why should I leave so soon? Could I not imbibe in this incredible atmosphere? May I not sample your adrenaline riddled glasses? Perhaps I could share in a takedown so careless that our prey had time to fear?"

"I have had enough of your insults little man! I can't stand how you household vampires look down on us! You're no better than us! We're all vampires here!" She yelled as she erupted from her chair. Aria waved to her bouncer.

Mark was confused as to what his next course of action should be. He thought they were there to make introductions but Eric's entire demeanor had changed since he saw the painting on the door. And now he had gotten the bouncer called on them in an unfamiliar underground lounge, surrounded by unknown and possibly unfriendly vampires.

The bouncer spoke as he approached, "Come on mr. monkey suit, your little girls not here!"

Eric could no longer contain himself as he leaned back in his chair. His left palm cradled his cheek as his lips began to part. The woman's expressions of anger and disdain turned to horror. Eric's smile had revealed itself. His serrated teeth pulsated with anticipation, and his fangs trembled with excitement. His eyes pierced the very soul of the creature in front of him.

Eric's mouth creaked open as he spoke softly, "You see, this is my problem with strays. You are too dense to comprehend the situation around you as it evolves, and you are certainly too short of temper to maintain even the slightest bit of composure at the mildest of insults. Had you maintained your composure, you would understand that your man has just given up the game and that no one should be approaching me."

The bouncer had approached Eric from the left and placed his hand on Eric's shoulder. "Time to."

These were all the words that Eric would allow him. As the hand made contact with his shoulder Eric rolled his eyes. As the bouncer dared to speak Eric unrested his cheek and sent his hand effortlessly through the bouncer's throat. He wrapped his fingers around his cervical spine and in one clean and violent motion, jerked down and behind himself. Aria couldn't help but scream in horror as her bouncer's head was so easily torn from his shoulders. Mark's blood went cold, he had never seen a vampire kill another vampire. Aria continued to cry and scream for help.

"Will you cease your incessant wailing?" Eric insisted.

In one motion, Eric's left leg kicked him and his chair backwards as his right knee knocked the table up. The chair and Eric came to a stop as the table leveled out as it fell. Once Eric decided the angle was correct he kicked the edge with his right leg, sending the gorgeous mahogany cleaving through Aria's sternum and into her lungs. She gurgled in agony as she was pinned against her booth. Eric then raised his left hand and began waving to the vampire in the white hoodie to come over. All of the other vampires were fleeing from such a horrific act. A vampire killing another was unheard of and nearly blasphemous to the strays.

"Mark, could you escort that gray veiny gentleman to our table, I'd like a word."

"Yes Mister Eric, one moment please." Mark scurried over to where the man was. He was still frozen with fear, and Mark was also forcing himself through each step. In a world of vampires he had the misfortune of finding himself in the company of a monster. And this monster was hunting Marcella.

Mark helped the man to his feet and guided him over to where Eric was sitting. As they walked Eric snapped his fingers at a waiter frozen at the bar of the lobby. Once the waiter was looking at him, Eric pointed at some empty glasses on the back shelf of the bar. He then waved the waiter over. The waiter quickly brought three empty glasses over. Eric retrieved a flask from his suit pocket and poured each glass till it was half full.

"Pull him up a chair please Mister Mark."

"Yes sir."

Mark pulled the chair up for the man and Eric pointed to it. The man took the seat and Mark walked around and sat next to Eric. Eric started to speak but was interrupted by the bothersome gurgling of Aria. Her blackened vampiric blood spilled from her mouth as tears ran down her face. She then began coughing and gasping as her lungs attempted to heal themselves.

"Do you mind? I'm trying to speak." Eric said as he gazed into the weeping eyes of Aria. He looked up for a moment as he let out an exasperated sigh. "I suppose I could move the table, but if I do I'm almost positive you'll start crying again." Aria shook her head. "Very well, but one screech or wail and I'll feed your heart to our new friend here." As Eric finished his sentence he grabbed the table and started slowly pulling it back. "Can't risk spilling our drinks, I'm sure you understand."

The table slowly pulling back allowed Aria to free her arm. She quickly grabbed her mouth and held it shut. The retching sounds of her ribs slowly reforming around the table as it moved would have been overwhelming enough but the pain of her nerves reigniting as they too rejuvenated was quickly sending her into shock. She held onto her mouth though, staring into the eyes of Eric, knowing the consequences should she disturb or interrupt him. The gaze returning her own was terror beyond her comprehension. His dilated eyes were unblinking, drinking in everydrop of her agony. The table moved so slowly she could hardly see so much as a ripple across the three glasses before them. Finally, it pulled free of her torso and her lungs sprung back, but Aria stopped herself. She knew to breathe slowly and quietly. The sudden changes running across the expressions of her face were not unnoticed by Eric. His horrid disfigured smile was on full display. He began to clap his hands in applause.

"Well done Miss Aria, you have impressed me! I truly believed you would slip just before the ribbon, but here you are!" Eric cheered as he pulled his flask back out and slid it across the table to Aria. "Take it all, it's yours! It's not too often I'm proven wrong Miss Aria, your self control and discipline are an unparalleled breath of fresh air! Mark, take notes."

Aria held her head down and did not speak.

"I believe I just gave you a drink and paid you a compliment Miss Aria." Eric stated as chills ran up Mark and Aria's spines. "Oh goodness I forgot myself in my excitement. You may drink and speak now, when spoken too, I must question your friend here."

"Thank you for your kind words and beverage, Mister Eric, I shall enjoy it while I await your address if you'll grant it at your leisure," Aria said.

"You see Mark, that is how you speak to your superiors." Eric laughed.

"Mister Eric we're all vampires here aren't we?" Mark spoke out of term before his brain could stop his foolish mouth. Aria quickly met his eyes in sudden terror.

"Which is why I said superior, not better, Mister Mark. As you improve upon your linguistic skills you'll soon be able to detect the nuances of speech." Eric turned his eyes to the veiny vampire. "Now you will tell me all you know of the girl I am seeking."

"You said you were looking for a son, sir." He replied.

"Yes and your genuine confusion at my blatant lie affirms my belief that you know exactly who I am looking for, and the blackened veins sprawling out of your eyes tell me you have seen her through eyes not your own."

The vampire's eyes widened. "Fuck." It was all he could utter. Aria was bewildered by the vampire's response to Eric. Eric had noticed.

"You really should keep your faces in the loop, when they feel undervalued or lied to they're far more likely to turn on you friend. You may speak Miss Aria."

"Riley what the fuck did you do? Who are they looking for?" She pleaded.

"Shut up Aria! Not another word!" Riley commanded.

"You got Steph killed you fucking moron! You tell them what they need to know, and you tell them now!" Aria began to scream, but she calmed her voice.

"He got himself killed, you dumb bitch!"

"Now Mister Riley, I will tolerate no such disrespect of the fairer sex. Now if you would be so kind as to comply with her and my request." Eric asked.

"How'd you even know?" Riley asked.

"You're too green at your craft. Where did you learn such a skill?"

"The Master taught me," Riley explained.

"So there is a stray vampire old enough to be teaching the forgotten vampiric arts?" Eric asked.

"That's right, and you have no idea what he's capable of."

"Were he capable of competently teaching his students I wouldn't have been made aware of such a possibility to begin with." Eric stated as he began to chuckle.

"And what makes you think that?" Riley wondered.

"He probably told you the black veins were a side effect of the dark magics, but what he didn't tell you is that it only happens if you under sacrifice for what you're doing."

"What do you mean? Explain!" Riley was suddenly furious.

"You used a spell to see through the eyes and guide one of your thralls, he didn't give you the time tables on the sacrifices. Those veins aren't a right of passage, they're what happened when the spell consumed whatever crow or dog you used and started eating the life force around your eyes."

"That bastard!" Riley shouted. Eric continued to laugh.

"Would you possibly be kind enough to tell me all you found?" Eric requested.

"I found a half breed at the outlets accompanied by two hicks from the country. They got into a new truck after she sensed me and had a panic attack." Riley explained.

"How did you let yourself be sensed?"

"I didn't, she's got some kind of heightened awareness. The two hicks did too, no way I got close enough, but sure enough, they saw me." Riley continued.

"Well I certainly appreciate your courtesy Mister Riley. I believe this adjourns our meeting, which leaves me in a precarious predicament."

Mark, Riley, and Aria's stomachs all sank at once. It was clear that Aria and Riley knew far too much. Eric began twirling his flawless gold mustache with his left hand as he thought.

"Aria, and Riley?"

"Yes!" They both answered in unison.

"You are both well aware that I could quite easily hunt you down wherever you hid correct?"

"Yes!"

"And you understand that you have no chance of regrouping with your little stray leader, correct?"

"Yes…" The terror was quickly consuming them.

"You see my problem is, that I am quite used to having to ruthlessly torture opposing house vampires to rip any nugget of information from them. By that time it's quite obvious I'm going to kill them, they just want the pain to stop." Eric explained as tears welled in Aria's eyes. "But you strays have simply given me everything I want, and haven't annoyed me to the point I think I should kill you."

"But you can't let us compromise your search," Aria spoke up as she lowered her head.

"Exactly! Mark, take their phones." Eric said.

"What?" Mark asked.

"We're taking them back to our hotel."

"What?" all three asked in unison.

"We can cut off their contact with the outside until we catch our quarry, then just let them go."

"Alright." Mark breathed a sigh of relief.

Chapter 5

Coal had awoken early this morning. He had opted to feed and water the chickens and dogs before sun up so he could shower before he and Marcella went to go shop for a new lawnmower. Coal had been borrowing his Memaw's bush hog but the drive ate up a lot of his time to bring the tractor over and back. He had eyed a large mower in his paper. It was large and orange. It was a sixty-one inch cut and had a bulldog for a logo.

Once he made it back in from tending his animals he went to the fridge for a glass of water. He could see the lights in Marcella's room were off. Of course it was still dark outside, but she certainly was a heavy sleeper. Coal couldn't help but wonder what kind of vampire slept in, after all, he thought, shouldn't they be awake all night? He could ponder it some other time, he thought to himself as he climbed the stairs.

He entered his bathroom and sat his clothes and towel over the toilet bowl. He sat on the toilet seat as he slowly creaked the faucet of hot water. Once the water had warmed up he cracked open the cold before turning it to the shower setting. He undressed and hopped in. He had just finished his pre-rinse and started to lather shampoo in his hair when he heard tapping on his shower door. He froze for a moment, then began tensing his arms as he stared at the blurry image on the other side. His eyes widened and he forced his breathing to steady.

"Coal, I think there's something wrong with my shower." Marcella's voice called.

"Nah, Carlos' crew does good work, let me finish up and we'll have a look." said Coal as he turned to look for his sugar scrub.

"Actually," Marcella began as she opened the shower door. "I thought we might shower together."

She had a clear look at Coal from behind. His legs were like tree trunks, and his ass was well defined. As she looked up at his back she could see the muscle hiding beneath his skin. Coal may have liked to eat, but Marcy could see the subtle ripples in his form as he moved. She could also see quite the curiosity. At the tops of his back and his shoulders, closer to his neck, were little off-colored dots on his skin. Some were raised and some were slightly pressed in. A few looked like tiny little rings compared to Coal's large frame. The majority were bunched up just below the back of his neck, a short distance below where a shirt would hide them. Marcella began to lightly stroke her right hand across the bumps.

Coal turned and caught her right wrist with his left hand and raised her arm above her hand as he pinned Marcy against the wall of the shower. He wasn't aggressive or violent, but rather firm and assertive. He didn't move with haste, he was gentle and deliberate. The sudden eye contact between the two of them made Marcella's chest buzz. There was now a churn in Marcella's stomach. She entertained the flirty idea of surprising Coal, but now that both of their naked bodies were so close she didn't know what to do. Her cheeks looked as if they could ignite at any moment. Coal smiled softly and leaned into Marcella's ear.

"Do you think you could close that door for me?" He whispered.

Marcella let out a squeak as she reached, trying to find the handle. Once she had, she grabbed it and closed the door. As soon as Coal heard the door click he moved his head down and bit Marcella's neck. Marcy's eyes glazed over as her knees began to buckle and her arms went limp. She recovered a bit and grabbed the back of Coal's head and began to press him against her neck. He continued to light bite until he started suck. Chills ran up and down Marcella and she started to push Coal's head downward until his lips reached her breast. He still held her wrist, but with his free hand he grabbed the small of her back and pulled her into him. The feeling of his tongue across her nipple as he sucked her breast made her moan with excitement. She pushed his head further and Coal began to lightly kiss her tummy as he worked his way down. He let go of her wrist and back and grabbed Marcy's hips firmly causing her to gasp. He lowered a few inches, but stopped just short of reaching Marcella's intended destination. Feeling the sudden resistance in the palm of her hand Marcella looked down.

Coal looked back at Marcy in complete anguish. In his excitement and surprise he had forgotten the drops of shampoo at the top of his head. He was reminded now that he was low enough for the shower to catch the shampoo and send the incendiary suds straight into the eyes of Coal. Marcella returned with one of shock and horror. Coal never broke eye contact, just clasped his lips together as he blinked very slowly. He brought in a deep inhale and Marcella began to laugh. Coal chuckled as he stood and faced the shower head and removed the soap from his eyes. He turned to look at Marcella as he held up his right index finger.

"Rain check?" He asked.

Marcella erupted into uncontrolled laughter, hunching over. As she hunched her laughter caused her to slip, landing on her shoulder. She let out a loud cough as she landed, causing Coal to lose his composure. He too began to laugh as he leaned his back against the wall and slowly slid down. Marcella rolled over on her back and propped her feet up against the opposite wall of Coal. Both continued laughing together.

Coal recovered first and stood. He helped Marcella back up to her feet. Once she was steady, he turned and washed the soap from his eyes. Once Coal could see he stepped out of Marcella's way so she could wash her hair. As she did, he scrubbed himself clean. Once Marcella's hair was washed she moved over to lather up as Coal rinsed off. Coal kissed her cheek as he stepped out of the shower to dry off. She blushed and smiled.

By the time Marcella had finished washing and stepped out, Coal was already in his room getting dressed. She pouted to herself for a moment, for missing the opportunity to get a better look at him. She wrapped her hair in a towel and started to make her way to her room. As she passed Coal she felt a sudden tug on the towel covering her body, causing it to fall. She turned rapidly as her face flushed red, only to see Coal adjusting his belt, turning slightly away from her.

"Oh wow, how'd that happen?" Coal asked as he turned his head to look at her.

Marcella looked at Coal's hands. They were both on his belt adjusting the length, but his smirk gave him away. "If you needed a better view you could've just asked." She said as she pressed her breasts together facing him.

"Damn" Coal stated.

"If you're a good boy you can touch."

"If I was a good boy we wouldn't be running late." Coal said as he started laughing.

As Coal finished his statement Marcella looked over at the clock to see that they were running twenty minutes late. Coal had wanted to go to the lawnmower dealer early so they could get things settled and be back in time to get the fence nailed before sundown.

"Oh, I'm sorry!"

"Nah, it's good, I'm having a blast."

Marcella hurried down and dressed herself. She left her room to see Coal starting his truck, waiting for her. She briskly walked over and climbed in. Once she was seated Coal handed her a smoked meat stick and a can of cold coffee.

"I thought we'd eat in town, but I figured you might want a snack."

"Yeah thanks!" Marcella said before tearing into the stick. She noticed that Coal only had himself a can of coffee. He had gotten both of them a can of Expresso with Cream. "You're not eating"

"Nah, I don't eat breakfast that often."

"You know it's the most important meal of the day Coal! Didn't your mom teach you to start your day right?"

Coal began to awkwardly chuckle. "Naw, I don't reckon she did. But I did get to start it with you so I reckon I'm workin on it." He winked at her.

Marcella could feel a tickle in her chest as she smiled back at him.

"Coal?"

"Yeah?"

"Are we moving too fast?"

Coal looked on and thought for a second. "What makes you think that?"

"I don't know, My dad always taught me to act right, I don't want you to think ill of me."

"Be a bit hypocritical, don't you think?" Coal answered.

"What do you mean?"

"Takes two to tango, darlin. Hell, maybe I feel a bit guilty for taking advantage of you." Coal explained.

"No, that's not what you're doing at all! Really!" Marcella burst out in a panic.

"Woah now, Marcy, it's ok. Why don't we just take this at whatever speed you want? Would that be ok?"

"But I think I like this speed, Coal."

"Then I reckon we keep on going then, right? Look, I know you been through a lot, but you can talk to me. About anything, really. Hell, I bet Jim-Bob has a spare ear somewhere, and Carlos can't really talk back."

Marcella giggled. "You're right. I'm just worried."

"Bout what?"

"Well, what if everything settles and we decide we don't like each other?"

Coal took another moment to think. "You know I was in the mud for a good 20 years before the dust first settled for me."

"But what if you get to know me, and I scare you away? You know I'm a monster, right Coal?" Marcella quivered as tears welled in her eyes.

Coal reached over and grabbed her hand. "Little honey, I met my fair share of monsters, You ain't one of'em.

"How do you know that Coal?"

"Hell, I know a lil bit about a few things, Marcy, ain't never seen a monster cry over what folk thought of them, not genuinely, at least."

"Aw, now my makeup is all runny." Marcella changed the subject.

"Truck's got a mirror in the visor, I'll slow down so you can touch it up if you want."

"Thanks." Marcella said as she pulled the visor down. She then grabbed makeup from her bag. As she fixed her makeup she looked back over to Coal. "So what kinda of lawnmower did you want?"

"I been eyeballin' this bigass sixty-one inch they got. It's got two-wheel motors and this thirty-eight horsepower EFI engine on it."

"Sounds like you did your homework."

"I have been waiting for this mower since I graduated."

"Awww and I get to be there when you get it. That's cool."

"That's destiny right there, baby."

The two both laughed together. Coal continued to drive until they reached the lawnmower dealer. They could see Coal's dream mower from the road. Its black front arms holding onto its orange wheels. Coal stared at the majestic bulldog logo staring back at him. They pulled into the shop.

Coal stepped in and was immediately greeted by a tall older man with glasses. The two exchanged handshakes and pleasant greetings.

"How you been, Kenny?" Asked Coal.

"Been doing well, what brings you here?" asked Kenny.

"Finally trying to order a lawn mower."

"Bout time, here step in my office, and we'll go over what you need."

Coal and Kenny stepped into Kenny's office. Marcella stayed in the showroom and began walking around, looking at the neatly displayed lawnmowers. She thought it was strange that they were color coordinated. There was a section of red and black mowers of all types and sizes, followed by solid yellow mowers, then the orange and black mowers. As she walked past the mowers, she found other pieces of outdoor equipment. There were saws, blowers, and trimmers of all colors. She continued to look and examine the wares until she came upon a door leading outside to a fenced-in area. She pressed forward to the outside and found herself surrounded by tractors and all their attachments and accessories. There, she could see a nice tractor that was also orange and black with the same bulldog logo. It had a cab, AC, and a radio. She read over all the specs and numbers on its pamphlet. She didn't know what horsepower really meant, but she thought it sounded cute. Marcella made her way back to where they had met up with Kenny and followed their trail to Kenny's office. Coal was sat in front of Kenny's desk, signing paperwork and preparing to write a check.

"They have a tractor with the same logo as the mower you said you wanted," Marcella explained.

"Ya'll got their tractors in stock now?" Coal asked.

"Yeah, they finally sent some over." Kenny answered.

"Well, let's go take a look, I might not feel like writing two checks," said Coal.

"Alrighty." Kenny agreed.

The two men got up from their chairs.

"Lead the way, Miss Marcy," said Coal.

Marcella took them to see the tractor she liked. When they arrived, Coal looked at the pamphlet and swung the doors open. He checked all of the features, then walked to the back and inspected the hitch.

"I need the tractor. Then I need the tiller, disc, bushhog, forks and grabber. You wanna make me a deal on all this?" asked Coal.

"I reckon since it's you, I can knock about fifteen percent off the total. You'll save plenty, and my accountant won't flip shit." Kenny explained.

"What about a maintenance plan?"

"I'll waive the shop fee and give you our preferred rate," Kenny answered.

"Sounds like a deal, let's get all this in writing and get her done."

The three returned to Kenny's office, and all sat down at his desk.

"Coal, I don't mean to pry, but a big buy like this won't put you in a bind, will it?" Kenny respectfully asked.

"Nah, seeing how these broken ribs put me out of work for a few more months, my settlement was pretty sweet, so I'm just getting all my shinies lined up before I start at a new company. Plus, I had a nice chunk of change of my own before they bout killed me." Coal explained.

"Well, that's great to hear. I just needed to make sure your memaw wouldn't kill me if I set this sale up."

"Naw, man, you should be safe."

"Alrighty then." Kenny chuckled.

Kenny began all the paperwork and orders for Coal's tractor.

"They make these in Arkansas too?" Coal asked.

"They build the whole mower in Arkansas. They get their tractors out of Korea, but they're still assembled stateside."

"Hell yeah." Coal smiled.

The paperwork was finished, and Coal signed the check.

"Come pick'em tomorrow, I'll have my techs start servicing them out and installing your accessories." Kenny explained.

"I appreciate it, man, we'll be seeing you then."

"See you then, good buddy, thank you for your business."

Coal and Marcella left the dealer and hopped in their truck.

"Where you wanna eat baby girl?" Coal asked.

"I don't know, what's good around here?" asked Marcella.

"What are you in the mood for?"

"Red meat."

"There's some type of Michelin place in town, they do red meat, I think."

"Ooo sounds fancy," Marcella said.

"That's the plan then."

Coal called ahead as they drove. They were in luck, as there was a recent cancelation for lunch and they could be fit in once they arrived.

"If I keep getting this lucky, I reckon I'll start getting scared." Coal chuckled.

"Why?" Marcella asked.

"Hell, when everything starts going my way, it tends to pull a one-eighty. I think I just get paranoid, you know." Coal explained.

"Relax, Coal, everything's great right now, let's just enjoy it."

They arrived at the restaurant and pulled into the parking lot, and stepped out. Coal opened the door for Marcella as she stepped out of his truck. They walked toward the front door. As they did so, a rental car abruptly pulled into the lot. The two payed it little mind and continued.

Two men stepped out of the car. A large man with nordic tattoos was accompanied by a smaller young man, who appeared to be sniffing the air. They immediately began following Coal and Marcella. Coal and Marcella showed their reservations and were shown in. They stopped for a moment to hear the maitre d stopping the two men.

"The chase has only just begun, young one now I have your scent!" Hrólfr called out.

Marcella froze in fear. Coal could see a tremor start in her hands and work its way up to her shoulders, then slowly down her spine. He couldn't imagine the thoughts crashing into her head. He did, however, know that a young lady was terrified, and he could not let that stand. He quickly turned his head to look at the muscular giant standing in the entrance, proudly smiling.

The smile shook for a moment, then began to fade away as the two made eye contact. Hrólfr stared into Coal's gray dead eyes. They were unflinching, Hrólfr stopped himself from flinching as violence itself emanated from Coal's gaze. Coal's pupils began to dilate as he slowly exhaled, gritting his teeth. As he did so, he squared his feet with his shoulders facing Hrólfr. He had raised his right hand to his back, the tip of his thumb lifting his shirt over his belt. Coal's fingers twitched in anticipation, and he broke the silence first.

"Does it look like we're running to you?" Coal asked.

Hrólfr was taken back. He searched for an appropriate response but was left wanting. He couldn't afford to fight Coal here in front of so many witnesses. His pup was still inconsistent after his transformation, so the collateral would be staggering. Hrólfr had lost himself for just a few moments and tipped their hand. He was confused. The young half-breed and a mere human should have broken at his very sight. They should have begged him to take them easily. This mortal most definitely should not have braced himself and made ready to fight in such a public forum.

"Looks like your half-breed's too scared to even move." the pup spoke up.

Coal shifted his gaze to the eyes of the pup, who visibly shrunk back upon making eye contact. Coal began to walk forward. Every step was smooth and deliberate, as Coal shifted his shoulders forward into a lean with his powerful stride. His right hand was still out of their view behind him, but his left was stretched and curled, ready to latch on whoever stepped to him first.

"Marcella ain't the one finna deal with you, why don't you just focus on me." Coal spoke calmly.

The restaurant had frozen with anticipation and fear alike. No one was sure as to what would happen next. The two men who had started the confrontation seemed to be losing drive and ground at once.

"Come on pup, now's neither time nor place, we will report back." Hrólfr commanded.

"You sure Rolf?" the pup asked

"Quite sure."

The two men began stepping back and Coal stopped his advance. They left the restaurant. Coal and Marcella were shown to their table. Coal profusely apologized for the issues the two men had caused. He was assured by the staff it was no problem. Coal lifted his menu.

"You see anything you can't live without?" Coal asked.

Marcella sat frozen. The waiter walked up.

"Can I start you off with drinks or appetizers?" he asked.

"Yeah we'll each have a soda, and can we get the steak tartare plate appetizer?" Coal asked.

"Certainly, sir."

"Did you know pigeons die when they have sex?" Coal asked Marcella.

Marcella suddenly looked up in shock and bewilderment. "What the hell? No, they don't!" she whispered.

"Well, the one I fucked did." Coal monotonously stated.

Marcella dramatically looked up at the ceiling, rolled her eyes, then began giggling.

"Now that you're back, do you know what you want?" Coal asked.

Marcella scanned the menu. "Ooo, I want this rosé lamb leg."

"Awesome."

"Have we decided on our entrees?" the waiter asked upon his return.

"Yeah, can I get this tomahawk plate and she would like the rosé lamb leg." Coal ordered.

"Ma'am you are aware that the rosé lamb leg feeds two?" the waiter asked.

Marcella's jaw dropped as she looked up at the waiter. Coal sucked in his lips as he leaned back in his seat.

"We're also going to need a bottle of wine, a good red, please." Coal requested.

"Right away, sir." the waiter said as he scurried off.

"Is he on the menu?" Marcella asked.

"No, but nerve-calming wine is." Coal laughed.

"You don't think I'm fat, do you, Coal?"

"I think you're the most beautiful woman I've ever seen, and even if you had rolls, I would only express the joy of having something to grab onto."

"See, that sounds rehearsed to me."

"You think the bomb squad just freestyles, or does he get to practice?" Coal joked.

"Bomb squad? You do think I'm fat, don't you!"

"Hell no, I could curl your little ass if I needed to, shit Marcy."

"Well, you might later." Marcy smiled.

Coal blushed a moment. "Yes, ma'am.

The appetizers were brought out. It was a plate of steak tartares. There were four pairs, and each pair was a different style.All the meat was a beautiful bright red, each with a quail egg rested in the dimple. Marcella's mouth watered at the sight of the crimson, quivering meat. She could feel her teeth start to shift and tried to hold them back.

"Get you a spoon and dig in, baby girl," said Coal as he followed his own advice.

Marcella listened and, grabbed her spoon, and took a large scoop from the nearest mince. The flavors bloomed in her mouth. The texture of the minced tenderloin coupled with the tartness of the dijon and capers hidden in it. This one's egg wasn't raw, it had been roasted in a dill-infused olive oil. She chewed slowly to savor such an incredible bite. They enjoyed the rest of the tartare plate just in time for their entrees to come out. They brought Marcella an entire leg of lamb rested atop a mound of mashed potatoes, garnished with roasted red potatoes. The smell of rosemary and walnuts wafted across the table. Coal was presented with his tomahawk smothered in a basil spice compound butter. This compound butter was also found in his baked potato atop a dollop of Greek yogurt.

Marcella could contain herself no longer and grabbed the leg, taking a full serrated bite of it. It was an explosion of flavor and satisfied her immensely as she glazed over. Her euphoria was interrupted as the waiter brought their bottle of wine. It looked expensive to Marcella, but it paired quite well with her lamb. They finished their entrees as the manager of the restaurant brought out two dark chocolate espresso brownie sundaes.

"I'm sorry, sir, I don't think this is ours." Coal spoke up.

"Oh, but it is; it comes with your wine as an apology for my waiter's mishap." The manager replied.

"Sir, that's not necessary, it was a simple mistake, no worries." Coal continued.

"I'm afraid I must insist, sir. We pride ourselves on our experience and service. I'm sure you may understand that any negative experience brought upon by our staff must be amended." The Manager explained.

"I certainly appreciate sir. Thank you so much. Coal said.

"Yeah, this looks awesome, thanks!" Marcella happily spoke up.

"We appreciate your gratitude and look forward to your continued patronage."

"Of course."

The manager stepped away, and the two began diving into their sundaes. Every spoonful was filled with an incredible balance of homemade vanilla ice cream and dark chocolate with an excellent note of espresso. The combined textures of the hot fudge and ice cream completed the experience.

Marcella looked up at Coal. "That was really nice of them!"

"Man, yeah, I might would make this our weekly haunt." Coal joked.

"This and the Diner!" Marcella laughed.

"Definitely."

The two finished their meal. Coal paid the bill and left a generous tip for the waiter. Coal could see Marcella grow nervous as they stood from their table. He wrapped his arm around her waist and escorted her to their truck. Once they were in and buckled up, Marcella breathed a deep sigh of relief. She then looked over at Coal, who was starting the truck and proceeding as usual.

"Do you have any idea who they were?" Marcella asked.

Coal looked behind them as he backed his truck out of the parking spot, then he pulled out toward the road. "Looked like some folk who forgot their place on the food chain, baby girl." He said.

"How can you be so calm, Coal! That was Hrólfr! He's my dad's pack lead!"

"Ooo, fancy." Coal chuckled.

"Are you serious right now?" Marcella screamed.

"Marcy, I really thought I would be scared. But I can't let you down. And when I finally made eye contact with the thing I had been dreading this whole time, they buckled. They're no different than any other motherfucker that preys on people they think are smaller than them, and I can't stand that shit, Marcy."

"Coal, you're just a human you have to be careful. Promise me you'll be careful!" Marcy begged.

"I'll be careful, baby girl, I promise. Relax, we gone get through this just fine. I gotta live long enough to figure out you ain't all that." Coal began to laugh.

"Oh fuck off! You couldn't handle all this!"

"Then let me get my hands on it!"

"Keep'em on the wheel, jackass!" Marcy barked.

"See, you backin down too!" Coal joked.

"Oh, you just wait till I throw it back!" Marcy egged Coal on.

"I'm literally begging you to." Coal continued.

"We have to nail the fences when we get back, baby sorry."

"Did you just call me baby?" Coal asked.

The two made eye contact for a moment, and Marcy blushed. Coal couldn't help but smile. Marcella held out her hand, and Coal grabbed it and held her hand the rest of the way home. They arrived home, and Coal performed his gately duties, then pulled up to the house. The two changed into their work clothes and nailed as much of the fence as they could before they lost daylight. They then went back inside and had leftovers for supper. They then played games until it was time to go to bed. Coal had gotten a text saying his tractor and mower were ready for pickup.

"You gonna teach me how to drive your big fancy tractor, Mr. Coal?" Marcy asked.

"Hell yeah, them things are awesome, I can't just keep it to myself." Coal replied.

"Is that our plan for tomorrow ?"

"Yeah, definitely, we're almost done with the fence, so we can wrap that up and then play with our new toys."

"Awesome."

The two went to their rooms and grabbed their sleeping clothes. Both met upstairs at Coal's shower.

"Excuse me ma'am can I help you?" Coal asked.

"Come on, Coal, you have the fancy shower! I'm a lady, you know!"

"I reckon we can share."

"Try not to be too excited to see me naked again, Coal, it's embarrassing." Marcella joked.

Coal laughed as he pulled his shirt off, and once again, Marcella could see all the little bumps on his back and shoulders. She rubbed them with her hand.

"What are these Coal?" Marcella asked.

"Ain't nothing to worry about, momma was just a real bad smoker." Coal answered.

Marcella thought for a moment and decided not to pry any further. She unhooked her bra and took it off with her shirt. As her shirt cleared her face, she could see Coal looking at her. She approached him and wrapped her arms around his shoulders. She pressed her chest against him. She gave Coal a kiss and swirled her tongue around the interior of his mouth. She became excited as he grabbed her above her hips and lifted her from the ground. She wrapped her legs around his waist, and they continued to kiss. Marcella pulled her head back and smiled.

"Maybe we should have taken our pants off first." She said.

"Or cut the water on so it could warm up." Coal added.

Both laughed for a moment. Marcella kissed Coal on the cheek and unwrapped her legs. Coal turned on the faucet, and both removed the rest of their clothes. Marcella stepped in first and shampooed her hair. She stepped aside so Coal could do the same as she scrubbed her body. Coal moved over so Marcella could condition. The two rinsed themselves off and got dressed. As they stepped out of the bathroom, Marcella looked over at Coal.

"You know I'm still kinda scared, would it be ok if I crashed here tonight?" she asked.

"Yeah, no worries, I can take the couch if you want."

"No, that's not really what I want, Coal."

"What you mean, Marcy?" Coal asked.

"I was hoping it would be ok if we like.. slept together?"

"Is that something you sure you're comfortable with, Marcy?"

"I really just want to be held right now.. by you." She confessed.

"Of course, baby girl, I got you." Coal said as he smiled.

Coal unfurled the covers and waved Marcy to bed. She crawled in, and Coal tucked her in and kissed her cheek. Marcy blushed and giggled like a little girl. Coal walked over to the other side and climbed in next to her. She scooched her back up against him, and he wrapped his arms around her. Everything melted away around her as she closed her eyes. She felt so warm and so safe in Coal's arms. She felt like nothing could reach her in the safe place she found herself in. She grabbed Coal's hands and held them as she kissed his forearm and drifted off to sleep.

CHAPTER 6

Mark had found himself looking over the city from the rails of his hotel suite's outdoor patio. Eric sat inside on his laptop, going over all of his emails. Mark looked at a text on his phone. He started his way toward the lobby. The front door of their room opened, and Hrólfr stepped in. He needed to speak with Eric, and Mark walked past him. He took the elevator down to the lobby and made his way to the hotel brasserie. There, the pup was waiting for him.

"Amund, what did you find?" Mark asked.

"We found your girl, Mr. Mark," Amund answered.

"And you two didn't take her?" Mark asked.

"We couldn't, she had a man with her!"

"A what?" Mark exclaimed.

"They were going into this fancy restaurant and we tried to follow them. Hrólfr jumped the gun and almost started a fight right there in public, cause he called Marcella out!" Amund explained.

"A human?"

"Yeah!"

"No human should have been able to challenge Hrólfr, let alone two lycans!" Mark began to lose his temper.

"Motherfucker we couldn't keep eye contact with him! You shoulda seen this fuckin dude. Lookin at us like he's the fuckin monster Mark." Amund ranted.

"You've gotta be full of shit!" Mark growled.

"Why do you think Hrólfr went straight to Eric after we sniffed around?"

"Why's that?" Mark asked.

"Hrólfr faltered dude."

"There's no way in hell."

"I'm fucking serious, bro! He was all smiles till that dude, and I can't stress this shit enough, stared us the fuck down." Amund stated.

"Hrólfr probably didn't want to cause a commotion in a public area," Mark explained.

"Yeah, whatever excuse he wants to give y'all."

"Fuck man. You get anything else?" Mark asked.

"Yeah, Hrólfr missed it but I caught whiff of his truck and the road he came from. Snapped a pic of his tag while Rolf was looking around."

"Damn Amund I'm impressed. You kept this from Hrólfr of all people?" Mark replied.

"Yeah, man, you said you were the best chance to bring Miss Marcy back peacefully, and she's always been nice to me, stood up for me a time or two even. I can't let Hrólfr track them down like he is now. Soon as he came to from our encounter, he's been super riled up, man, his prides like super fucked right now." Amund explained.

"Good call. Sorry for my temper, you did good, really good." Mark complimented.

"It's all good man, just bring her home safe bro. I hate it out here, this isn't our turf and there's too many different types of smells in these parts." Amund lamented.

"Course I will man, what do you mean different smells though? I'm curious."

"Like you know those two strays Eric brought back, there's some like them around a few sewers or basements, but there's also a few areas that smell like them, only super rotten," Amund spoke.

"Vampires don't rot, though?"

"Exactly, but I seen some books in the father's library about how there's some magic type shit that can corrupt them real bad. Like that veiny dude has a hint of rot to him but he's got nothing on some of those places. Some of the humans don't smell right either, this whole place is fucked as far as I'm concerned. Hrólfr says he feels like we got watched at some point."

"I don't like the sound of any of that," Mark commented.

"Yeah, same, like bring her home so we can fuck right off," Amund said.

The two men finished their plan to track down Marcella without Eric and Hrólfr. They stayed and drank in the lobby while they waited long enough for Eric to be briefed on the situation. Eric and Hrólfr spoke in the room.

"So you are saying that this human had a presence that gave you pause and you could not recover Miss Marcella?" Eric asked.

"There's no need to rub it in Master Eric," Hrólfr replied.

"No, I'm not rubbing in Mr. Hrólfr, I trust your instincts implicitly. Therefore I must have perfect clarity regarding anything or anyone that would give you pause."

"My apologies, Master Eric, I spoke out of term in ignorance," Hrólfr responded.

"No need for apologies dear Hrólfr, I should have approached the subject more tenderly, you are no doubt embarrassed, and to have it occur before your pup could only add fuel to the flame."

"Yes sir, Mister Eric."

"It is nothing to be ashamed of, there are humans with such a violent presence that you have described, him aside, have you found anything else?" Eric asked.

"No, the pup sniffed around the parking lot for just a minute before we drove off."

"Fair enough. I'm ordering room service, let me know if there is anything I can order for you."

"A burger will suffice."

"Excellent choice. I'll be out on the patio awaiting our supply drop, so if you could listen for the room service I would appreciate it."

"Of course sir."

Eric stepped out to the patio and greeted his two captives. He wasn't in the mood to pry for intel. He was awaiting his drone delivery so he could show them the vastly superior blood the household could produce. He hoped that the greener grass would bring them to the otherside with little friction. Knowing that strays had taken an entire city was unacceptable to Eric, and he was already planning to bring them down. He had communicated his concerns with the father via email and was awaiting a favorable response. He knew that finding Marcella was a top priority but there were other operatives suited to the job. He was also aware now that the stray faction had taken an interest in the young Marcella and as far as he was concerned this was an open declaration of war upon his house. It was a war he would gleefully prosecute on behalf of the father.

It was only a matter of time before the hounds honed in on Marcella. Soon she would be safe and secure with her father. Eric trusted that Mark would have devised a way to reach her before the rest of them, and without some extreme circumstance she would no doubt see the error of her ways and rejoin the household. If not, Hrólfr could be quite persuasive when necessary.

He could hear the buzzing above his head as the supply drop arrived. It came with a wonderful cooler filled with packets of well curated blood. Eric unhooked the drone and it flew off to a car below. The car drove away unseen back to the household. Eric pulled a packet and carefully poured three glasses for himself and his new friends. They were hesitant, until Eric took a sip then followed suit.

"That's delicious!" exclaimed Aria.

"We thank you dear Aria. And is it to your liking Riley?" Eric asked.

"Yes sir, best I've ever had," Riley replied.

"Excellent. I'm sure you're both wondering why I've taken you captive." Eric began.

"Because we complied with all your demands right?" Aria asked.

"You are partly right Miss Aria, it did help to get your foot in the door." Eric explained.

"You need people who know the area and the local stray chapter so we can help you bring it down and establish an outpost for your household right?" Riley asked.

"You are quite intelligent, Mister Riley, I am very impressed."

"Thank you, sir," Riley responded.

"You can't expect us to just turn on our chapter for some fancy blood!" Aria blurted out.

"If you give me a formal acceptance into your household, I'm in," Riley said, placing his hand on Aria's shoulder.

"How could you, Riley?" Aria asked.

"I was an unwanted accident! You think I'd pass on a chance to be accepted into a real household?" Riley retorted.

"But…"

"Shut it Aria! You've always been everyone's favorite, none of'em gave a fuck till they figured out I could use the arts and look where that got me!" Riley explained as he waved his hand back and forth in front of the blackened veins in his face.

"Can I please have some time to think about it Mister Eric, to go over some details maybe?" Aria pleaded.

"Of course, Miss Aria, and as for you, Riley, I will speak to the father on your behalf and report back with the news. Do mull things over in your heads, after all, this is an excellent opportunity to work with someone like me," said Eric. "Now, let us enjoy our drinks before Mark joins us and ruins the mood." He continued as he picked out a different label from the cooler and began pouring a fourth glass.

"You can be quite the ass Mister Eric!" Mark laughed as he stepped on to the patio.

Eric held up the freshly poured fourth glass and extended it to Mark. "Your favorite if I'm not mistaken Mark."

"I resend the previous notion." Mark joked.

Mark sat at the table next to Eric. He swished the glass then took a sip. Eric then grabbed his own glass. The four continued to drink until total Darkness had fully enveloped the town and the majority of the businesses had closed.

"Mark, I believe I will stay behind and watch over our captives if you wouldn't mind taking the pup out on patrol." Eric requested.

"Of course Mister Eric," Mark answered as he stood from the table and entered the hotel room.

Chapter 7

Marcella awoke from the best sleep she had had for quite some time. She rolled over to see Coal starting to lean up. He had woken up five minutes before his alarm and was silencing his clock. He hadn't noticed Marcella and when he turned she closed her eyes and pretended to still be asleep. She was far too comfortable to be roused up and the chickens could wait. As she lay there Coal leaned down and brushed her hair off from her face. He kissed her forehead and tousled the strands on top of her head.

"Sleep tight babygirl, I'll handle everything today." He whispered.

Coal got out of bed and dressed himself for the day. He handled the morning chores and called a friend of his. He started cooking breakfast and was nearly finished when Marcella made her way downstairs.

"Morning hun-bun you sleep well?" Coal asked.

"Yeah, I feel great. What's for breakfast?"

"Sausage biscuits and eggs."

"Smells amazing, what time are we picking up your stuff again today?"

"Prolly, after lunch, Kenny'll give me a call when all the accessories are installed." Coal answered.

"Cool, you still want to teach me how to drive the tractor?" Marcella giggled.

"Hell yeah, it'll keep you in the AC longer and out of the sun."

"Thank God." Marcella laughed.

"Yup, I got a buddy of mine heading down here in a bit to handle some business with, oh and T. Rell's ole lady and some of her girlfriends are going out tonight and she wanted to invite you." Coal explained.

"You mean Miss Latisha? I'd love to!" Marcella said with such excitement.

"Awesome, you can plan your outfit while me and Crane go over some work orders."

"How do you have so many friends, Coal?" Marcella asked.

"Hell, I got a story for all of'em. I grew up with Jim-Bob, he's a brother to me."

"Could you tell me the ones about Diego and Carlos?"

"If you'll tell me a story about you." Coal said.

Marcella paused for a moment. She didn't feel completely comfortable talking about her life as a halfbreed, not even to Coal. She was afraid of judgment, and more so turning Coal away from her. She however, wanted to know more about Coal and his merry band. She needed to know what kind of people they were.

"Deal."

"Well me and Diego met in college, and became fast friends." Coal began.

"Boooo, that's not worth one of my stories. Cheater!"

"So when he graduated he worked for his dad's construction company for like a year before his dad just gave it to him. His dad wanted to go home to their ranches. Unfortunately, he didn't do a great job with the handoff, and a few things got mixed up. Like Carlos' work visa and a few other guys, but they didn't have Carlos' history. Well, the timing couldn't be better because the company had just broke into what I like to call the 'rich white neighborhood' market,"

"Coal you're white."

"Yeah but I work for a living."

"But you don't?"

"Not right now, cause some rich dude tried to kill me."

"Right."

"Anyway, one of their rivals had a cousin in the state department or some shit, so when Diego fumbled the visas that bitch sicked the dogs on'em like a week after they ran out. Carlos had worked real hard to rise up the chain on his own merit, but... If they woulda picked him up there was a solid chance that he'da been thrown in the pen for a hot minute. Diego told me he had turned his life around, and if Diego respected him it was good enough for me so I offered my trailer. I think me and Carlos wound up living together for near bout a year. They're both the reason this house is so fancy."

"What do you mean?" asked Marcy.

"Well when my case was all handled o'course I was using their company to build my house. Diego threw my plans away and designed it himself. Then, whenever a job site wouldn't use a full pallet of something, or a part was shipped wrong or warrantied, Carlos would load it up and bring it by to see if it matched anything. That got me all the cool tile in the master bathroom, the shower in the guest bath, my badass fridge, and this professional stove we all love. All the other building materials wound up knocking a quarter of the costs off the whole build. Pipe is expensive by the way."

"All that cause you let Carlos stay with you?"

"We also share a passion for game chickens. It was actually Carlos that got me all the automatic coop doors. He didn't want me bending over after my accident. That's also why I sell them birds half off, and send them freebies that I think they'll like."

"That's so sweet."

"Yeah, they're great dudes. Your turn." Coal said.

"Let me think of one." Marcella leaned back for a moment and pondered. "It's kind of hard to be honest Coal."

"Booo, cheater!" Coal laughed.

"Hey, that's not fair! All your stories are sweet and wholesome! I grew up with vampires!"

"Fair enough, but storytime!"

"I got grounded one time for interrupting one of my dad's right hand's meeting."

"How?"

"Well I was still kind of young and we hadn't learned that I could eat human food, or that I would freak out if I got hungry. I was binging some rom-com so I didn't realize how long it had been since I had drank a packet. I got so distracted that my stomach started cramping, so I started making my way to the kitchen. All of a sudden my mouth just starts watering and I pick up the smell of blood coming from the hallway leading to one of dad's backrooms. It was the smell of fresh blood. So out of nowhere my teeth come out and I'm on all fours tracking this scent down. So now I'm rapidly approaching this closed door, but I'm super hungry so of course the best option was to jump at it instead of opening it. So I knock it down. When I look up there's Eric talking to some guy sitting in a chair, but the guy was human, and bleeding. So like, I lunge at him, and Eric, straight up, kicks me in the face."

"Dude just kicks a baby shark in the face?"

"Knocked all my little baby shark teeth out of my fucking jaw, Coal. So the dude sitting down panics and starts flailing in the chair and tips it over and knocks himself out. Eric was so pissed. He said I had delayed his interview by at least an hour. I tried to explain that I was so engrossed in my rom-com, but he wouldn't have it. He told my dad that until his current assignment was done if he saw me on the TV, he would throw it at me."

"That seems a little harsh for a teen, right?" Coal asked.

"It was a sixty-inch plasma Coal. More than a little harsh."

Coal began laughing at the shock in Marcella's voice. Marcella did not find it nearly as funny. Coal quickly realized his mistake and stopped. Both stared at each other awkwardly for a moment.

"So what are you and your friend doing when he gets here?" Marcella spoke up,

"He's here to check out that saw log. I hired him to carve some toys and accessories from it."

"Like what?" she asked.

"A solution to our upcoming vampire problem."

Marcella's face went blank. A cruel reality had once again struck her. The saw log that Obadiah had brought was ash, and this friend of Coal's was most likely a woodcarver. She didn't know what to say or even what to feel. She had only told Coal that she ran away from home, he had no idea why.

Marcella hadn't run away from an evil and abusive household, she had run from her annoying ex and overprotective father. It had finally clicked that Coal was making sure he was ready to fight monsters and, by extension, kill Marcella's friends. She realized that Coal thought of vampires and lycans as monsters that preyed on humans. Marcella also knew that he wasn't entirely wrong in his assumption, and he could very well be killed to prove a point or to simply clear a path for her. Coal was a strong human, but he was no vampire hunter. He certainly couldn't hold up against Mark, let alone Eric or anyone that her father could have sent.

Marcella sat as Coal pulled the biscuits from the oven and threw sausage patties on her plate from the skillet. She hadn't spoken for a few moments. She had begun to think of her father's hunting dogs ripping Coal to shreds or Mark draining him in front of her. Tears began to run down her cheeks.

"What's wrong, Marcy?" Coal asked, seeing her on the verge of breaking down.

"I've killed you, Coal." she let slip quietly.

"What?" He asked again.

"I've killed you."

"Might need some explaining, baby girl." Coal chuckled.

"They're coming for me, Coal. You can't stop them, and it's all my fault."

"Hell, I might just surprise you."

"Coal, just let me go. Let me go home. If I apologize I know I can convince daddy to let you live." Marcy pleaded.

"Baby, I can't let you go back to that."

"To what, Coal? You don't know me! You don't know where I come from! You just think I'm some little half-breed damsel for you to save!" Marcella began to yell.

"Miss Marcy, please don't yell at me, I'm sorry." Coal shrank back for a moment.

Marcella couldn't recognize his voice for a moment. He didn't sound like the loud ruffian she had come to know. He almost sounded like a little boy whose feelings had been hurt.

"Coal, you don't understand, you're getting ready to hurt people who I grew up with, and some who helped raise me."

"You said they were hunting you, Marcy."

"I ran away from home Coal. Just not a bad one." Marcy explained.

"They sent those weird dudes to wrestle you down."

"They were just thralls Coal, human servants to vampires. Drained little playthings really." She continued.

"They had one eat the other two, Marcy. They've got bigass dudes calling you out in broad daylight."

"That was the best opportunity for that thrall to prove himself Coal, it was a chance for him to take a huge step towards being turned. And the big man and his friend were two of my dad's prized hunting dogs. And Amund has always been a good friend to me, and I'm sure he just wants me safe at home."

"Then what did you run away from?"

"I was just mad at Mark and Dad, they had been lying to me about how we source a lot of our blood packs. So I broke up with Mark and ran away." Marcella answered.

"So you're not running from people who are trying to hurt you?" Coal asked.

"No, I just got so mad at them I needed to leave."

"And I was a convenient little rebound? Or what?" Coal asked in painful confusion.

"No Coal, it's not like that." Marcella tried to assure him.

"Then what was it like Marcella?" Coal asked.

Marcella's eyes welled up, and she leaned back in her chair. "Please Coal, please call me Marcy. I'm still your Marcy. Don't call me Marcella."

"Then explain yourself, Marcy."

"I had been running away for days Coal. I couldn't face my dad after being gone for so long. I was a mess, and you just came out of nowhere with Jim-Bob. You were fearless and huge! I was in a storybook for a moment. Then you opened your home to me, introduced me to your friends. You were all so nice and genuine, no ulterior motives or secondary objectives. And a man liked me for once without knowing my father. I didn't want to leave, and I don't want these feelings to go away."

"They don't have to Marcy."

"They do Coal, I can't see you get hurt, I can't let you or friends get dragged into this any further. Dad's a good man, I know he'll see reason."

"Then I'd lose you before we even got a first date. Fuck all that noise."

"Yeah but we had a good first kiss, we've had a good few days and I'll never forget them."

"But I'm greedy sumbitch and I'd like plenty more of them days."

"I do too Coal. I do."

"Reckon it's settled then, ain't it."

"It's not that simple Coal" Marcella looked into his eyes. "It's not just your decision either."

"I tell you what Marcy, you think on it and whatever decision you make I'll respect, but you gotta give it some real thought and you gotta give me a real chance, after that it's on you."

"You want that date night something fierce don't you Mr. Coal."

"Hell yeah I do, and I want to keep rubbing off on you till you talk like that all the time."

"The hell'd I just say?" Marcella asked. Her eyes widened. "Oh good lord no I need to leave."

"Nah I'm pretty sure you just agreed to hold out for a date night."

"You sure you're right about that?" Marcella asked.

"Hell yeah I'm right I can't remember a time I was goddamn wrong."

Both began laughing, and Marcella agreed to have their first date. Coal was happy to have the chance to prove himself. He thought she was beautiful, and he appreciated her honesty and straightforward personality. He needed time to rethink his strategy. He had believed the things chasing Marcella were simply monsters in the night. It had never truly occurred to him that these were the same monsters that raised her, or the ones that she grew up with. He could accept killing creatures of darkness but the thought of killing things close to Marcella made him sick. Even if he knew that they may have been willing to put him down, he still couldn't quite grasp the state of being necessary to take their lives.

"Coal, are you ok?" Marcella asked.

"Yeah babygirl, I'm fine."

"Can I ask you something Coal?"

"Yeah?"

"What made you like this?"

Coal appeared flustered and confused for a moment, "Like what?"

"I don't know, like, how do you stay so focused? Or, how are you so composed, I know that there's a lot going that's on you, but you don't even seem fazed." Marcella explained.

"I know the secret hunbun." Coal joked.

"What secret?"

"Never matters what kind of fight you're in babygirl, long as that head stay moving and you keep swinging you can find a way through it."

"That has to be the most oversimplified bullshit I have ever heard. IN MY LIFE." Marcella explained.

"You rebounded with a simple man Marcy, I'm not sure what you were expecting." Coal smiled.

"You're not even a rebound, you wanted to save a damsel and I wanted a hero." Marcella retorted.

"Damn, that sounds pretty simple."

"Oh fuck off."

Both began laughing again. They stopped when they looked into each other's eyes. Coal could see the neon orchids blowing in the breeze of Marcella's gaze. He didn't know why he had fallen for this woman so hard or so quickly. He wanted to know her, everything. More than that he felt comfort with her, she was someone who didn't know him or his family, and liked him for who he was. She saw him as a man, and as someone she could come to.

Coal was much more difficult for Marcella to read and comprehend. She struggled to see through the storms beyond the portholes. Thunder and lightning emanated from Coal, and yet despite the clouds and wind, all was dry. She thought he was incredible, unwavering, and kind. She wanted to sit down and discover the forge in which this steely man was created.

There was a knock on the front door and an uppity voice could be heard behind it. Coal stood from the kitchen table and walked over to greet his guest. As he opened the door a tall gangly man stepped in. He wore short shorts and a wife beater. He had long blonde hair and oddly smelled like a skunk.

"Sup dude, how you living?" He asked Coal.

"Living the dream, Crane, how you been?"

"Solid, bro, it turns out folks around here love most of my carvings and sculptures."

"Hell yeah bro, that's great to hear. Let me introduce you to Marcella, Marcella this is Crane. He's the best wood worker around."

"Don't talk me up bro, she's too pretty."

"Pretty sure she's mine." Coal chuckled. As he spoke Marcella could once again feel her stomach flutter.

"Lead with that bro, I'd be bragging not making introductions," Crane replied.

"Fair enough."

"Now let me see that big log you been hiding big boy," said Crane.

"Do what now?"

"I'm tryna get my hands all on your wood bro."

"Right in front of Marcy bro come on?"

"It's fine bro I'm wearing socks."

"Are you?"

"No Shows baby."

"What on earth are you two on about?" Marcella interrupted.

"Don't worry about it babygirl, he's a good buddy of mine." Coal explained.

"I have never met this man before in my life, he promised me candy online," Crane said. Both Coal and Crane had erupted in laughter before he could finish his sentence. "So where's Jim-Bob?"

"He's coming over Saturday." Coal answered.

"Aight, sweet bruh what're ya'll up to?" Crane asked.

"Got some chorin to handle. You're more than welcome to join if you want." Coal answered.

"Hell yeah, I need some brewskis with the boys."

"Everything alright?"

"Yeah, yeah, just been dealing with the high end clients here lately and I need to chill and recenter with the homies." Crane explained.

"We got you, bro."

"Hell yeah, now show me the log and we'll get after it."

"Right this way."

Coal led Crane down the hill while Marcella stayed at the house. She went curled up on the couch, pulling a blanket over herself. She began browsing the streaming services on Coal's gaming console. She had almost settled on a show when Coal's cell phone started to ring. Coal had forgotten to bring it with him as he took Crane to the saw log. She picked it up.

"Coal my man, we got your equipment ready rock and roll, whenever you ready for pickup." a voice explained through the phone.

"Awesome, he's on a project with a friend of his at the moment but I'll go let him know!" Marcy replied.

"I appreciate it, have him call us when y'all start up this way."

"Sure thing!"

The man hung up the phone, and Marcella got up from the couch. She left the show she was interested in hovered. She then put her shoes on and started down the hill. As she approached the barn in front she slowed for a moment. She knew that on the other side of the barn was the log, Coal and Crane. Marcella was curious as to what Coal had planned so she decided to creep up to the wall of the barn and eavesdrop on the two men. She held her ear against the wall and listened. The two were mid conversation already.

"Righteous bro, nah I can make some sick designs with some wicked silver trim on these things. Half of this'll be done in no time, but I'ma make these babies fuckin' lit boy!" Crane exclaimed.

"I appreciate it man, you got an estimate on the time?" Coal asked.

"Bro, I'll put you in the front of the line and no-life these bad bitches. I'll have them in your hands when I come to get fucked up saturday my dude." Crane explained.

"Sweet bro. You ain't gotta put in the overtime though my boy, no need to rush." Coal said.

"Nah man, I never get to work on that raw badassery, I'm just fucking stoked you feel me?"

"Yeah, I feel you."

"Anyway, the important questions." Crane began.

"Your pay?"

"Nah that's not important right now, I need to know what liquor we need."

"Man whatever you want, I got Jim-Bob coming over after his shift tomorrow and we doing a quick lil run, so we gone have some good liquor." Coal explained.

"Oh shit my boy. Aight say no more I'll bring a lil fancy fancy for ya lady and some mixers for that sweet nectar."

"Sounds like a plan, bro."

"Hell yeah, let me bring my mill down here and I'll get to work on this log, all this ground hard pan?" Crane asked.

"Yeah you won't bog down around here, it's all safe."

"Sweet, sweet."

"You need any help?" asked Coal.

"Nah, my boy, I like the serene loneliness of the craft, you know?"

"Sure thing, I'll leave the back door unlocked, stay hydrated amigo."

"I will broseph, no worries."

The two men exchanged a pound hug and Coal started his way back up the hill. He looked over at Straton who was staring at the barn. He continued past the first lean-to, not noticing Marcella. Marcella began to creep slowly behind him as he left her view walking past the center structure of the barn. She continued under the lean-to and began to round the corner of the center of the barn.

As she rounded the corner and before she had time to respond she could feel her wrist being grabbed. Marcella was quickly yanked into the barn and twirled around before being pinned against a wall, facing her assailant. Her right hand was held firmly against the wall above her head, and her left was firmly, but gently pressed against her stomach. She once again found herself lost in a gray storm over blue oceans. They were unblinking and focused. She could feel her heart beating, as if it were trying to tear its way out of her chest. She may have been frightened for a moment, but upon seeing and being pinned so quickly by this man her chest now fluttered for different reasons. The man leaned down and calmly spoke in Marcella's ear. His crisp voice seemed to tingle in her hearing, sending goosebumps down her neck.

"You know it might just be a little rude to sneak up on a man on his own property." He said as he lifted Marcella's left hand and pinned it against the wall next to her right. "It could be dangerous too, you know?"

"How so?" Marcella whimpered.

As soon as she had finished her question the man bit through the goose bumps on her neck, catching every nerve. This caused Marcella's knees to buckle, and she balled her hands into fists as she rubbed her thighs together. Her eyes then glassed over and her body went limp as she let out her soft moan.

"Oh, fuck Coal."

She could hear a deep chuckle as Coal released her wrists and she slid down the wall. He leaned down and scooped her up like a little princess. As he started his way up the hill he held her tight as she lightly patted his chest with her little fists.

"That's not fair, you can't bite vampires." She quietly mumbled, still feeling glassey.

Marcella had finally come to as Coal had made his way up the stairs and to the back door. She leaned up and kissed his bearded cheek.

"You can let me down now, I think I can walk."

"No problem."

Coal slowly let Marcy out of his arms, making sure she could catch her footing. Marcella pulled Coal's phone from her pocket.

"I think Mr. Kenny called, they said you were ready to rock, but for you to call him before we started his way," Marcella explained.

"Awesome, that means we'll have time to teach you how to drive a tractor before it's time for your girls night."

"It's not my girl's night Coal, I'm just hanging out with Latisha and her friends."

"Yeah, but I really want you to make new friends around here."

"Why's that?"

"So it's easier to convince you to stay." Coal chuckled.

"You make it pretty easy yourself," Marcella said as she started rubbing the spot on her neck where Coal had bitten her.

"I try. Well, let me go grab the keys to the truck and trailer hitch and we can be off."

"Aight, I'll guide ya'in" Marcella froze as the words left her mouth. She looked over to see Coal giggling to himself. She didn't know if it was the double entendre or the horrible accent which had escaped her that made him laugh, but she was quite distressed by both.

She waived Coal in as he backed his truck up to the the trailer. Coal hopped out and unlocked the hitch. Marcella lowered the trailer on to the ball and hopped into Coal's truck. They went down the drive and stopped by the gate. Marcella hopped out and opened the gate. Coal pulled the truck through and Marcella closed the gate. She hopped back into the truck and they drove off toward the outdoor dealer.

"How did you know I was following you?" asked Marcella.

"Do what now?"

"When you pinned me against the barn, how'd you know?

"The dog gave you away."

"Damn, and I was so sneaky too."

"Very."

"So what are you doing tomorrow?" Marcy asked.

"I'ma head out to the woods for a hot minute, see where I want to drop some feeders and set up some food plots. Now that I'll have a tractor, I can just record plots real quick."

"Oh, cool. I think I'm gonna try to catch up to your character on our RPG if that's ok with you."

"Sure thing babygirl."

When the two had arrived at the dealer, Coal pulled in and backed his truck up not too far from the gate. They went in with their receipts and waited in line. In front of them was an older gentleman and his young grandson.

"Can I load the tractor up this time, papa?" the child asked.

"It might be best to let the professional handle it, little buddy." the man answered.

"Oh, please! I never get to load the tractor."

"Well, if it's ok with them, I'll let you."

"Thanks, papa!"

The grandfather paid for the tractor service and the clerk called for a tech to show them to their tractor. The two followed the tech to the back lot. The grandson skipped happily behind the two men. Coal handed the clerk his receipts and the clerk signaled over to another tech to go fetch the equipment. Coal and Marcella then went back outside and let down the trailer gate.

Coal looked at the old pickup to the left of his truck, and then at the trailer behind it. The trailers gate was on the shorter side causing a slightly steep incline up hill. The gate was also on the bulkier side causing a large bump from the lip to the ground. The tech brought Coal's new lawnmower out first. A forklift drive loaded his extra accessories and left to bring the tractor.

Coal and Marcella could hear the grandson giggling as he drove his grandfather's tractor. He carefully lined it up with the trailer behind the old pickup. He then began to drive forward, and the front tires hitting the lip of the gate shook him a bit, but he pressed on. However, once the back tires hit the lip, the boy was shaken again, causing his foot to ride the clutch. The tractor quickly began to slow up the hill, but the child, not wanting to stop on the hill, quickly let his foot off the clutch too quickly.

"Shit." Coal said under his breath.

The grandfather began to holler out in distress as the tractor reared up as if it were a raging bronco. Marcella froze as the child began to scream, and the tech dove from behind the tractor. With not a second to waste, Coal erupted into a dead sprint toward the tractor. As he ran toward the trailer, he propelled himself up and his right foot forward from the ground, catching the rail of the trailer. Using his right leg, he launched himself forward with all his might, catching the grill of the tractor. The sheer force and weight of his body wrestled the front of the tractor back to the trailer with a resounding impact as the trailer shook. As the tractor landed, it began to roll forward onto Coal.

"Shit, shit, shit." Coal murmured as he scrunched and pulled his legs quickly between the front wheels of the tractor.

The tractor barely stopped before it pinned Coal to the front of the trailer as the scared child leapt off to the arms of his grandfather. The seat safety quickly killed the engine and Coal pulled his lower half from under the tractor and made his way to the two family members. The scared grandson was still crying a bit, but he was trying to push through it.

"Hey, hey lil man, it's ok bud." Coal comforted him. "It's all over, and look you even got it to the front of the trailer. Good job lil man."

"I'm really sorry sir! I just wanted to show papa I could drive the tractor! Honest!" the grandson bawled.

"And you did little buddy! Look! All we gotta do is throw it in park and tie it off." Coal continued. "Now come on, bud let's show you how to strap'em down, what'd ya say?"

"Yes sir." The child said as he began to regain his composure.

"Awesome, you got that covered grandad?" Coal asked.

"Yes sir, we'll take it from here." He answered.

The grandson's eyes suddenly widened as the tech pulled Coal's new tractor off the yard and began to load it.

"Can we ride that tractor papa?" he asked.

"No now, I think that's the nice man's tractor, you'd have to ask him." the grandfather answered.

"Yeah, I could use a spare hand." Coal answered. "I gotta show Miss Marcy over here how to drive it first and when she's used to it I'll give you a call."

"Thank you sir!" the grandson replied.

The grandfather gave Coal his business card. "I can't thank you enough sir."

"No worries bud, I'll be seeing y'all round." Coal said.

The grandfather went to their trailer to strap down their tractor. The tech had just finished loading Coal's new tractor and walked up to him.

"All right sir, is there anything else I can help you with?" the tech asked.

"I'd hate to ask man, but could you strap these down for me? I gotta go get your bosses first aid kit right quick." Coal requested as he revealed the palms of his hands. There were jagged cuts on his hands and fingers where he had latched onto the grill of the tractor. The tech's eyes widened as he looked, he the looked over to see that the grill of the tractor had nearly been yanked from the frame.

"Yes sir no problem!" he answered.

"Thanks, man!" Coal replied.

Coal could see the panic forming in Marcella's eyes and he held his finger in front of his lips as he began walking back into the dealer.

"Kenny, bud, can you help me out real quick?" Coal asked holding his hands out in front of him.

"Shit, Coal, step in my office quickly," Kenny replied.

Coal and Marcella stepped into Kenny's office as Kenny pulled down a large box. He laid the box on his desk and popped it open. He pulled out a bottle of disinfectant and a tube of ointment.

"Hold'em out, son, this next part ain't too fun," Kenny said.

"What does he mean Coal? Why would you say that?" Marcella asked losing her calm.

"Relax Marcy, it's fine. Here, watch." Coal explained as he held his hands out.

Kenny poured a large helping of disinfectant onto the cuts on Coal's palms and fingers. Coal remained unfazed. Kenny the took a q-tip and dabbed ointment onto it. He then patted the q-tip onto the cuts. Once all the cuts were filled with ointment Kenny bandaged them up.

"This from that old tractor grill?" Kenny asked.

"Yes, sir." Coal answered.

"You up to date on your shots?"

"Yes sir."

"You oughta be all set then, good work out there Coal."

"Preciate it Mr. Kenny." Coal said, he then looked over to Marcy. "Come on sweet pea, let's roll on out of here."

"Sure thing," Marcy answered.

Coal shook Mr. Kenny's hand again and headed back to the truck. He opened the door for Marcy. She climbed into the truck and Coal stepped around and got into the driver's seat. He buckled up his seatbelt and looked over at Marcy, who was staring back.

"Everything alright?" Coal asked.

"Are your hands ok?"

"Yeah, why?"

Marcella looked blankly at Coal, dumbfounded. She hadn't been around regular humans often, but she knew that cuts and disinfectant both hurt. There Coal sat, smiling at Marcella and happy to have his tractor and mower in tow.

Marcella couldn't help but be impressed by Coal. She realized that he hadn't saved her in a vacuum, and that if he saw a problem he simply acted. She could feel a weight lifted from her shoulders. She now understood that she hadn't dragged Coal into anything, and that he simply saw a problem and acted. There was a certain genuineness about him now. She no longer felt that she was just some damsel in distress for him to save, but that she was someone who he was happy to help out of a bad situation. She did, however, wonder what Coal had been through to so quickly assume she was fleeing abuse. Coal had pulled onto the road as she thought to herself, and the drive had become painfully quiet.

"Coal?" She asked.

"Yes Marcy?"

"You thought I was running away from an abusive home didn't you?" Marcy asked.

"I did." Coal answered

"What would make you think that?"

"Well, you were running away from strange men trying to grab you, and you said you were running away from your dad if I remember correctly."

"Is that the only reason?" Marcy questioned.

"I mean, it looked like simple math to me." Coal chuckled.

"Do your hands hurt Coal?"

"Nah, they're pretty fine."

"Coal, they're cut up and Kenny doused them with alcohol. There's no way they don't hurt right now."

"Babygirl I'm fine, really." Coal assured her.

"Why don't you let other people see you hurting Coal?" Marcy asked.

"Cause Marcy, folks don't need to see you bleed. It ain't like I needed to make them two feel worse about that youngin's mishap." Coal answered.

"You know if we're gonna start dating soon you can't hide anything from me."

"I won't babygirl." Coal laughed. "Want some music?"

"Yeah, let's hear your playlist."

Coal turned up his music as they drove home. Once they got home, they repeated the gate ritual. Coal pulled behind the house by the barns. Marcella helped him unstrap the tractor and mower.

"You gonna teach me how to drive these?" Marcy asked.

"Yeah, but I hope it's okay with you if I'm the one who unloads them." Coal said, smiling as he waved his hands in front of himself.

"Yeah, I guess I can wait a little while," Marcella said, giggling.

Coal let the trailer gate down and hopped on his new zero-turn. He parked it in the non-chicken barn. He then climbed into the tractor and backed off. He then swung the door open and waved Marcella over. He turned the tractor off and pulled the parking brake before jumping out.

"Well come on babygirl." He smiled.

"Wait for real? Right now?"

"Yeah, you want to play on the tractor before you go hang out with Latisha and her girls right?" Coal asked.

"Yeah, you're right. This might be fun." Marcella said. She had thought Coal had been joking the entire time. At no point did he think this big southern man was going to let this little ole gal run his tractor. She Stepped up to the metal beast, and climbed up onto the seat.

"The cab's too small for you though Coal. How are you even going to show me anything?" Marcella asked.

"That's what this here Oh Shit Handle is for." Coal said as he climbed halfway up the cab. He right foot in the stirrup and his left toward the front of the handle. His left hand held the metal handle toward the front of the cab, and his right arm wrapped tightly around Marcy. She blushed slightly and subtly leaned into him.

"This doesn't seem safe Coal." Marcella protested.

"Relax, long as you don't sideswipe nothin I'll be alright."

"I'll remember the brave man you were." Marcy joked.

"Just don't tell Jim-Bob I cried."

"Deal. Alright so explain please." Marcy demanded.

"Right, so, this one is way more simple than some of the older models. So your break is that pedal on your left, then on your right you got forward and reverse pedals. There's no clutch or gear stick, really just the throttle and parking brake is all we gone worry bout. So turn your key one click clockwise."

"Ok," Marcy said as she turned the key.

"Nice, now crank the AC right there. You can also see that flashing red icon right yunder?"

"Yeah what's that?"

"That's the parking brake light, it's gotta be in park to start."

"Is that this big stick on my right?"

"Nah that's the fork stick. The park is on your left, this orange nob."

"Ok, so do I push it down?" Marcy asked.

"Not yet, turn the key further clockwise and start the tractor. Remember next time this a diesel so you gotta let it heat up before you crank her."

"Alright," Marcy said as she cranked the tractor.

"Now you can let the parking break go. Ease the throttle about halfway up, we not haulin ass just yet."

"Alrighty."

"Ok, she's automatic so you don't have to worry about shifting anything, just work the pedals. Remember you got a fork up front and a bush hog in the back, and let's stay away from anything expensive for a while."

"Ye of little faith!" Marcy laughed.

"Almost none." Coal laughed.

The two spent the next hour and a half running up and down Coal's field and land. Marcy was careful not to sideswipe Coal off the tractor. The two laughed together as she hit bumps a little too fast or took turns a little too sharp. Coal pointed out the fuel gauge and Marcella drove them to the spare barn by the lawnmower. The two hadn't quite disembarked.

"You pick up pretty quick Miss Marcy. You have fun?" Coal asked.

"Yeah, that was way more funner than I thought it'd be," Marcella admitted as she rubbed her hands on the dashes next to her seat.

"Everything ok?"

"Yeah, I was just seeing if this chair was big enough to pull you on top of me." She giggled.

"I wish, but I'm more scared of where the steering wheel wound wind up."

Both began laughing. As they did they could hear a band saw start up through the wall. Coal stepped down, and held his arm out. He helped Marcy down as she left the cab.

"I reckon we'll wave to spare poor Crane's ears." Coal said.

"From what?"

As Marcella asked Coal quietly brought his hand back and the quickly forward, giving Marcy a crisp slap on the ass. Marcella's cheeks blushed immediately and Coal laughed.

"No fair, if I knew you wanted that we could've stayed in the house!"

Coal continued to laugh, and looked over at the now pouting Marcy.

"It's better if it happens spontaneously before the first date. I wouldn't want you to think I'm just some dog with a bone." Coal joked.

"I bet that dog's bone is big enough for a baby shark to chew on."

"What?"

"What?"

"Miss Marcy, I declare!" Coal chuckled as the two made their way up the hill into the house.

"I'm just a woman Coal, what am I supposed to do with all this man?" Marcella began to laugh with Coal again.

Coal looked down at the clock on his phone. "Not a lot right now, you've gotta start getting ready." He said as he showed Marcy the time.

Marcella looked, then suddenly grabbed Coal by his belt and pulled it to her waist. "Guess I'll have to do all this man later then." She said as she leaned up on her tip-toes and pulled Coal closer. She gave him one passionate kiss and swirled her tongue about his mouth until their tongues met, and she twisted around his. She then finished her kiss and pulled back, winked at Coal, and skipped off to her room to get ready.

"Damn." Coal said as he smiled.

Marcella took a quick rinse and put on one of her nice dresses that matched her favorite bag that Coal had bought her. She checked to make sure her sunhat matched her nice gray dress. She put on a nice lustreglass lipstick. She double checked herself, then left her room to rejoin Coal.

Coal could scarcely believe his eyes. Marcella's orchid eyes were flawlessly framed by her lacey black sunhat and shiny pink lips. Her gray dress fluttered just below her knees. She was smiling at Coal so brightly he could feel his chest sink. It was a feeling he only had on rare occasions and only in the presence of Marcella.

"Is it too much?" she asked.

"If you think so, I'd be more than happy to help take some off." Coal joked.

"If it wouldn't make me late, I could slip these off," Marcella said as she pulled up her skirt, revealing her sheer-laced panties.

Coal visibly blushed. "I don't reckon I'd last long enough to make you late if I'm being honest, Miss Marcy."

"I don't think one round would suffice, Mister Coal," Marcy smirked.

"I might would surprise you now."

"Sir, sir… get your keys." Marcella chuckled.

"Yes, Ma'am."

Coal grabbed his truck keys then held the door open for Marcella. He then showed her to the truck and helped her in. They then drove off.

"I got the gate." Coal said.

Coal hopped out of his truck and opened the gate, got back in, pulled the truck through, then closed the gate. He climbed back into his truck and Marcella greeted him with a kiss on his cheek. They then began the drive to town.

"So what are you gonna do while I'm out?" Marcy asked.

"Me and T. Rell are gonna chill out at a pool house not far from ya'll." Coal answered.

"Oh, cool. You practicing for Carlos comes back?" Marcy asked.

"Nah, that'd be a waste of time. I just play for fun and lord knows T. needs practice." Coal replied.

"Oh, Jim-Bob's not coming?"

"Jim-Bob's already there." Coal chuckled. "They have a half ass arcade with like two games he likes."

"Awesome. I really hope Latisha likes me."

"If she didn't, odds are you wouldn't be going. I don't know her too well but if T's granny approved she might just be a saint. Course she'd have to be to put up his wild ass." Coal explained.

"Okay, I guess I'm just nervous. I really want to make some friends, but I want your friends to like me too."

"My friends don't have a great deal of choice babygirl." Coal laughed.

Marcella giggled in response. The two sat for a moment and Coal turned up the music. They drove for a while before they arrived at the club to meet Latisha and her friends.

"Now, if there's any trouble, Latisha knows to call me or T," Coal explained.

"Oh no, it didn't even occur to me that I have no way to reach you Coal."

"Yeah, I'll grab you a phone tomorrow now that I think about it." Coal said, "For now, Latisha's got a good head on her shoulders, she'll have things on lock for you."

"Alright."

"Alrighty then babygirl. Be safe! Have fun!" Coal cheered.

Marcella stepped out of the truck as Coal waved goodbye. She could see Latisha with her friends outside the door. She waved to them and Latisha waved back. Marcella walked up to the group.

"Hey girl! Glad you could make it!" Latisha said.

"Hi, yeah, super glad to be here!" Marcella responded.

"Well we're happy to have you! This is Jenine, Ashley, and Harmony. This is Marcella y'all," Latisha introduced.

Jenine was a short and bulky white girl with teased up blonde hair. She wore a denim dress with a nice pair of beige flats. Ashley was a tall and thin pale woman with pink dyed hair with blue highlights. She was stitched into a tight blue and red dress that stopped well above her knees. Harmony was a black woman of average height. She wore a tank top accented by an external black corset that pushed up her large breasts and highlighted her broad shoulders. Below the corset was a pair of tight black leather pants. Lasha was wearing a navy blue dress that stopped below her knees. She wore a new pair of leather cowgirl boots.

"Well howdy Marcella." greeted Jenine.

"Hi!" exclaimed Ashley.

"Damn it girl, between you, Tish and Ashley, I ain't getting no dick!" shrugged Harmony. "I mean hey girl!"

"Minnie you don't want no kinda man up in the club on a wednesday." Latisha joked.

"Oh all the good ones at church witchu?" Harmony chuckled.

"Girl don't play with me." Latisha laughed. "Look I can take a day every once in awhile to chill with my friends."

"Yes, you can, darlin, now, if you don't mind I'd like to get drunk and dance," Jenine said as she started toward the door of the club.

The women entered the club together. It was a girls night so there was no cover charge. This club was known for its large dance floor. It had a stage in front of the dance floor set up with lights, screens and an extensive DJ booth. Music with hard bass was already playing and colors streamed from the stage lights as various cover arts flashed across the screens. Ashley pulled Marcella into the crowd and began dancing on her. Marcella could see Jenine and Latisha head to the bar, where Jenine ordered a double shot of Jack and downed it, and quickly asked for another. As Marcella danced with Ashley she scanned the crowd to see Harmony toward the back of the club dabbing up a gentleman in a hoodie. After they finished their greeting Harmony began walking toward the dance floor as she lit what appeared to be a hand rolled cigarette. As soon as the cigarette was lit Harmony began eyeing the tallest single man on the floor and called out to him. When he looked over to her she threw her arms to the side and began shaking her breasts as she laughed and approached him. His eyes grew wide and he smiled and began bobbing his head. When she reached him, Harmony turned around and began twerking on her new mark, never stopping the billowing smoke from her mouth.

Jennine had downed three vodka red bulls before joining them on the dance floor. Latisha held a Coke and followed Jenine. They had only been dancing for an hour when Latisha found Marcella on the dance floor.

"I'm sorry, Miss Marcella, I had no idea it was gonna be one of these kinda nights," Latisha yelled.

"What do you mean?" Marcella asked as she continued dancing.

Latisha pointed behind Marcella. Marcella looked over to see Jenine on her knees in front of Harmony, who had undone the front of her corset and lifted her tank top up. She did it in a manner that caused her breasts to squeeze together, with a nipple slipping just below her top. The crowd cheered as Harmony leaned back, pouring a bottle of whiskey between her breasts. Jenine was below, grabbing Harmony's leather pants and swallowing all the whiskey that flowed off of Harmony's size F tits.

"Oh my." Marcella chuckled.

"Good lord," Latisha said as she rolled her eyes.

The girls all continued to dance for an hour and a half. Marcella was getting along well with her new friends, even if they hadn't had a chance to talk much they had made plans to meet either saturday or sunday for a brunch. Marcella, Latisha, and Harmony had found a table and sat down.

"Fuck, I'm too tired for dis man. Shit, even if I brought a man back, I don't think I could put this thang on him." Harmony ranted as she tried to catch her breath.

"Girl, we thought you were finna Jenine home for a minute." Latisha laughed.

"Girl, I might, you know me, I can only go home after a successful hunt. I just gotta be finding me the right quarry." Harmony said.

"Lord have mercy." Latisha exhaled.

Marcella laughed, and as she did, Harmony looked over. Harmony's coffee skin glistened with sweat, but her eyes were red from her smokes on the dance floor.

"Whatchu laughin at girl? I might take you home and see if that porcelain cracks, baby. I'm a conqueror!" Harmony guffawed.

Marcella and Latisha both erupted in laughter with Harmony.

"Yeah, she's definitely coming to brunch," Harmony said. "Either saturday or after church sundie."

"Oh yeah, you have to join us, Marce! It'll be so much fun." Latisha seconded.

"Oh, I want to, but I have to make sure Coal doesn't have any plans," Marcella explained.

As the girls continued to talk at their table, A slender figure walked into the club. He was a tall man of 6'5". He had bright and fiery red hair that was undercut hair. He had a red hollywoodian beard to match. He had a form-fitting walnut husk leather cafe racer jacket. His hands were in the pockets of a pair of black denim pants over balmoral leather boots. He inhaled deeply through his nose as he entered the club. He looked over and made eye contact with Marcella, then looked over to the bar where he walked.

The tall red haired man was followed by a slightly shorter, handsome, and roguish man. He too had a slender build, and was clothed in a black leather blazer with black dress pants with onyx leather oxford shoes. He was cleanly shaven with a gelled curly undercut. He followed the red head to the bar.

Marcella's face changed to one of shock and worry. She wondered how she could be so unlucky. On the night she could unwind with her new friends, her old friend, and her ex had finally tracked her down. Coal was nowhere to be found, and Marcella didn't know what to say to Latisha or Harmony.

'I'll be right back, guys, sorry!" Marcella said as she rushed up from her table and began walking toward the exit next to the bathrooms.

As Marcella moved through the club and dance floor Amund tapped Mark on the shoulder. When Mark looked at him Amund pointed to the exit by the bathroom. This did not go unnoticed. As Mark began to make his way to the exit, he was followed by Latisha and Harmony. They had almost made it to the exit behind Mark when Amund stepped in front of them. He immediately stumbled back and slapped the metal door catching the attention of a nearby bouncer.

"Woa bitch, you can't just grab my cock like that!" He yelled.

"The fuck you just say, you pasty ass freckled fuck!' Harmony yelled.

"Bitch you might look fine, but you can't be grabbing my shit like that!" Amund yelled again.

"Harmony, we've talked about this!" the bouncer shouted angrily as he walked up to them.

"Piss off, Deandre! This boy lying through his teeth!" Harmony argued.

"Bullshit, this lil hoochie done walked up and slapped my dick and asked if the carpet matched the drapes!" Amund explained.

"Harmony baby, you can't keep doin these boys like that now!" Deandre yelled.

"Sir, this man is lying we were following our friend out the exit!" Latisha insisted.

"You can't just lie for your homegirl like that! She gotta be in on it, man, up in here dick grabbing!" Amund continued.

"What would T. say about this Tish? Girl, y'all need to get on up out of here!" Deandre ordered.

"Deandre, please!" Latisha pleaded.

"Nah, you know T. Rell's my boy, I can't let you put him through this, now ya'll gotta get up out of here," Deandre said as he began gently showing the two women the door. The front exit, to be specific.

Marcella had leaned on the wall of the club to try to regain her composure. She had hoped that they hadn't seen her and that she had made a clean getaway. She stood back on her feet just in time for those hopes to be dashed as Mark stepped out of the exit.

"Hey Mars, it's been a minute." Mark casually spoke.

"What are you doing here?" Marcella asked.

"Looking for you."

"And what about Amund?"

"The very same," Mark answered. "Your little rebellious phase has lasted long enough Mars, we need you to come home."

"You don't need me to do anything Mark! And if all dad sent was you, clearly I'm not needed!" She sneered back at him.

"Cut the old man some slack, he sent someone way more qualified than me. I just cheated and used Amund to find you first." Mark explained.

"Oh and other than the two hounds who did he send hm?" Marcella asked.

"Eric." Mark solemnly said as he held eye contact with Marcella.

Marcella's heart dropped in an instant. It felt like it had bounced off every organ inside her as it fell. She knew Eric well, he was her father's right hand and rightfully so. He was fairly young for a vampire of his status and had proven himself capable beyond his years. Marcy knew the colder side of Eric as well. He had earned his seat at the table by quelling or eliminating various stray incursions and camps. He maintained the security and future of the house as he liked to say. Marcella couldn't believe her father would send Eric of all people to find her.

Part of her wanted to give up, and go home. She almost took comfort in Marks worried face, and she was nearly glad to see Amund doing well. Maybe in some way she was homesick, but she was so conflicted. She began to think of the new friends she had made, and the interesting characters she had met along the way. When she pictured Coal's smiling, bearded face her chest began to burn. She had no longer simply ran away from home, she had begun a journey. She had escaped the shackles of her vampiric household and had found people who happily supported her. In only a week's time these people, these humans had shown her more kindness than she had ever known. She couldn't leave them just yet.

"I can't go with you Mark. I think I may have found something here, I can't leave just yet." Marcella softly spoke.

"What did you find Mars? We don't even have time for this! You have no idea what's going on here!" Mark said. As he spoke, his voice began to rise gradually.

"I found other people! And maybe even a new house!"

"The fuck do you mean a new house? With that human? Mars baby I can't even…"

"Don't you call me baby!" Marcella screamed at him.

Mark was taken back for a second, but his anger brought him forward. "The fuck you say to me? Don't call you baby? What do you think you're acting like right now? Huh? Do you have any idea of the shit I've seen go down on your behalf over just a few days? You're coming the fuck home!"

"The hell I am you son of a bitch! What the fuck do you even care! You couldn't be bothered to chase me then, now that dad's put you on the job suddenly you give a fuck? Fuck you!"

"I thought you needed space you stupid bitch, Damn it all! How the fuck was I supposed to know you wanted to throw everything away after one fucking fight!"

"Throw everything away? What were we Mark? Do you even know? Cause last time I checked you were too chickenshit to ever look me in my fucking eyes and tell me you wanted me!" Marcella yelled.

"And what? Your new human told you he did? We making life fucking decisions on atta'girls now Mars? Your half brained bullshit has put us in so fucking deep! I'm fucking over it and you can forgive me later! You're coming home!" Mark bellowed as he grabbed Marcella by the shoulders. When he did Marcella used the palm of her hand and delivered a painful blow to Mark's face, breaking his grip.

"I'm not going anywhere Mark. You can't make me. Dad can't make me. I finally made my own decision and if you can't handle that you can fuck off." Marcella said. She spoke in a low calm tone, and she thought she was holding herself together. Mark, however, could see her eyes begin to twitch. Her shoulders rolled on their own and her fingers pulsated with anticipation. He knew she was agitated, but he was taking her back.

"That's fucking it Mars you're coming with me!" Mark snarled. He grabbed her by the collar of her dress and yanked her toward him. "That new toy of yours is dead fucking meat and you can explain all this shit to your dad," he growled through his teeth.

Mark loosened his grip as he felt a sudden sharp pain in his torso, just above his stomach. It quickly grew to an unbearable tearing sensation that rippled through him as his body processed what had occurred. He looked down to witness Marcella's hand slowly pulling out of a hole just below his ribs. She had shown her claws and driven her hand straight through him. A part of Mark knew that they had both crossed a line, but in some way he was grateful that he wasn't staring at his own heart.

Blood began to bubble from his mouth as he spoke, "Mars? What the fuck?"

Marcella used her left hand to push Mark off of her right. He coughed small gobs of blood as he landed on his back. Until this point Mark was just foolish enough to believe that he could somehow win her back, that she would see through his blunt disposition and harsh temper. Marcella had speared straight through that hope.

"I'm not letting you intimidate me, and I'm sure as hell not letting you threaten anyone who's helped me. Now I'm gonna leave you in this alley way steaming like the pile of shit you turned out to be, and I had better not see you or any of Daddy's lackeys again." Marcella commanded.

Mark opened his mouth to protest. Marcella hushed him by quickly flicking her right hand, sending splashes of Mark's blood into his own face. Mark closed his mouth, and simply stared at Marcella. He had never thought that she could be so capable. She was slowly retracting her claws as she wiped the remaining blood from her hand. Marcella walked out of the alleyway toward the front of the club.

Mark crawled backwards and hid himself next to a dumpster and a few garbage bags. He checked to make sure no one could see him and tears streamed down his eyes for a few moments. He finally had an opportunity, and yet he had failed to tell Marcella his feelings. He had let his temper stop him from communicating and Marcella was leaving him yet again He never used a chance to tell her how incredible she was, or how she would light up any room she walked into. She had been the only one to truly understand and care for him and he had pushed her away. The crushing weight of his responsibility fell upon him as he realized he had blown his best chance to get her back to safety. Marcella didn't even know about the strays that were hunting her. She was now going through her days with no idea of the danger she was in. The wretched part of Mark almost pushed a smirk through. "Let her new precious human save her." He thought to himself.

As Marcella rounded the corner she was stopped by Latisha and her whole group. She tried to hide her hand but it was too late. All of her new friends surrounded her in a panic. Latisha grabbed her forearm as Jenine frantically searched her purse. She pulled out a package of napkins still sealed in plastic. Harmony pulled a bottle of vodka that she had hidden under her breasts and she and Jenine began to quickly clean what they thought to be a wound. Ashley stepped past them slightly, grabbing a bottle of pepper spray from her clutch. Latisha saw that the girls had the situation under control and went to find a bouncer or a doorman.

"Girls girls, relax! It's not mine! It's not mine!" Marcella tried to explain as Jenine and Harmony scrubbed her arm.

"It isn't? It's not!" Jenine looked up at Marcella in shock.

"Hell yeah lil mama, cut that bitch!" Harmony burst out laughing.

Latisha came with a massive doorman. "He's in that alleyway!"

"No sir! It's fine! Don't go in there!" Marcella pleaded.

"Don't you worry miss, everyone's safe." the doorman explained as he pulled up his blazer revealing a taser. He pulled the taser out of his pocket as he approached the alleyway.

"No you don't understand, please! Those men are dangerous!" Marcella continued.

Her words fell on deaf ears. The doorman walked into the alleyway. As he did, Amund stepped into the alleyway from the club. Amund could smell Mark's fresh blood and looked straight at him. Mark had done his best to hide but anyone actively searching would find him with ease. Amund let out a deep sigh as he looked to his left at the large suited man walking toward him.

"Fuck bro, we blew it!" Amund said, his eyes darting back at Mark. Mark had begun to fade away from blood loss. It wasn't enough to kill him, but it would force him into stasis for a while. "Ahhhh, fuck."

"Ayo, I got some questions for you!" the doorman called out.

"Fuck me man," Amund yelled looking up. He took a deep breath and turned to face the man approaching him. "Look, you just let me grab my boy here and we can move on."

"No sir, the authorities are already on the way, I'm going to need you to come with me."

"Well, I can't do that now, can I?" Amund nervously laughed.

"Then I suppose we're going to have to do this the hard way."

"Hard for who, bud?" Amund said as he squared his shoulders and legs.

"Not me." the doorman casually spoke as he thrusted his taser toward Amund.

In the blink of an eye Amund had used his right hand to backhand the taser out of the doorman's hand. Afterward, Amund quickly stepped forward into his opponent. As he stepped in, Amund folded his right hand back toward his chest and swung his elbow into the jaw of the doorman, knocking the suited man out instantly. As the doorman fell, Amund quickly swiveled behind him, grabbing his head and back. Amund gently lowered the man to the ground and patted his bald head.

"Good effort there buddy," he said. Amund looked over to see Marcella and her friends staring at him in horror. He smiled at Marcella and gleefully waved his hand at her before turning back to the alleyway. He briskly jogged over to Mark and picked up his unconscious body. He then ran out of the opposite side of the alleyway.

"Who the hell was that?" Latisha asked.

"They're some guys I knew before I came here and met Coal," Marcella answered.

"We gone need details girl!" Harmony erupted.

"The red head's my old bestie and the other guy's my ex."

"Girl." Harmony exhaled.

"I thought Ashley made choices," Jenine remarked.

"Yeah, me too!" Ashley agreed.

The girls all stared at Ashley a moment.

"Well this has been a fun and eventful night! Can't wait to do it again girls!" Ashley said breaking the silence.

"Yeah, we finally got some excitement." Jenine chuckled.

"Maybe next time I can cut a bitch." Harmony continued.

"Well I'm glad you're all happy, I'm calling T," said Latisha. "We'll start plans for next week ladies."

"Even me?" Marcella shyly asked.

"Of course!" Latisha answered.

After about thirty minutes the girls could see T's challenger and Coal's truck pull into the parking lot. The men stepped out and T. Rell walked up to Latisha.

"Did my bae have fun tonight?" he asked.

"I sure did sweet thang, Coal help you get any better at pool?"

"Shiet no girl. I thought my boy was finna pop a blood vessel, for real for real." T. said.

Marcella ran up to Coal and gave him a big hug then kissed him on the cheek.

"Did you and Miss Latisha hit it off?" Coal asked.

"We sure did Mr. Coal! We already making plans for next week!" Latisha piped up.

Marcella wore a large smile as she looked up at Coal. "Yeah everything was awesome!" She turned over to Latisha. "Thank you so much for inviting me! I had a great time! It was awesome to meet you all!" She waved goodbye. Coal opened the door for Marcella and she climbed into the truck. Coal closed the door and Latisha approached him.

"Get that girl a phone so I can add her to the group chat!" Latisha demanded.

"I'm heading that way tomorrow." Coal answered.

"Good, now I'm gonna give T. the down low on everything that happened tonight, and he's gone give you a call, ok?"

"Umm, yes, ma'am. Is everything ok?" Coal asked.

"You just go on and get some rest Mister Coal. I'll have T. call you tomorrow." Latisha responded.

"Alrighty then. Welp, reckon I'll be seeing y'all next time. Thanks again for taking Marcy out, I'm sure it meant a lot to her." Coal said.

"Sure thing! Anytime! And we'll be seeing you round, Mister Coal!" Latisha waved.

"Take it easy, Big C! I'll hit you up after work tomorrow! Later!" T. Rell said as he opened the door for Latisha.

Latisha sat in T. Rell's car. T. hopped in the driver seat and the two were off. Coal opened the truck door for Marcella, and she climbed into the passenger side. Coal hopped into the driver's seat. Marcella sat quietly in thought. Coal pulled out of the parking lot. The couple listened to music all the way home.

It was late when they arrived, and Coal began winding down to get ready for bed. Marcella did the same. Coal laid in his bed and turned his fans on, he then began watching the TV. Marcella curled up against him. He ran his hands through her hair, then kissed the top of her head.

"So everything was as fun as you hoped babygirl?" He asked.

"Yeah, the girls are so nice and fun. I'm really hoping I won't scare them off though." Marcella answered.

"I'ont know bout that hun they looked pretty tough."

"Yeah, they're pretty cool." Marcella smiled.

Coal let out a yawn, "Aight sweetums I reckon it's about time we turned in for the night."

"Yeah I agree," Marcella replied as she yawned.

Coal Turned out the lights and wrapped his arm around Marcella. The two relaxed and comfortably fell asleep in each other's arms. They were once again blissfully unaware of things they had set in motion.

CHAPTER 8

Amund had thrown Mark in the back of their car and told him to keep pressure on his wounds. He started the car and began driving.

'We can't go back to the suite, Amund." Mrk whimpered.

"Yeah, no shit dumbass. You think I'm explaining that gut wound to Eric and Rolf?" Amund hissed.

"Hang on, I'm looking up a motel real quick."

"There's an old roacher just down the road, don't smell like anything we know or know of. You'll be safe there."

"Surely you don't expect me to sleep in bed bug central, do you?" Mark asked.

"I didn't expect you to get fucking skewered and blow our whole fucking op either! Roaches or get the fuck out!" Amund yelled at Mark.

"Shit, let me out!"

"Naw bitch fuck that! I changed my mind, you sleeping with the roaches." Amund said as he pulled into the lobby parking. "Wallet."

"What?"

"You think I'm paying for your fuckery? Wallet." Amund answered.

"Man, I can't catch a fucking break tonight," Mark said as he reached into his back pocket.

Mark handed Amund his wallet, and Amund walked into the lobby to get the a room.

"Man fuck this," Mark said as he struggled to sit up. He opened the passenger door and began slowly walking away from the motel.

"Oh nah bitch, you thought!" Amund yelled, seeing Mark making a sad effort to escape. He ran at Mark full sprint. As he neared him, he ducked low to the ground and lifted Mark into the air as he tackled him. Mark could feel his wounds reopen as Amund brought him back down to the ground, grinding his side into the pavement. Amund grabbed Mark by his collar and dragged him back to the car. He swung the door open and threw Mark into the back seat, slamming the door behind him.

Amund drove them around the motel until he found their room. He parked outside the room next to the door and helped Mark into the room. It was an awful beige, but at least there were two beds. Amund helped Mark lie down in the bed, which appeared to be the cleaner of two. Once Mark was comfortable, Amund went back out and opened the trunk of their car. He took the two coolers in it and brought them into the motel room. He opened one and tossed one of the packs to Mark, and began putting the rest in the minifridge.

"Eric said those were your favorite, right?" Amund asked.

Mark looked down at the pack, and they were. "Yeah, why'd you bring so many?"

"I seen something like this coming a mile away," Amund replied as Mark began to drink.

"Does no one have faith in me?" Mark said sounding exasperated.

Amund began imitating Mark in a whiny crying voice, "Does no one have any faith in me?" He stopped and returned to his own voice. "Bitch we are in a motel because you pissed off your ex and she fucking lanced you."

"You don't understand, she…"

"No, no" Amund interrupted. "You don't understand Marky boy. You on some rose color type shit. When I figured out she had a new man I shoulda pulled the plug on your bitchass and told Eric."

"The fuck you mean by that?" Mark asked.

"I mean, your fragile little ego got shit on, and you went and fucked up!" Amund answered. "I put money on that shit Mark. She prolly told, you know, brought up that other dude and you blew the fuck up like a fucking two year old!"

"She needed to understand what was at stake, Amund!"

"Man who the fuck you arguing with? You needed to communicate that shit! Not just boss her around like she was your little squeeze." Amund explained.

"What make you think I used to boss her around?"

"She did dumbass. We grew up together. You don't think I don't every stupid fucking thing you pulled. Hell, I don't even know why her father bet on you, but shit, I bet he never really talked to her either."

"Well, if you two were so close, why didn't you go talk to her? Huh?" Mark asked.

"Cause I fucking agreed with her!" Amund exploded.

"You what?" Mark winced back.

"Yeah that's right! Motherfuckers called every mothafucking shot in her life and when she made her own decision and bailed out you all lost your fucking shit. You don't even know her, you dumb bitch! The fuck was her favorite pack you self centered prick? She got a favorite color? Nah you don't know shit! You were some little piss ant nobody that got a pity job then landed the big dog's daughter. Fuck you!" Amund finished.

"Is that really what you think Amund? Am I just trash to you?" Mark asked.

"Mark you dumbfuck, you asking about how I feel about you when I'm tryna get you to think about how you made Mars feel to runaway. If you ever decide to pull your head out of your ass we might just be boys afterall." Amund explained as he pulled a Guinness out of his own cooler. He popped the tab and gulped half the can down. "Once I think you can fend for yourself I'll head out and get this shit handled."

"I thought you agreed with her."

"I still fucking do, but I can't let her get caught up by that witchy fucker, so I'm gone have to finish what you started. I'll jump her boy when he's off alone and drag her back." Amund said.

"What will we tell Eric?" Mark asked.

"If we fail, not a fucking thing Mark. Our little solo strategy has put us on one." Amund answered. Amund began to push buttons on his phone.

"So how are you gonna handle Mars' man?" Mark asked.

Amund finished with his phone and sat it on the bed next to him. He then picked up the remote from the nightstand between his and Mark's beds. He turned the TV on and began scanning through the channels.

"Hello? Plan?" Mark asked again.

"Oh, I heard you. I'm just not including you. Your fuckery might jump over to me."

"Oh come on, that's not fair bro!" Mark defended.

"Can I watch some TV and recenter? Like mah dude one of us has to be focused and ready. Spoiler, it's not you." Amund retorted.

"Yeah, yeah, you're right. Fuck I guess I'll just try to rest."

"Good idea, bleeding stopped?"

"Yeah, for the second time!" Mark retorted.

"Think smarter or run faster, my boy," Amund replied as he began to laugh at his own joke.

Mark closed his eyes and tried to clear his head. He was exhausted and his wound wasn't healing as quickly as it should have. Amund tackling him certainly didn't help matters, but Mark knew that was his own fault. He rolled around a bit until he was comfortable and dozed off. He awoke for just a few moments to a knocking on the door. He saw Amund walk up to it with Mark's own wallet in hand. He took a bag from a young man at the door and tipped him a twenty from Mark's wallet and closed the door. Amund opened his bag and there was a large carry-out box from a local steak house.

"Haven't you taken enough already?" Mark asked dramatically enough for Amund to know he was joking.

"I don't carry cash, bro. I ordered with my card online, though, if it makes you feel better," Amund answered. He opened the box to an incredible porterhouse with mashed potatoes. He pulled out a second box filled with steakhouse mac and then yet another box, this one filled with a sweet potato creme brulee.

"Can you eat all that?" Mark asked out of genuine curiosity.

"I gotta carbo load dude. Can't get drained on the hunt tomorrow, might fuck up any opportunities I get." Amund answered. "You think you'll be healed up good enough in the morning for me to make a move?"

"Yeah, I'm good enough right now if you think you're ready."

"Nah, dude, it's night. The human's probably curled up with Mars right now, in their own home. If I break in they'll have time to ready up for me. Plus, I can't take Mars." Amund explained.

"You really can't take Mars?" Mark chuckled.

"If we were both trying to kill each other, probably, but I got a real handicap here, dude. Plus, the man spooks me. You'd have to see him. People should naturally be scared of Rolf, man."

"Yeah, I thought that was a little concerning, too," Mark said.

Mark's cellphone began to ring. He looked at the caller ID to see Eric's number staring at him. He took a deep breath and showed Amund.

"Fuck no, we'll have good news tomorrow. Turn that bitch off," said Amund.

"I don't know if it's a good idea to leave him in the dark like this."

"God no, fucking stupid idea, but we're in too deep now. Only way out is to keep digging till we see the light."

"Fuck, you're right."

CHAPTER 9

Coal had once again awoken before Marcella. He leaned over and kissed her forehead before getting up. His schedule was clear for the day, and he was looking forward to scouting out the woods on his property. He was also ready to break out his tractor disc and try and set up some food plots to attract some deer. He set out to feed the chickens and handle the dogs.

Marcella woke up an hour after Coal. She stretched and yawned loudly. She put on some comfortable clothes and went to the kitchen to start breakfast for Coal and herself. She may not have been a chef, but she could preheat an oven and throw premade biscuits in it. The open fire stove still scared her and she planned on having Coal teach her how to fry eggs and bacon when he got in from the chickens.

When Coal opened the back door to come inside Marcella rushed over to welcome him in. She hugged him and kissed his lips.

"Come on, I've got biscuits in the oven!" Marcella happily exclaimed.

"Awesome! I'm starving." Coal said.

"Yeah, can you show me how to fry eggs and bacon? I'll make you a full breakfast tomorrow." Marcella said as she clasped her hands together and swayed from side to side.

"Sure thing baby girl, grab me that flat iron and a stick of butter." Coal said as he lit one of the eyes.

Marcella put the flat iron over the fire and handed the butter to Coal. Coal opened the tip of the stick and began smearing it over the iron as it heated.

"Once you got this buttered up you can throw the bacon on there." Coal explained. "I like to finish the bacon, re-butter the iron and fry the eggs in the grease. You like your yolk hard or runny?"

"Runny please?" Marcella requested.

Coal let the bacon finish frying and he re-buttered the iron and cracked four eggs onto it. He lightly salted and peppered the eggs. "When you want'em runny you only let it fry on each side like two minutes. The white'll be done, but your yolk will be nice and runny."

"Oh, cool."

Coal finished frying everything and dumped the eggs on their plates next to the bacon. The two sat with each other to eat. Coal made a quick cross over his chest and began jamming a biscuit. Marcella did the same, copying Coal.

"So you said you're looking in the woods today?" Marcella asked.

"Yeah, there orta be a few good spots to sow some clover and radishes. Try to attract some deer to the property." Coal answered.

"Oh, neat, and what are we doing with the deer?"

"Eating them."

"Oh," Marcella said as she quietly stared at Coal for a moment. "What do they taste like?"

"Let me call a buddy, and I'll show you sometime soon. Gotta be tasted to be believed." Coal answered.

"You really do have a buddy for everything!" Marcella giggled. "And you said it was ok if I stayed home today and caught up on our game?"

"Yeah, baby girl, no worries!" Coal replied.

"Thanks, baby!" Marcella said.

Hearing this, Coal smiled and blushed. When Marcella noticed, she laughed girlishly, which made Coal smile wider. The two were happy together despite the circumstances. Coal made his way into the woods.

As Coal trudged deeper in, the sweet smell of the pines filled his nostrils. The trees swayed gently in the breeze. Coal looked about for clearings with light sun to plant his clover and radish plots. He also searched for clear paths that his tractor could reach. It was apparent he needed to clear out a great deal of underbrush, but the briars hadn't grown to the point that they were a hindrance. He didn't believe that it had grown so tall that his new Bad Boy couldn't mow through it. Coal stopped for a moment just to soak in the natural ambiance around him. The birdsong carried gleefully on the wind, and the babbling of a brook could be heard in the distance. Coal made mental notes of his terrain before adventuring further. The leaves crunched crisply beneath the weight of his steel toes, and the branches grasped longingly at his cargo pants.

"Good Lord above." Coal whispered to himself.

As he approached the next clearing he wished to investigate, he could see it. In the gleam of sunshine, there lay a perfect branch. Its base was thick and flat, and ways up the length, another stump jutted out at a perfect handheld angle. The rest of the branch tapered off perfectly straight and consistently. Coal knelt beside it. He decided that he was compelled to take it back with him to show Jim-Bob its perfection. They may not have been children anymore, but a perfect gun-stick simply could not be wasted.

As Coal giggled to himself, he could hear the sudden cease of song in the air. It was now a lonely, cold breeze. It had been hot, save for the shade, and this new breeze felt off to Coal. The sudden quiet was inescapable, and the emptiness of the wood echoed around him. He could hear a sudden eruption of paws charging from the distance. The woods and leaves crackled under the beast's stride, alerting Coal of the direction from which it was coming. Coal looked to his right to see the monstrous beast lunging at him. He quickly ducked and turned, letting his hiking pack take the brunt of the impact and claws. The creature's claws caught the railing of the pack and threw it off balance, causing it to fall as it landed. The sudden jerk pulled Coal's pack hard to his side and sent him to his knees. As he turned and stood to look at his assailant, he also unbuckled the straps of his pack and dropped it as he lifted himself from the ground.

He was now gazing upon the thing's monstrous form. It appeared to be a horrid cross between man and wolf. Fur slipped between tears in human flesh, and as the muscles of the creature shifted in its wretched movement, the flesh tore from its host as more muscle and fur revealed itself. It had emerald green eyes that seemed to pierce straight through Coal with a wicked intelligence. Its front legs were too long for any canine's, and they ended in ripped hands with claws shredding through the tips of its fingers. Its head was large like that of a pit bull, but its snout was long and filled with fresh teeth that seemed to have just exploded from the creature's wretched maw. It walked on all fours as it collected itself and turned to face Coal. Its eyes widened, and it snarled as if to taunt Coal. As it did so, its own blood spilled forth from the cuts made by its fresh teeth.

"Hell naw, buddy, fuck that." Coal said as he quickly reached for his back belt loop.

The creature looked at him with varying degrees of confusion. The human should have been terrified and unable to move, let alone maintain eye contact. The deadly calm of Coal was cause for concern, the creature thought to itself, but it was far more concerned with what Coal was reaching for. Surely, this man knew that no mere pistol would be enough to bring it down.

As Coal drew from his back there was a distinct shaking sound. It all became clear as Coal produced a large canister attached to a pistol grip. The creature squinted its eyes in confusion as Coal unleashed the flood.

The creature's roar and rage quickly devolved into yelps and whines. Yelps and whines became cries. Coal looked on in bewilderment but never relented the deluge. As it rained down upon the beast, it writhed in agony. The burns and smells permeated its highly keen senses. Its incredibly honed sense of smell was sure to be its downfall, and the only way to dull its senses was to revert. The beast began to shrink back as its fur and mass sloughed off. It frantically ripped its excess flesh from its face in an effort to get the spray off as he cried. What was once a monstrous creature was now a tall, red, red-haired man in the fetal position on the ground.

"God fucking damnit! What the fuck is that?" he cried.

"Bear Mace," Coal answered.

"Ahhh, what the fuck are you doing with bear mace? Fuck it burns!" the man screamed.

"We're in the backwoods, brother. Why are you surprised?" Coal asked.

"They're your fucking woods dickhead!"

"Not if something bigger'en me thinks otherwise." Coal said as he shook his bear mace in front of the man.

"Fuck you motherfucker!" The man shrieked.

"What's the matter, bud? Never been maced before?" Coal asked.

"AHHH, HAVE YOU?" the man cried out.

The man had decided he had bought enough time as his vision had cleared, and his smell had finally burned out. Coal had never encountered a creature like him, so there was no way he could account for his incredible recovery time. The man suddenly lunged at Coal, wrapping his arms around his waist, and had shifted himself behind Coal. Before he could set his legs to supplex, Coal had quickly crouched and used his powerful arms to break the man's grip. Coal grabbed the man by his wrist as the man's grip broke, and started to twist his arm as Coal turned to face him. The man wrenched his arm from Coal's grip. Coal's left hand followed the man's arm back to him, and before the man could react Coal had sent his fingers and palm into the mouth of the man and clamped down on him with his thumb. The man wanted to use the golden opportunity to bite off Coal's fingers but Coal was already yanking the man. Coal used his incredible strength to pull the man back to himself and deliver a vicious blow with his right hand to the man's temple. As the man's head swung back Coal released his jaw and grabbed the wolf flesh still attached to his collarbone and shoulders and pulled him back in to deliver a devastating right elbow. This horrific blow sent the man to the ground and as he bounced and tried to form a guard Coal had quickly stepped past it. Coal found his left leg between the man's right arm and leg. The man was too slow to close his guard as

Coal quickly raised his right leg and stomped the man in the face. The man quickly closed his arms around his face so Coal elected to stomp his stomach. The man curled into the fetal position to protect what soft spots he could and Coal continued to stomp his side and kick his back with his steel toes.

"Come on, man fuck! I give! I give!" The man cried out in agony. His cries and pleas were interrupted by coughs and sniffles.

"Who the fuck you think you are?" Coal asked.

"I was sent here to pick up our heiress!" he coughed.

"You're that little fucker that was with that Viking prick!" Coal realized.

"Little?"

Coal raised his leg to stomp him again.

"No, no, you're right, that was me!" the man interrupted.

"Fuck, where's the big one?" Coal asked as he picked up his mace.

"Nowhere, nowhere! I came alone."

"And why's that?"

"You're gonna kick the shit outta me if I answer, dude!"

"I'll kick the shit outta you anyways!" Coal said as he began slowly stepping on the man's clearly bruised and broken ribs.

"AHHH FUCK! Ok man, OK!."

"Come on now, let's hear it."

"I was gonna smoke you and try to talk some sense into Mars."

"And you came alone?"

"Dude, Rolf's just here to bring her back; I didn't want to sick that pagan fuck on her. We've always been friends, man, but I just want her back safe."

"And you thought killin me was the best plan?"

"Literally yes, ain't a fuckin reason for her to keep this shit up with you gone." The man explained.

"You must be Amund." Coal said as he began to calm.

"You know me?" Amund asked.

"Yeah, Marcella said you were always a good friend to her. Said you'd just want her home safe."

"Bro, yes! You have no idea what the fucks around here!" Amund exclaimed.

"I got a few ideas. Come on then, no point in you laying around naked and catching a cold." Coal said as he reached his hand out.

Amund flinched at first, but he realized that Coal's offer seemed to be genuine; he took his hand, and Coal helped him to his feet.

"You just explode out of your clothes when you change?" Coal asked.

"Nah, they're this way." Amund pointed, he then picked up Coal's hiking pack and started to hand it to him then jerked it back and stared at it.

"Everything alright?"

"The fuck's this thing made out of?"

"I ain't too sure." Coal answered as Amund handed the unscratched pack back to Coal.

"That's some bullshit, can't even cut through a fucking pack, man."

"That really what you're complaining about right now?"

"Bro, as rough as the change is, you'd think the fucking monster claws would cut a fucking backpack!"

"I don't know, man. Badlands makes some pretty good shit."

"Fair enough. Hey, what are we telling Mars?" Amund asked.

Coal stopped walking and thought for a moment. "That we met, had a minor disagreement, and then came straight home to talk it out with her."

"Deal."

The two men continued through the woods until they found Amunds clothes. Amund dressed himself, and the two started back toward the house.

"Oh shit." Coal said. Amund stopped. Coal pulled out his cell phone and began calling.

"What's up, dude?" Amund asked.

"My dogs are out." Coal whispered.

"Bruh, I don't think a couple of dogs will be a problem." Amund joked.

"You ain't seen these." Coal whispered, "Hey baby!" He said as Marcella picked up his house phone.

"Hey, hun! I found the house phone!" Marcella answered on the other side.

"That's great, sweet pea, can you put up Briggs and Straton for me, please?" Coal asked.

"Yeah, baby, is everything ok?"

"Yes, dear, we just have a guest on the way." Coal answered.

"Ok, sweetie! I'll get them!"

"Thanks, baby! Bybye." Coal hung up.

"You two are fucking disgusting." Amund snorted.

"Maidenless comment." Coal laughed.

"Never heard her bubbly, and I don't think I've ever been more uncomfortable."

"Maidenless behavior." Coal joked.

"Fair enough, show me the way home, brave knight."

"Oh shit, hang on a sec." Coal said as they past the clearing where he had been ambushed. Coal jogged over and groped his perfect stick.

"Dear sweet fuck." Amund exclaimed.

"I know, right!"

"It's fucking perfect!"

"Exactly!"

The two men awed over the stick for a few more seconds before continuing to Coal's house. When they arrived, Amund looked around at the chickens, barns, and house. He thought it was a very nice homestead. It was secluded but not too far from the towns. Coal took the lead and went up the stairs first and opened the door.

"Babygirl, while I was out I found a puppy you want to keep him?" Coal called out as he entered the back door.

"Ooo, a puppy!" Marcella exclaimed as she shot up from the couch and turned to look at Coal.

Coal stepped aside as Amund stepped into the house.

"Amund?" Marcella asked in happy confusion. Her face quickly changed to a teeth clenching grimace. "Amund!" She snarled.

"Whoa now sweety pie he's cool!" Coal assured her.

"What the fuck are you doing here?" She asked.

"I thought you said you guys were friends!" Coal insisted.

"Until he lead Mark straight to me at the club last night!" Marcella shouted.

"He what? You what?" Coal was utterly bewildered.

"I thought Mark was our best shot at getting you home, Mars!" Amund tried to explain.

"That's what the fuck you get for thinking, Amund!" Marcella hollered at him.

"The fuck was I supposed to do dipshit? You dipped in the worst fucking area possible! Every fucking corner reeks of fucking rot and some type of evil shit! There's black magic vampires in this bitch Mars! I want us to go home!" Amund yelled back.

"I don't want to go back Amund! The one person who was consistently good to me just lead dad's fucking killers straight to my new boyfriends house!" Marcella argued.

"Hell yeah," Coal whispered to himself, "Oh wait, shit."

"I came alone, Mars. Mark and I went to the club without telling anyone, and I left Mark at the motel," Amund said.

"Yeah, but you still brought him to me while I was out trying to make new friends. You think I wanted to sober up with him losing his temper and screaming at me while threatening my boyfriend?" Mars asked.

"I don't what you want Mars fuck! I'm surrounded by fucking humans that don't smell right making eye contact like they fucking know me! Eric's already smoked one fucking vampire! He took two more hostage and one's fucking weird with that black shit on his face! I'm barely holding it together here Goddamn! I'm only here for you!" Amund erupted.

"Don't feed me that bullshit Amund!" Marcy snapped.

"Cut the boy some slack Marcy." Coal interrupted.

"Don't you dare take his side!" Marcy growled at Coal.

"Now little missy you take that tone with me and I'm slipping worcestershire in your next biscuit." Coal calmly explained.

"You wouldn't dare!" warned Marcella.

"Mars, I don't think I'd try this one," Amund spoke.

Marcella looked at Amund in confusion. Amund had always been a formidable lycan. Though he was young for his prowess, he was considered prodigious. As Marcella took a moment to inspect him, she began to see the cuts and bruises that had yet to heal on his face.

"Oh no, what happened to your face, Amy?" Marcella asked as her anger turned to concern for her childhood friend.

Amund and Coal made eye contact, and Amund looked at Marcella sullen. Marcella looked at Coal perplexed until it suddenly clicked to her.

"Holy shit." She said.

"Look, we had a minor disagreement and moved past it babygirl. He's really just here trying to help." Coal explained.

"I should know that, I just… I just…" Marcella stumbled through her words as tears began to well in her eyes.

"You feel hurt and betrayed babygirl, and that makes you angry. It's ok though sweetheart we can work through it, you just have to understand that your friend here made a well intentioned mistake." Coal explained.

"I know he did, it's just so frustrating. Fuck I'm so angry right now!" Marcella cried out.

"Why don't you go take a break, keep tryna catch up on your game sweetpea, me and Amund will just talk outside. We can talk when you work through some of those feelings ok?" Coal guided. He could tell that Amund was dear to Marcella and didn't want her anger or confusion to cause a painful outburst.

"Ok, ok. I'll calm down." Marcella said as she went back to the couch.

Coal showed Amund the back door, and the two men stepped out and sat on the patio furniture.

"Where's this Mark boy at?" Coal asked as soon as the two were sat comfortably.

"You know I can't tell you that man."

"Bullshit, you can tell me here and now."

"Dude, I can't just let my boy get staked, I can't betray someone like that," Amund explained.

"I promise you I'm not gone kill'em." Coal insisted.

"What would you do then?"

"I'm gone get my boy, and we gone pull up and beat his ass." Coal explained.

"You know you can't just beat up on a vampire right? I might would get you killed telling you."

"You let me worry bout them details. Write it down."

"Fine." Amund agreed. Coal went in for a moment and returned with a notebook and a pen.

"So what's your plan now?" Coal asked.

"No fucking clue. We failed the Op so we sure as shit can't go back to Rolf and Eric. They'll cancel our cards if we don't report in. Fuck."

"Look man. I got a trailer on my old property, it's just a single wide but I take good care of it." Coal informed Amund.

"The fuck you'd do that for us for?"

"Cause you're Marcy's one loyal friend and some other down on his luck dumbass who I'm gone beat the shit out of. I feel responsible."

"Yeah, that's really my only option. I guess I'll swoop in and get Mark after you rough him up. When will that be exactly?" Amund asked.

"Probably Saturday, I can get your number and call when we're on the way."

"Sounds like a plan."

Coal reached out and shook Amund's hand.

"You know, you seem pretty mature for a dude our age, like how you handle Mars' outbursts." Amund lead on.

"I had to grow up pretty quick and get a hand on my temper even quicker." Coal explained.

"Coulda fooled me." Amund joked.

"I put on a good act." Coal laughed. "You smoke?"

"Socially."

Coal went back for a moment and returned with two of his vanilla coffee cigars. "Socialize."

The two men lit their cigars and leaned back in their chairs. It was too early for sundown, but too late for any chorin. The two men continued to smoke in silence until Marcella joined them, beers in hand. The three then sat and watched the chickens while they drank. When the sun had fallen they went back inside. Amund sat at the kitchen counter, and Coal handed him and Marcella another beer before going outside to let the dogs out. Once Coal had left Marcella looked over at Amund.

His emerald gaze gave her shivers. He had now fully recovered and his predatory eyes had revealed themselves. He slowly inhaled through his nose and examined every inch of Marcella, then the room they were in.

"What do you think you're doing Amund?" Marcella asked as her hands began to tense and her fingers began to pulsate and twitch.

Amund closed his eyes for a few seconds and when they opened, they were human. He exhaled through his mouth. "Just checking on you Mars." Amund continued to look around. "He seems nice, and he keeps a clean house."

"He's great. He's giving, and understanding."

"I'd have to agree, I just hope he can keep you safe," Amund said.

Coal came back in through the back door. "Well, shit, now that the dogs are out, I reckon you'll have to sleep on the futon, fuc,k I shoulda thought that my bad."

"Is the futon comfy?" Amund asked.

"Jim-Bob swears by it," Marcella answered.

Coal pulled out the futon in front of the TV. He brought blankets out a chest in the guest room.

"If you have any problem sleeping I'm logged in so you can watch whatever you want. We're probably gonna crash upstairs. I'll see you in the morning!" Coal waved goodbye as he and Marcella walked up the stairs.

Chapter 10

Amund awoke to the sound of sizzling coming from the kitchen. He stood up, still in his clothes from yesterday. He folded the blanket and sheet, then packed the futon back in. As he did so he could see Marcella in the kitchen. She was in a white tank top with a pink bra beneath it. She also wore her Daisy Duke's with comically large pockets sticking out below where the shorts ended. She was flipping patty sausage when she noticed Amund.

"No way in hell some hick's made a homemaker out'a you Mars." Amund chuckled aloud.

"That hick took me in and has been nothing but nice to me!" Marcy sneered.

"Whoa now, little philly, I ain't mean you no harm," Amund spoke in his worst possible accent.

"You ain't from round'ere are ya boy?"

Amund's entire back seized up on him as chills ran down his spine. The low drawled out growl behind came as a horrifying surprise. Amund turned around to see a large bearded man behind. The man's legs were just past a shoulder apart and his arms were wide, hands flexed and ready to grab at anything.

"Jesus fucking Christ, you have got to be the scariest fucking thing I've ever seen." Amund barely got out.

Coal closed the back door behind himself and erupted in laughter.

"I don't think he's used to getting snuck up on like that, hun. Go easy on him." Marcella giggled.

"How the fuck's he move so quiet, Mars? Where'd you find him at?" Amund asked.

"This is my house, man. Where'd you think?" Coal laughed.

Amund stared into space for a moment. "Fair enough."

"I got all the chorin done early today, just in case the trailer needs a little spiffing up when I drop you off." Coal explained. "We can roll soon as we finish breakfast if you want."

"Yeah, if you think it'd be ok if I caught up with Mars for a little bit after," Amund said.

"Sure, brother, no problem. Sausage and biscuits again?" Coal asked.

"Yeah, I learned how to make that white gravy packet, too!" Marcy replied.

"Aw, hell yeah." Coal smiled as he loaded a plate.

"That smells awesome, Mars!" Amund added.

The three sat down at the table. Coal said a quick prayer over the food, and they began eating together. Amund carefully observed the two. Marcella looked to make sure Coal was enjoying her cooking. She smiled at him when they made eye contact. Coal was tearing through his biscuits and gravy like he hadn't eaten in days. Amund took a few bites and found them to be tasty. The three finished their meal and then sat at the table.

"So, how did you two meet?" Amund asked, breaking the silence.

"Dad's thralls were chasing me, and when Coal saw them, he and Jim-Bob jumped in to save me," Marcella answered.

"How?"

"We thought they were wild methheads, so we beat their ass and gave Marcella a ride, then she gave me the full story." Coal explained.

'And you believed her? That easy?" Amund asked

"Yeah, dude, she can shoot them fangs out on cue." Coal said.

"Ha, shit, I forgot about that." Amund chuckled. "Welp, I've seen all I need to see." Amund stood from the table. "I'll go wait by the truck."

"Sure thing, bud, let me wash these dishes, and I'll be out there," replied Coal.

"I got the dishes, hun. You can go ahead and help Amund," Marcella said as she shooed Coal out the door.

"Aight, thanks babygirl!" Coal waved goodbye as he stepped down the stairs of the front door.

Coal unlocked the truck with his key fob. Amund climbed into the passenger seat, and Coal hopped into the driver side. The two pulled out of the drive way, stopped at the gate, then pulled through. Coal's old trailer was only a few miles down the road, but they had to make a stop by where Amund had hidden his car. Coal pulled over to the side of the road. Down a small cut-out path sat a coyote tan MX-5.

"That's me hiding up there," Amund explained.

"You got that diff locked up?" Coal asked.

"With aftermarket coilovers and a few giggles in the console," Amund answered.

"Not bad." Coal smiled

"It gets it done when I need it to," Amund said. "Let me hop in and follow you the rest of the way."

Amund hopped in his car and followed Coal to his old trailer. It was a single wide, and it was almost freshly pressure washed with the weeds and grass cut back. It had a nice wooden deck with a grill on it. The two men stepped out of their vehicles.

"Man, you took good care of this place!" Amund exclaimed as he looked around the small property.

"Yeah, it ain't a lot, but I made it look good."

"Hell yeah. I'll lay low. You just let me know after you and Mark have had a little heart-to-heart, and I'll swoop in and pick him up."

"I'll be sure, too. I think we're just chilling Sunday, you want me to give you a ring then?" Coal asked.

"Sounds like a plan," Amund replied.

Coal nodded and got back in his truck. He took the short drive back to his house. Coal thought about his remaining plans for the day leading up to his date with Marcella. The chicks weren't big enough to separate just yet, but he could go ahead and clean the dog kennels while they were out. Crane was still hard at work on their project, and Jim-Bob wouldn't be over till Saturday evening.

When he arrived home, Coal said hello to Marcy, who seemed content playing their RPG game. He went to his barn and found his pressure washer. Once it was hooked up by the kennels, Coal turned the gas valve on, choked it, and crunk the washer. Briggs and Straton wouldn't even look at the kennels until late in the evening, so Coal was welcome to wash down everything. He pulled all the plastics out and hosed them off, then went into the kennel with a shovel.

Once the kennels were clean, Coal decided it would be a good time to rate some of his chickens. He walked through the teepee yard checking the health and quality of his fowl. It wasn't long after the last time he had culled this generation's yard and all of them remaining birds still appeared to adhere to Coal's strict standards. Coal breaathed a sigh of relief. Although the thought of a full deep freeze was enticing, he didn't enjoy culling any of the birds he had hand raised.

There were still a few hours until he needed to get ready, and Marcy had taken up his console. With all of his chores done for the day he opted to kill his remaining time with a nap. He checked Marcella's progress before walking up the stairs and laying down. He reached over and set his alarm. He closed his eyes and began to drift off. Despite the apparent challenges, soon, he would be taking a beautiful young lady out on the town for a night. He still wasn't sure if she had decided that that would be their only night together, but he wouldn't let the possibility deter him from making the most of what could have been their last moments together. He was determined to win her over, and he thought he had already proven himself against that which hunted them. Still, he would have to respect her decision, but the thought of her leaving filled him with a strange sense of sorrow. He had thought himself able to fade away to slumber quickly, but his mind had begun to race with all the possibilities. After a half hour, he finally quieted his rampant thoughts. He drifted away.

Coal awoke to the sound of his alarm. He shot up from his bed and silenced his clock. He grabbed his towel and washcloth to take a shower. He quickly pulled the outfit he had picked out and laid it out on his bed. He took his shower and made sure to deep clean himself. He smoothed his skin out with a sugar scrub, and when he stepped out, he followed up with a coconut shea butter lotion. He grabbed his straight razor and edged his beard cleanly off of his cheeks, then took an electric razor to clean off his neck. When he exited the shower into his room he donned a pair of light gray slacks, cinching them in with a Versace belt. He topped it with a corsica semi-spread polo. He finished his look with a swiss watch and a burgundy high-shine oxford shoe. The medusa head shining from his belt provided an intriguing focal point. He took two spritzes of his favorite cologne and headed downstairs.

All while Coal was getting ready, Marcella was also finishing her makeup. She had applied her favorite bright coral pink lustreglass lipstick from Mac, which was framed by the brand's studio powder foundation. She had clad herself in a shoshanna bentley lace and faux leather minidress, which she accented with Fendi leather traced heel booties and Wolford velvet de-luxe thigh highs. She beamed as Coal came down the stairs. She had seen him wearing decent clothes, but she had never seen him cleaned up and putting in an effort. She could smell the notes of rum and vanilla from his cologne, followed by the hints of coconut from his scrubs and lotion.

Everything looked different about Coal, the way he walked and even the way he stood. The way he smiled so arrogantly made Marcella excited. He had transformed from a southern slouch to an upright stallion. She watched his eyes gleam as he looked at her. She wondered what he saw in her at this moment. She had carefully planned out her outfit from what she could, and she was wearing her favorite makeup and brands. She worried that he would not like the things she had picked out. She had also worried if he had reservations, given everything that had happened. Marcella struggled to process everything on her own. She had no girlfriends that she knew well enough to talk her up or calm her down. Even Amund would almost be a welcome input but she didn't get his temporary phone number, and she hadn't been to town with Coal to get a cell phone anyway.

Coal, for all his composed demeanor, could only barely stop his legs from shaking. He stood before the most beautiful and intriguing woman he had ever met. Her outfit was so well composed, and her face seemed to gleam there in front of him. He froze before her, too nervous to take her hand and show her to his truck.

"How do I look?" Marcella asked as she twirled in front of him.

As Marcy twirled Coal could only stand in amazement. Her calves were well toned and accentuated by her heeled booties. Her tight thighs hid beneath her skirt. He struggled to meet her eyes. They looked as if they were the rarest flowers on earth, and they looked at him so longingly. Coal had never felt wanted in such a way. He had always had the camaraderie of the men he considered friends and brothers, but to feel something so romantic brought him so much joy and anxiety.

Coal pushed through and took Marcella's hand and looked deep in her eyes. "Those orchid eyes are a hidden treasure and a key to what I believe to be happiness, And you are a bewitching mystery wrapped in lace and leather, and if were the last I would ever see of you, I would cherish the moment, and lament that I would stand firmly against your wishes just for the opportunity to see you again."

Marcella's chest felt as if it would burst as she held back tears. She didn't know why it was they fought so hard to escape her eyes, but she knew no one had ever held her in such a regard. There, a humble man stood in awe of her. He wanted only her. Every challenge, foe, and title alike melted away from her. There was a blue-gray smoke that hid the fire in Coal's eyes. She knew they burned only for her in that moment, and she felt like a true lady as his hand held hers.

"You wouldn't ever let me go, would you?" Marcella smiled.

"Iron itself would be envious of my grip." Coal said.

Coal suddenly pulled Marcy into him, and gently kissed her lips. She wrapped her arms around him and pulled him even closer as she kissed him back. Coal pulled away and smiled at her.

"We really should eat first." He chuckled.

"I suppose so, Mister Coal." Marcy stepped back and smirked as she pulled up her skirt revealing a cute pink bow pinned to the strap of her sheer lace panties. "Would you like to start with dessert?"

Coal took a deep breath. "Sorry, Miss Marcy, but they are very strict with the reservation times."

"Alrighty then, but make sure you save room."

"Yes, Ma'am."

Coal opened the front door and escorted Marcella to his truck. He helped her in. They drove off toward the city. The sun was starting to set, and the sky glowed with pink and orange.

"So where are we headed?" Marcella asked.

"Well, I remembered you like lamb, and I had a buddy that works at this high-end Persian restaurant, so he got us reservations on short notice." Coal explained.

"Short notice? I thought you planned this days ago?"

"Yeah but you typically gotta make reservations like a month in advance for this place." Coal replied.

"How do you have so many friends that can just get you into places?" Marcella asked.

"I'm nosey and helpful," Coal laughed.

"Did you rescue him too?" Marcella snickered.

"Nah, he was goin through culinary school, and he needed guinea pigs. We were in the same dorm, and I can eat anything, so it worked out pretty well. Plus, Obadiah's dad's always been a solid metal worker, so Jim-Bob and I got him a knife set to say thanks for feeding us."

"So you guys kept in touch."

"When we can, he stays busy at his job, but we're still friendly. I'm pretty happy he still uses them knives after all these years. He let me know when I called him, and I'll need to tell Obadiah later 'cause I'm sure that'll just tickle his dad."

"You guys are so sweet." Marcella smiled.

"If you say so, baby girl."

"You know I really like when you call me Marcy or baby girl," Marcella said shyly.

"I'm pretty fond of saying it myself."

Marcella leaned over and kissed Coal's cheek. They weren't far from the restaurant now. The truck was now weaving about traffic in the city. They pulled into a parking garage next to a luxury hotel. Coal stepped out of his truck and circled around and opened the door for Marcy. He held out his hand and helped her out. The two then made their way into the Hotel. The restaurant occupied the roof.

The couple took the elevator up, and when they exited, they were greeted by the maitre d. Coal showed her their reservations and she took them to a secluded balcony. There was a singular table set in black linens and lit by a candle. The view of the city was extensive. Skyscrapers lit up the night sky, and the gleams of headlights illuminated the highways and streets below. The clouds had gone to bed for the night, and the starry night pierced the veil of the city's glare. They seemed to be eating at the tallest building in the town.

Coal's fear of heights only had seconds to make him uneasy, for when he looked at Marcella's gleeful amazement, all of his worries vanished. She leaned over the rails, looking at everything below, then she gazed at the stars above. Coal would have been otherwise unaware of all that surrounded them had it not been reflected in Marcella's glimmering eyes. His smile brightened his face next to her as they watched the city together for a few minutes.

The two took their seats and looked for their menus. As they did so a tall Arab man approached the table with a bottle of wine in hand.He showed the label to Coal and Marcella. He removed the cork and poured their glasses before placing the wine on the table.

"The wine was opened to breathe four hours prior to your arrival. You will notice that there are no menus present. This is because, as my honored guest, I will be taking care of you this evening. Rest assured, great care has been taken with regard to your preferences. Amuse-gueules will arrive shortly." He explained.

"Thank you, sir." Coal nodded.

"My pleasure." the man replied. He gave a quick bow and made his way back to the kitchen.

"Who was that?" Marcella asked.

"My buddy Farhad." Coal answered.

"You said your buddy worked here," Marcella whispered.

"Well, yeah, he's the head chef, but his uncle owns the place."

"Are you serious?"

"Yeah, he's a real humble dude outside of work, but when you're in a place like this, you're paying for an experience." Coal said.

Marcella swirled the wine in her glass. "Consider it experienced." She said just before she began to taste.

Farhad returned with a tray of decoratively assembled appetizers. Dolma was surrounded by triangles of pita bread. Hummus and a blended aubergine bake were on the border of the pita, and finally there was a small pomegranate cheese ball. Farhad described the arrangement and its origins, as well as the flavor profiles. Once his presentation was over he thanked the couple again, and explained that the entrees were to arrive within thirty minutes so that they could take their time to enjoy the different elements of the platter. He gave a quick bow and returned to his kitchen.

Marcella and Coal began sampling the plate before them. Everything was carefully crafted, the dolma exploded with eastern spice and pizzazz, while the aubergine bake slowly exuded complexity and depth dripping from the tip of the bread that was dipped in it.

"So what's your story, Miss Marcy?" Coal asked as he reached for another grape leaf.

"What do you mean?"

"I've only heard you talk about one real story, I'd really like to get to know you." Coal spoke.

"I was born after one of the darkest feasts in our household's current history Coal, I like you, I really like you. But I'm still running from a lot right now, and I'm still scared to open up about a lot of it. I don't mean to be rude, but I don't think it's something you could really understand." Marcella tried to explain.

Coal leaned back in his chair with a slightly puzzled look on his face. His lips were closed but he licked the front of his teeth as he pondered. He took in a sizeable breath before looking into Marcella's eyes. "You know I spent the first sixteen years of my life in abject terror. Never knew peace a day in my life, you ever seen me sign for something?"

"I have."

"How you spell my name babygirl?" Coal asked.

"C O A L," Marcella answered. "I had wondered about that, but I didn't know how to ask.

"I was born in december. I was an unwelcome lump in my mom's stocking, at least I reckon that's how she put it."

"That's horrible Coal."

"That's life hun, I ain't choose it, but if I run from it, I let it make decisions for me. And I'll be damned if I ever let them bastards make another decision for me."

"Coal, I'm sorry, I didn't know."

"Now babygirl there ain't nothing to be sorry about. The only reason I'm telling you this is because I might be quickly falling for the incredible woman I've come to know as Marcella, and I don't think you should relegate yourself to the thing that Marcella is running away from, cause when you do, it gets to steer where you're headed as long as it's behind you." Coal explained.

"And I guess you just naturally gained all that wisdom?" Marcella retorted.

"Nah, see I met the sheriff while he was still a regular officer when they moved me in with my meemaw, and when I started acting out, he hunted me down and held me while he gave me the same lesson."

"You might just be the only one I can open up to Coal, maybe that scares me a little." Marcella responded.

"Babygirl, that's fair enough, I just want you to understand that I'm here when you're ready."

"When my dad decided he needed to solidify the household's position, and regain a firm grasp over our resources and territories, he gathered every candidate the household had to offer at the time and attempted a mass conversion. Because there were so many, and the inherent bloodlust that taints our lineage, the candidates that couldn't turn fast enough were devoured by their friends on sight. This quickly spilled into the surrounding town. Unaware of the possible side-effects of gorging himself so indulgently, my father returned to my mother to relieve the night's stress. I was conceived that night. My official title to the vampires of our household, is the heiress of the blackest generation. I'm also lovingly called the queen of the feast by the members of the blackest generation."

"Are Eric and Mark members of those guys?"

"No, Mark is a younger mistake, like vampire young, he's a little older than me. Eric came a few years after, but he was a special case and a gift from some super mystery vampire." Marcella said.

"Your dad didn't send any of the blackest generation to find you?" Coal asked.

"No, because of the resulting feast so early in their inception, the entire congregation from that night is tainted horribly. My dad only uses them as enforcers and shock troops. They are way too violent and quick to anger. Plus they have terrifyingly fast metabolisms so they have to be kept close to the manor to be sustained. Most business they conduct has to be planned logistically well in advance."

"Still wouldn't they be concerned for you? I don't mean you're one of them, but you are, well, one of them." Coal tried to wrap his head around them.

"I was always their favorite little mascot, so there's no way dad told them I ran away."

"Awww, that's so cute. I could see you behind them with little pom-poms." Coal laughed.

"You'd just want to see me in a cheerleader uniform."

"Or that mini skirt and nothing else. So what kind of relationship did you have with your so called, brothers and sisters?" Coal enquired.

"The blackest generation love me as their little sister, the rest of the household had mixed feelings. I could never get a real read on Eric though." She explained.

"How could they have mixed feelings about you?"

"I was the immediate named heiress of the house and my fathers pride and joy. Most were jealous, then there was Lucah."

"Lucah?"

"He fucking hated me. He was dad's right hand until I came around, and then when Eric took his position, the bastard still found a way to blame me!"

"What a dick!"

"I know!" Marcella exclaimed.

The two began laughing together. Farhad emerged with a large pot of slow cooked pomegranate legs of lamb. He moved the candle in the middle of the table and sat the pot between the two. The smell of the pomegranate molasses and orange filled the air. Marcella's mouth began to water. Farhad simply bowed and walked away.

The two began to both eat from the pot in the center of the table. The sweet molasses cut by the citrus of the orange was simply immaculate as the mint and ginger slowly snuck its way onto their palates. Marcella chewed slowly and hummed to herself as the flavors overtook her. Coal was also indulging in a large helping of the lamb and sauce.

"So how'd you meet T. Rell?" Marcella asked.

"Through Obadiah surprisingly."

"How on earth?"

"T. used to roll with a rough bunch. There came a day when they wanted to escalate and his boys at the time jumped an old man down the street from the diner. T. Rell tried to stop them and wound up in the hospital with the old man. That was Obadiah's grandaddy, so after the old man spoke on T's behalf, Obadiah tracked down the thugs."

"And what happened then?"

"Have you seen Obadiah? He walked in on them all playing pool and beat them all half to death. Afterward, he came to me to see if I could get T. a job at the factory to get him away from all that bullshit. Then he went and told T. Rell's grandmama on'em."

"So Obadiah's a sweet guy after all then?" Marcella laughed.

"He's a damn hooligan when he drinks but he's got a heart of gold." Coal replied. "So what's your dad like?"

Marcella stopped and thought for a moment. "To everyone at the manor he was a stoic two century old vampire, but to me he was either distant or just a goober."

Coal almost spit up his wine. "Don't reckon I ever heard anyone call a vampire a goober."

"Well he always tried to be a fun silly dad when he could, but he was always so busy, or just really aloof about the whole 'having a daughter' thing. Like, I know it's silly, but I feel like he should've been the one out here looking for me. Like, does he just not care?" Marcella asked in painful confusion.

"You said he sent his right hand and your ex to come and get you, didn't he?"

"Well, yeah, he did."

"Look, sometimes folks underestimate people's tantrums and breakdowns. There's every chance he thought you were throwing a fit and didn't give it too much attention, but he was still worried so he not only sent his best man, but also your friends to comfort you."

"You know Coal, I never really thought of it like that. Maybe he just didn't take me seriously." Marcella pondered.

"Parents rarely take their kids seriously, dude is two hundred years old, you are definitely still a baby to him."

Marcella laughed a bit, "Yeah, I guess you're right."

"Course I'm right, I can't…"

"Remember a time you were wrong?" Marcella smiled.

"Well, none off the top of my head." Coal chuckled.

"So what's your Meemaw like?" Marcella asked.

"Oh, you have to meet her Sunday." Coal answered.

"Fucking what?" Marcella looked up in shock.

"Aw shit, did I forget to mention that?"

"Well, hell yeah, you did, Coal!"

"Well, if the date didn't go well I wasn't gone have to worry bout'it now was I?" Coal joked.

"Oh it was going well Coal. Was." Marcella taunted.

"I'd say it's going great, cause you're still coming home with me." Coal smiled.

Marcella blushed, and failed to find a witty come back. Farhad came to her rescue as he emerged with dessert. He held two ornate glasses decadently filled with saffron rice pudding. The light reflected off of its golden color and illuminated the rose petals serving as a garnish. As the two marveled over their glasses Farhad vanished.

Each small spoonful was delicate and smooth. The two savored every taste slowly. It wasn't too long until the glasses were empty. Coal leaned back in seat, and Marcella sipped her wine.

"So where did you learn to fight?" Marcella asked.

"What do you mean?" Coal questioned.

"Come on, Amund might be a little dramatic, but he's definitely no pushover." Marcella continued.

"Yeah but I got the drop on him with that bear mace." Coal answered.

"The what?"

"Bear Mace. We got a couple of bigass black bears in these woods." Coal continued.

"So when Amund tried to hurt you?"

"I hosed him down, I think he's got like super senses even for a werewolf, so he had to change back to lessen everything."

"So you're just gonna handle all your supernatural problems with outdoor accessories?" Marcella joked.

"Yes."

Marcella burst out laughing. She was completely dumbfounded by Coal's simplistic approach to everything that could be coming for them. He genuinely believed he could handle any problems that reared their ugly heads. She thought he was so endearing and genuine.

"You're really not scared Coal?" Marcella quietly asked.

"I might have been startled for a while, but I got my head on. I'm not as good with surprises as Jim-Bob." Coal answered

"Yeah, other than when we first met, you've been pretty level-headed, how is that?"

"Nasty temper runs deep in my family, so I'm a little more methodical in my approach to things, but when I get surprised, I still go back to my defaults." Coal explained.

"I haven't met any of them yet, your family that is."

"Nonsense, you met Jim-Bob, and you'll meet meemaw next week." Coal replied.

"Yeah, but I've talked about my dad a lot, I don't know anything about your parents though." Marcella prodded.

"You ain't never gone meet either of'em, so I don't really bring them up."

"Oh, ok then."

"So, what do you think we should do next while we're on the town?" Coal asked.

"Honestly, after the check comes I wouldn't mind going home and curling up. We can just stream a movie if you want." Marcella answered.

"Alright then, sounds good to me."

As the two finished speaking, as if it were magic, Farhad appeared with the check in his hand. Coal pulled his card from his wallet and handed it over to him. Farhad took the card and backed away through the curtains. He promptly returned with the receipts. Coal wrote the tip and signed one before handing it back.

"Thank you very much for your patronage and continued support, kind sir. We hope you have both had a wonderful evening and will join us again soon." Farhad said graciously.

This time instead of backing away, he turned around. As he turned Coal could see the three knives he and his friends had gotten Farhad years ago. They looked as new and well maintained as the day they gave them to him. Coal smiled as Farhad left his view. Coal looked over to Marcella who had also noticed the knives and was joyfully grinning. Coal held out his hand.

"Shall we retire for the evening?" He asked.

"I think we shall, Mr. Coal," Marcella answered as she blushed a bit.

She took his hand and the two made their way through the restaurant and into the elevator. They then made their way into the parking garage. Everything was well lit to be so late at night. Coal opened the truck door for Marcella. They then began the ride home. Marcella watched the city lights fade away as the truck began weaving around the curves of the back roads. The music was turned up to pass the time, and Marcella was left thinking to herself during the ride. She watched the trees and powerlines zoom by as they passed them.

Marcella couldn't help but feel torn about her whirlwind romance. She had known the man for a week, but somehow it felt like she had always known him. He was open and honest with her. She appreciated his endearing forwardness, and ability to communicate. Her chest fluttered as Coal's truck slowed to turn into their drive. She had plans for the night but wasn't sure if Coal felt the same way, and her nerves were quickly giving way to a build up of anxiety.

Coal hopped out of the truck and opened the gate. He then pulled the truck through, stepped out, then closed the gate again. He climbed back in.

"Man, I have got to get some eclectic gate openers." Coal exhaled.

"Maybe you'll buy them quicker than you finished the fence." Marcella giggled.

"Quicker than WE finished the fence ma'am." Coal retorted.

Coal pulled his truck into the drive in front of the house. He stepped out and around to open Marcella's door. He took her by the hand as she exited. The two began slowly walking up the steps. Coal opened the front door and held it for Marcella as she walked through. They both stood in the empty house for a moment when Coal flicked the light in the living room on.

"You know, tonight was a pretty good night Marcy. You given any thought to…" Coal was interrupted when Marcella gently pressed her fingers against his lips. She was looking into his eyes. He could tell she was nervous. Her eyes were slowly welling up as she searched for the right words to say. Maybe she was searching her feelings for what she really wanted. She suddenly snapped out of her nervous lock and wrapped her hands around Coal's head and brought him to her.

Marcella kissed Coal passionately, forcing her tongue down his throat before he could even fully comprehend what had happened. When he realized, he grabbed Marcella's waist and brought it to his. Marcella grabbed Coal by his belt while turning, backing up toward the stairs, dragging Coal with her. She turned again, hurrying up the stairs toward Coal's room, stopping to wait for him in his doorway. Coal rushed up to meet her, as she threw the door open and waved her finger to tell him to follow. He did so and stopped after entering the room.

"Are you sure this is what you want Marcy?" He asked.

Marcella grinned triumphantly as she unzipped the back of her dress, "You tell me." The dress fell to her ankles revealing her black laced bra and panties. She tugged on the pink bow at the center of her panty strap as she fell backwards onto Coal's bed. "Come and get it baby."

Coal approached her and reached his hands out to pull Marcella's panties down. She swatted them away and grabbed his hair as he leaned down. The two made eye contact as Coal looked at her in confusion.

"I've already tried to eat you. Time to return the favor and show me what your teeth do," Marcella demanded as she forced Coal's head between her legs.

Coal understood the assignment and bit the pink flower on the strap and yanked the lace from Marcella's hips, then to her knees, then off from around her feet. Coal grabbed Marcy's left leg and began kissing at her ankle, working his way up.

"Aw how sweet," Marcella giggled.

The moment Coal reached her inner thigh sweet kisses turned to one quick, ravenous bite. Marcella squealed as her legs jerked. As Marcella recoiled in sudden shock Coal wrenched her legs open. She only had a moment to gasp before he was down on her. His tongue plunged deeply within her, and he worked his way up, finding the pearl in an ocean of pink. Marcella moaned as the tip of Coal's tongue played with her. She never imagined she was so sensitive. She let out an even louder moan as Coal lost grip with his right hand and sunk a finger into Marcy, just below his tongue, thrusting it back and forward. Coal was aggressive but gentle. He couldn't believe how tight Marcella was as she suddenly gripped around his finger. Marcella quickly wrapped her legs around Coal's head, and grabbed his hair again with her hands. Coal responded by picking up the pace with his tongue and finger, sucking and flicking her pearl and energetically fingering her. She squealed as she began violently thrusting her hips back and forward, grinding on Coal. The two were fast in their grinding tumble. Marcella grew louder, wetter and faster by the second.

"Ah, fuck!" She squealed out as she released herself into Coal's beard. Her legs went limp and she released his hair as she fell back. Coal stood and admired her for a moment, when she regained her composure, sitting up and looking at him. "Take your pants off!"

"Yes ma'am," Coal smiled.

When he did so, Marcella was taken back by the size of him. She knew Coal as a man was nothing short of massive, but to see him fully erect was mouthwatering to her. She had to have him. Before he could start unbuttoning his shirt she lunged forward grabbing it by the collar. She slung him onto the bed and before he could register, she had mounted him. She let out a shocked gasp as Coal's cock stretched through her. She gripped onto him with all the strength in her legs as she began unbuttoning his shirt. She lost her patience halfway and ripped the last of his shirt open. She then unbuckled her bra, unveiling her bouncing breasts and pink nipples. She grabbed Coal's right hand and placed it on her chest as she began grinding.

"I'm all yours baby, just please take me." She begged.

Coal lightly groped her breast before violently grabbing her hips with both hands. He began thrusting into her with all he had. His powerful legs bounced her rapidly on top of him. He didn't know what had come over him, but she was so tight he couldn't help it. Whenever he would pull back she seemed to suck him straight back in as Marcella's pussy grabbed every vein on Coal as he continued to thrust. She pulled him up to her to kiss him as she rode.

"Oh God, come on baby! Make me yours!" She cried as her legs began to shake. With one great thrust she seemed to snap. "Oh fuck yeah, shit!" She screamed. "Come on, you gotta mark what's yours baby!"

As she demanded, Coal shifted his hands to her back and began to scratch. As he did so, Marcella bucked back and slapped him.

"I'm not some little southern belle bitch you brought back from prom!" She yelled as she grabbed Coal's hair. "You fucking claw me like an animal!"

Coal knocked her hand away from his hair and yanked hers. She squalled like a panther as he pulled her into him and bit into the nerves in her neck. Marcella's eyes rolled back as chills shot through her. She let a light squeak as her pussy clamped around Coal even harder. Coal wasn't finished. He took his hands and dug his fingers into Marcella's back and cleaved down. Marcella's loud squeals quickly turned into a low growl as squirted into Coal's lap and began quivering on him. Coal became excited as Marcella seemed to vibrate on top of him and began thrusting as fast and hard as possible, with renewed vigor. He grabbed back onto Marcella's hips and held her in place so he could thrust even deeper. His cock began to throb and pulsate inside Marcella and Coal sped up even further.

"Oh shit, Oh fuck," Coal began to moan.

"Come on baby! Faster, oh fuck me! Fuck me baby!" Marcy squealed.

"I'm close, baby. What do we do?" Coal asked.

"Come in me baby! It's mine! I want it all! Oh fuck!" She moaned in answer.

"You sure?"

"Oh god, all of it! Fill me up, baby. Oh, fuck me! Fuck me! Harder!" Marcella squealed.

Marcella grabbed Coal and squeezed as hard as she could as she began thrusting back against him. She could feel his cock engorge itself.

"Oh fuck yes, baby, give it to me!" She screamed out. As she did, Coal could no longer hold it back. He exploded into her. Their laps were left soaking wet and sticky. Marcella quickly dismounted from Coal and brought his legs of the side of the bed as she went to her knees.

"What are you doing, sweetie?" Coal asked.

Marcella grabbed Coal's member as she looked back at him and began to stroke. "It's not enough, I need more!"

"What?"

"I've wanted to taste you so badly since the last time I sank my teeth into you!"

"What?" Coal asked in shock just before Marcella sucked her lips around him. "Oh… fuck."

Marcella bobbed her head back and forth as quickly as possible. She stroked him with her left hand and played with his balls in her right. She used her long tongue to wrap around Coal as she bobbed. She could feel him begin to throb in her mouth again, so she quickened. The thought of him satisfied excited her, and she needed to taste him.

"Oh shit, baby, I'm really close." Coal warned.

Marcella smiled and hummed happily as she sucked harder and faster. At the last moment, she squeezed his balls as he burst into her mouth. It was more than she anticipated as it began streaming down her chin. She released Coal and drew back to look at him. As they looked at each other, she opened her mouth, showing that it was so full of Coal's cum that it was dripping down her chin. She stuck out her tongue towards Coal and swirled it around, savoring him. She closed her mouth and let out a loud gulp, then opened it again to show that it was empty. The second orgasm had seemed to deplete Coal, but seeing Marcella's feverish joy had brought him back stiff.

"Oh fuck yes," Marcella said as she caressed his erection with his finger. She climbed onto the bed facing directly away from Coal. She remained on her knees, but she pressed her chest against the bed and then brought it towards her knees as her back arched. Her face turned to look at Coal as her two fingers spread herself open to invite him in. As she did so, Coal could see his white liquid break from her princess pink slit and run down, then between her fingers. "Just one more round, I'm begging you!"

Coal turned and climbed up before grabbing Marcy by the ass and wrenching her back onto his rod. He could feel his and her juices pushed around and out of her as she moaned once again. From this position, he could use his arms to move her around more freely. Marcella Could feel his grip tighten around her in anticipation. She clenched around Coal's meat.

"It's the last round, baby, I need you to fuck me harder than anything before," Marcella begged. "I'm all yours, baby, hit me! Bruise me! Fuck I need you so bad right now!"

Coal nodded his head and pulled Marcy back as he began viciously pounding her. Marcella reveled in the sound of Coal's hips colliding with her ass and the sensation of his balls slapping against her clit. Coal had gripped her ass so hard it was already starting to bruise. He grunted as he thrust full force while simultaneously pulling Marcella into him, forcing his cock deeper and deeper into her. He could feel every wet bump and rivet inside Marcella's tight pussy. Everything about her was a dream. What were loud claps now sounded like splashes as Marcella rapidly fingered herself as Coal plowed her with all his might. She couldn't feel her legs anymore, only the incredible sensation of Coal's shaft desperately searching for her womb. She couldn't squeal anymore, and her moans were almost inaudible. She was on the brink of unconsciousness as Coal began pulsating and throbbing again. He was once again renewed as he grew closer and closer, thrusting faster and harder.

"Oh fuck, baby, I don't think I can take anymore! Fuck!" Marcella cried out.

"Nah baby you started this. Be a big girl and finish it!" Coal roared as slammed against Marcella and slapped her as.

"Oh fuck, baby, please, I'm trying!" Marcella squealed.

"Come on, be my good girl!"

"I am your good girl, I'll be a good girl! I'll be whatever you want!" She yelped.

"Say it, baby! Say you're my good girl!" Coal commanded as he slapped her ass again.

"Ooo," Marcella squealed and tried to catch her breath. "I'm your good girl! I'm your good girl! I'm your good girl! Fuck me! Fuck your good girl! AAaahhh!!" Marcella screamed as she squirted and began shaking vigorously. The shaking sensation was too much for Coal and he sped up for three more rapid and powerful thrusts before erupting. Marcella's eyes glassed over as Coal filled her. She could feel his cum running down her legs as he pulled out. As Coal pulled out the sudden sensation gave him one last pump that fired across Marcella's back. She slumped forward until she was fully laying on the bed. She wiped the white fluid from her back before rolling over on her back.

"My bad pulled out a little early." Coal apologized.

"It's fine, I saved room."

"What?"

Without breaking eye contact, Marcella smiled and winked at Coal before wrapping her tongue around her fingers and licking them clean. She swallowed and stretched out on the bed.

"Fuck I love you." Coal exclaimed.

"What?"

"What?"

"Coal, you know you can't say shit like that if you don't mean it!" Marcella said in shock and fear.

Coal brought in a deep breathe as Marcy's eyes widened. She had never felt so many feelings or so much anxiety at once. She didn't know why he would say something like that. The sex was incredible, but she didn't think it would possess him like that. Did he mean it? Or worse, did he not mean it?

"Hell, Marcy, I do think I love you." Coal spoke up, interrupting her thoughts.

"How the fuck do you know that Coal?" Marcella asked.

"I just so happened to have had a long time to get to know myself." Coal answered as he lay down next to her and gently placed his hand on her hip.

"You can know you! What about me? What do you know about me?" She asked as tears formed in her eyes.

"I know you're a sweet girl who had a weird lot and made the most of it. I know your smile lights up a room. I know you suck at RPGs and that my dogs took to you faster than anyone, not Jim-Bob. You've been scared but showed nothing but kindness and concern for the men that saved you. And I feel like the more I get to know about you, the more I'll learn to love." Coal answered earnestly.

Tears ran down Marcella's face as she buried it in Coal's chest. He wrapped his arms around her. "I love you too, Coal. Fuck! I love you too!"

"That's the best thing I've ever heard, baby girl. Why don't I turn off the lights, and we can cuddle and sleep together?"

"Please, baby. I just want to fall asleep in your arms right now."

Coal got up and walked over to the switch and looked back at Marcella, taking in all her beauty as she smiled at him. He turned the lights out and returned to her. He wrapped Marcella in his arms and the two slowly drifted off together under the covers. They had discovered they were in love, and would dream of each other as they rested peacefully.

Chapter 11

Coal woke up early as always. When he opened his eyes, his arms were still around Marcella's naked body. He hugged her tightly, before getting up. She lay there still sleeping. He kissed her forehead before dressing himself and starting his chores. He worked in double time. Jim-Bob would arrive soon. Jim-Bob had wanted to run errands of his own, but upon hearing Coal's report of the situation he decided he could put them off. Coal had just finished letting the dogs loose before Jim-Bob pulled up.

"What's the plan?" Jim-Bob asked as he exited his Kia.

"We can't kill the fucker, so I've opted for a plan to teach him a valuable lesson."

"Well, what's the plan, Coal? Damn"

"We finna hit up the grocery then whoop his ass." Coal explained.

Jim-Bob looked on at Coal in confusion. "The grocery?"

"Man, just hop in the truck, it'll all make sense soon." Coal said.

The two got into Coal's truck and drove off towards the city stopping at the grocery. Coal went straight to the produce aisle and bought several cloves of various garlics. The two checked out and returned to the truck.

"Where to next?" asked Jim-Bob.

"We gone pay him a visit." Coal smirked. "That wolf boy told me where he's holed up at."

"Easy money then?"

"Yup."

When the two pulled into the parking lot, they could see the sheriff's car waiting for them. Coal climbed out of the truck first.

"How are you today, Sherriff Lance?" Coal asked, smiling.

Lance spit the dip he tucked away onto the ground. "Don't reckon it gets any better, does it?"

"No, sir."

"And may I ask whatch'all doin here?"

"Just a quick house call, nothing else, really." Coal answered.

"Bullshit. Don't you lie to me, boy, I can read you like a damn magazine."

"I'm here to whoop a man's ass, Sherriff. He done threatened me and my girlfriend." Coal explained.

"Ain't no fucking man hiding in that hotel, boy."

"What do you mean?"

"I got a call for a man gettin speared in the chest outside a club and getting whisked away by another man. We tracked'em here. Ain't no fucking man on this earth get speared like what your little girly did too'em an live."

"How'd you know it was Marcy?" Coal asked as worry began to fill him.

"Think club alleys ain't got cameras?"

"Oh fuck, who knows?"

"Fuckin' shame their security drinks on the job. Spilled beer all over the fucking computers."

"I can't thank you enough, sheriff."

"I know. Now why ain't you staking that fucker lying up in there?" the sheriff asked.

"It's so complicated."

"The fuck it is, boy. That's her ex up in there, and she don't want her friends killing each other. Question is, why you listening?"

"How'd you know?"

"Audio surveillance. Spilled a lot of beer."

"Fuck man, I'mm trying."

"Look here Coal, I'm giving you a lot of leeway here. You handle this shit how you think's best, but if it spills over I'm gone have to drop the hammer on'em" Lance explained.

"Yes, sir, I understand."

"Bullshit, now one fucking whiff of escalation outa these pale fucks, and you best call me."

"Yes, sir, I understand."

"Good, Jim-Bob, get the fuck out here you got work to do, son." The sheriff said as he snapped his can of copenhagen long cut with his wrist. He then loaded a pinch into his lip as Jim-Bob crept out of the truck. "You keep my boy straight, you hear?"

"Yes sir, I got'em," Jim-Bob replied.

Sheriff Lance strolled over to his sheriff's car. He reluctantly got into his car and started it. He spit into his bottle and looked over to Coal and Jim-Bob. He tipped his hat to them and drove off slowly.

"Alrighty, what we got now, Coal?" Jim-Bob asked.

"This." Coal answered as he opened the back door of his truck. revealing a new pack of crew socks next to the large amount of garlic. Jim-Bob began laughing to himself as he grabbed a sock off the pack and began filling it with garlic. "What's so funny?"

"I'm about to beat the shit out of a supernatural predator with a fucking garlic sock." Jim-Bob giggled.

Mark was lying in his bed, staring at the ceiling. His stomach still hurt, and his feelings were sore. He thought of everything his temper had cost him, and he wondered what he could do to get it under control. He had never been so stressed. He hadn't heard from Amund for near a day, and he had no idea what they would tell Rolf and Eric. He lay there, just weighing his options.

Mark's hotel door suddenly exploded from its hinges. Mark leaned up to face his attackers, but before he could react Coal had pelted him in the face with a large clove of elephant garlic. The horrible smell made him sick to his stomach immediately and he felt woozy. He was quickly brought back to a full state of consciousness as Jim-Bob quickly wove around Mark's bed and mightily swung a sock at Mark. Mark was thinking and reacting as rapidly as he could, but he couldn't stop himself from staring at the sock rapidly approaching his face. It made no sense until it did. As the end of the sock collided with Mark's face the garlic within it cracked open and filled the room with its wretched essence. Mark had no time to dry heave for as soon as Jim-Bob had struck his head, Coal had struck his stomach, and as Mark recoiled in pain, Jim-Bob struck his balls.

Mark was suddenly filled with rage and attempted to lunge at Jim-Bob. Jim-Bob grabbed him by his shirt and slung him into the hotel room TV before continuing the beatdown. Mark tried to stand his ground in front of the TV, but Coal gained momentum, approaching him from the other side of the bed and kicked Mark's chest. The impact sent Mark forcefully into the TV, causing the screen to shatter and dig into Mark's back. Mark fell to the ground as the TV fell on top of him. He tried to throw the TV at Coal, but his vision was blurred by the garlic fumes burning his eyes. Upon wasting his only possible shield, Mark was quickly met with the continued volley of garlic socks, now bolstered with the occasional steel-toed boot.

Mark was very disoriented by the silence of his assailants. Blow after blow, but no words to be heard. Their faces were likened to stone and emotionless. It appeared as if it was merely business to these men. Mark had curled up into a fetal position in an effort to cover his stomach. The garlic had done its work, and Mark had become utterly helpless. The blows stopped all at once. Mark tried to peep through his hands, when quickly, he felt a large hand grab him by the hair and pick him up. His defensive egg unfurled as he was effortlessly lifted until he met eyes with his attacker.

The eyes that met his were gray and dead, but they seemed to harbor a deep seed of violence. They gazed back at Mark for a few moments, sizing him up, piercing through his very soul.

"Who, who the fuck are you?" Mark wheezed.

"You ambushed someone very dear to me while she was out with her friends. I'm here returning the favor. You threatened her. You threatened me. You sicked your dog on me. Now I think it's time we came to an understanding." Coal calmly spoke before flinging Mark to the second bed of the motel.

Mark sat up on the bed and watched as Coal calmly walked over and sat on the bed in front of him. Jim-Bob made his way to Mark's side and stood over him.

"Speak your piece, boy." Coal demanded.

"Boy? Just who the fuck.." Mark exclaimed before being violently interrupted by a blow to the side of his head. Things spun around for a bit before Mark could once again meet Coal's eyes.

"I've been kind enough, but my patience has run its course. Now explain yourself while I'm still letting your jaw remain in place. You understand?" Coal asked.

"You're Marcella's new man. Oh fuck, oh god! Amund!" Mark began to panic.

"Amund will be on his way in just a bit. We reached an accord. Same as I'm trying to do with you." Coal explained.

"Jesus fuck. I got sent with Eric, Rolf, and Amund to bring Marcella home. After your run-in with Rolf spooked him, me and Amund thought it'd be best if we tried to get to her first, without the other two. I tried talking some sense into her, but when she wouldn't listen, I lost my composure a bit. And when she mentioned you, I lost my shit." Mark told his story.

"So you thought it'd be best to change it up and threaten her?"

"Fuck no, that shit just happened, man. I didn't mean for any of this shit to happen. Before all this shit, I was all set up to make her mine and try to live happily ever after in that big fuckin vampire house."

"What didn't you mean to happen?"

"We got in a fight about how vampires source their food. She's all about that, only the willing bullshit. I'm not a super fan of hunting humans down. I mean, look what happened to me, but the types of people who just offer themselves up are fucking weird."

"She ran away over a fight like that?" Coal asked.

"If I'da kept calm and left it, we'd still be home, but I couldn't wait to get back at her and tell her where her precious daddy gets all these fuckin blood packs from."

"And she ain't like the answer and hauled ass." Coal inferred.

"In the blink of an eye. Told me what she thought of me right there and dipped on the ride home." Mark explained.

"So what's your plan now?"

"I don't fucking know, man," Mark broke down, "I wasn't built for this vampire shit, man. I don't know what to tell Eric, no one at the fucking manor respects me, and the closest thing to a friend I have don't even fucking like me, man."

"Hell, he's on his way to save you now. Tell you what, when your little pity party runs out of cake, why don't we all sit down and hash this out before y'all try to talk to Eric?" Coal suggested.

"Yeah, man, I'm sorry, I just need time to think about shit, you know? But yeah, let me regroup with Amund, and we'll get a plan going, OK?" Mark asked.

"Sounds good, Mark. Y'all welcome to stay as long as you need, courtesy of Marcella. Amund'll call me when y'all have a plan. We're cooking out tonight, and if you can behave yourself, you can join, but you need to understand one thing. I eat plenty of garlic, so it's readily available, you hear." Coal explained.

"I understand. I'll see about it, just let me get my head easy."

"Alright then, we're gone roll out, and Amund should be right behind us. You get your head on right and try to take it easy." Coal waved. And just like that, Coal and Jim-Bob were gone.

The two men were now in Coal's truck. Coal let the windows down as they drove out of the motel parking lot. As he drove with his left hand, his right opened and sifted through the center console until he pulled out one of his cafe' cigars. He lit it and puffed deeply. The notes of coffee and vanilla tickled his senses while the nicotine calmed him.

"You need anything while we're in town?" Coal asked.

"We need any sides or drinks?" Jim-Bob returned the question.

"Nah, the freezer's pretty packed, should have plenty to feed everybody and have leftovers."

"Sweet, we should be good then. Who all's comin'?" Jim-Bob asked.

"Crane, T, T's fiance, you, Marcy, Lance when he gets off, Amund, and maybe Farhad. We gotta feed him after he set me up real good for my date."

"Hell yeah, how'd that go?"

"One of the best nights of my life." Coal answered.

"Hell yeah, bro, what you thinking?"

"Think I'm in love, Jim-Bob." Coal said.

"Sweet."

Coal continued to drive until they reached home. Jim-Bob hopped out of the truck and opened the gate. Coal pulled through, and Jim-Bob closed the gate. Jim-Bob climbed back into the truck, and Coal pulled off to the house. The two hopped out and made their way up the stairs, then through the front door. When they stepped in, Marcella was sitting on the couch, playing her game.

"Fuck, I forgot to get her a cell phone, bro." Coal remembered.

"Monday, my dude," said Jim-Bob.

"Welcome home, baby! Hi Jim-Bob!" Marcella waved when she saw the two.

"Morning, sleepyhead." Coal smiled.

"I'ma go start defrosting shit before I throw up." Jim-Bob joked.

"Yeah, I gotta go check on Crane." Coal explained.

Jim-Bob began pulling the meat from the freezer. Coal went down the hill to see Crane. Marcella began cleaning the kitchen and patio. Jim-Bob joined her once everything was set out. As they finished cleaning, they could see Coal and Crane walking up the hill to join them. Coal grabbed beers for everyone and they sat and visited for a minute until they could hear a car pulling into their drive.

"Yooo, where the burgers at?" Amund called out as he exited his car.

Coal stepped out of the front door. "It ain't time for them yet. You want a beer?"

"Hell yeah!" Amund answered as he began quickly stepping up the stairs.

"Where's Mark?" Coal asked.

"Y'all fucked him up pretty badly, He dropped his tough guy act after you two left."

"That was him acting tough?" Coal asked as Jim-Bob began cracking up. "Shhh, that's his buddy!"

"Shit, at least you're laughing behind his back," Amund said.

"You ain't laugh in that boy's face, did you?" Coal asked.

"Nah, I'm mostly joking, you beat me pretty badly, too, remember?" Amund reminded Coal.

"Fair enough. Come on, let's get you a beer." Coal finished as he opened the front door for Amund.

Two hours had passed and T. Rell was pulling in at the same time as Lance. Coal greeted them all and started the grill. Farhad texted that he would need an open fryer for a recipe he wanted to try. Jim-Bob pulled out a tall propane stove top, and a large pot with oil. Lance cooked gumbo inside while he watched over a pot of greens. Coal grilled hamburgers and chicken breasts while Jim-Bob handled the fries and tator logs.

Farhad pulled in where he could fit in, then walked around to the back of the house, waving at Coal and their friends. He had a large bag of frozen balls. He darted up the stairs and started on the propane stove top. Once it reached the temp he was happy with he dumped his bag in.

"I can't wait for you to try these Coal!"

"Whatchu got in there, Farhad?" Coal asked.

"I call them Hajis." Farhad answered.

"I don't know bout that one, bud."

"No, my friend, They're halal jalapeno poppers!" Farhad exclaimed.

"Fucking how?" Lance asked.

"It's heavily battered jalapenos stuffed with cream-cheese and lamb with spices. It's an explosion of flavor, I promise you, my friend!" Farhad explained.

"Hell yeah. Hey, man, I meant to thank you for last night," said Coal.

"And I thank you for the generous tip, my friend, anytime."

"Don't play, Farhad, I'll take you up on that offer!" Coal joked.

"It would be my favorite game, sadeeq. I can only pray the night ended well." Farhad hoped.

Coal smiled, "Man, you pulled through for me, man, she might be the one."

"You fill my heart with joy, brother. We feast in celebration!"

Coal laughed with his friends. "Yeah, buddy, let's get to grilling."

"Where's your new old lady anyhow?" Lance asked.

"I think she's catching up with Amund a little more, prolly see'in how Mark's makin' it." Coal answered.

"Ah, wait, I thought you handled him?" Lance asked.

"We just educated him a lil." Coal replied.

"Aight, but if he ain't a good student, I'll have to tutor him," Lance said.

"Yeah, I feel you."

"How you living Big C?" T. Rell hollered as he burst from the back door, hands filled with beers.

"The dream lil cuz, where's yo boo at?" Coal asked.

"She with Marcella and that ginger dude, Y'alls date go smooth?"

"Yessir."

"Hell yeah." T. Rell smiled as he tossed the boys beers. "Shiet, keep her big cuh, Latisha thinks she pretty cool."

"Oh yeah?" Coal asked.

"Foreal Foreal, on the low she like one of the only friends I'm really down with you feel me?" T. Rell said.

"Whatchu mean, T?"

"Bruh-bruh, that Harmony lady crazy, and the others might be cool, but they a lil too wild when you get'em together," T. explained.

"Hell T, you get all of us together, excluding the sheriff, you got a real problem on your hands, cut'em some slack." Coal laughed.

"Yeah, you right, you right. But Harmony still be grabbing on dudes."

"Fair enough." Coal nodded.

"You boys wouldn't believe the number of calls I get when she goes out to them clubs. Hell, I think Deandre's bout tired of her shit. The bouncer at the main club downtown?" Lance said.

"That bro be having that Job-like patience man I'm telling you." T. joked.

As the men laugh and exchanged stories, Coal stepped over to the grill and flipped the burgers that Jim-Bob had started. Farhad checked the time on his jalapeno poppers, and Lance rushed back in the house, remembering his gumbo. Marcella had crept outside, and, while no one was watching, hugged Coal around his waist from behind. She nestled her head in his back as her arms interlocked. She then let go and walked over to his side. He looked down at her and smiled. The burgers were done, lance was bringing out the pot of gumbo, and Farhad was tonging out his poppers. Jim-Bob brought out the greens and fries while Crane set up Coal's radio. T. Rell went to Latisha's truck and returned with a cornhole set.

Once everyone had finished eating, they exclaimed their shock at Farhad's latest creation and thanked Coal for inviting them all. They then paired of into to teams for cornhole. Marcella and Coal, Jim-Bob and Crane, T. Rell and Latisha, and Farhad and Lance. Amund assumed the role of shoutcaster and referee. Everyone laughed and drank as they played, but as the little cornhole tourney continued, it became clear that Farhad, who was stone sober, and Lance would clean house. Coal and Marcella came at a close second, followed by T. and Latisha, then Jim-Bob and Crane.

"I don't think I've ever seen anyone throw like that, or that accurately," Lance said in shock as they tallied their last points against Coal and Marcella.

"It's all in the wrist, my friend," Farhad said as he waved his hand.

"It's all that practice throwing knives at the sous chefs, I'm telling you!" Coal laughed.

"I would never throw knives at the sous chefs! They are too expensive!" Farhad exclaimed.

"Plates then?"

"Of course not! I throw the cheapest thing I can find!"

"Which is?" Marcella asked.

"The smaller sous chefs!" Farhad erupted into laughter.

The group of friends laughed with each other while the four contenders made their way back onto the patio. They gathered around in their chairs and continued to drink.

"Backyard camp?" T. Rell looked to Coal and asked.

"Yeah we been drinking for a while. I got some tents in the storage closet." Coal answered.

"What's a backyard camp?" Marcella asked.

"When everybody gets too plastered to drive, so you start pitching tents cause there ain't enough beds." Coal replied.

"Prolly be a bad idea to drink and drive, I feel like the sheriff would catch you pretty quick for some reason." Crane joked.

Lance laughed heartily. "Yeah, I'd save that for next weekend, I'm taking a trip out to the cabin."

"Nice," said Crane.

Coal went into the house and grabbed the tent rolls from the closet. He and the men helped each other pitch the tents. They then began readying a bonfire in the middle of the tents.

"Bruh, you got marshmallows and shit in the cabinets?" Jim-Bob asked.

"Do you remember where I keep them?" Coal asked back.

"Hell yeah, I'm on it," Jim-Bob replied as he ran up the stairs.

Everyone had gathered around the fire, and Marcella leaned on Coal. Latisha had curled up with T. Jim-Bob returned with the smore supplies and began passing out sticks. The group was winding down for the night. It was a calm and cool contrast to the heat of the day, and the frogs and crickets had begun their choir practice, hidden in darkness. The chickens had gone to roost, and even Briggs and Straton had taken the night off. The friends continued laughing and smiling around the fire for a time, and slowly but surely, one by one, they crept into their tents. They curled up, with stomachs full and bodies warmed, drifting into restful sleep.

CHAPTER 12

"It is a cruel world that mistakes arrogance for hubris," Eric said as he exhaled a pillar of smoke from his hookah. Riley sat alone across from him, he looked at Eric, awaiting his explanation. "Too often, these people misunderstand that arrogance is an unearned sense of superiority, that one simply entered this world better than the rest. They should all learn that hubris comes from a much darker place, a bitter one. A place that was equal or even less than everyone else until it clawed its way to what it had envisioned to be its peak." Eric stood from his chair and looked over the rails of the hotel balcony. He could see various cars pulling around the hotel. "I have never believed myself to simply be superior to those around me by birthright. I was born for this. My parents themselves were hand-selected to bring me into this world, and every moment since my conception, I have fought, learned, and climbed. Forced to prove myself worthy of a position I had never known." Eric took a sip from his blood-filled glass. "I killed them, Riley. I have killed them all with my incompetence. I knew they were too young, too foolish, and yet I, in error, saw a bit of myself in them and was convinced they were safe. How could mere strays bring down vampires from my noble house? And yet, I have killed them. We are always eager to jump at the opportunity to prove ourselves, so we waste all of our time looking for them instead of preparing for them. I knew Mark and Amund would prove themselves and bring Marcella home. It was an incredible opportunity to prove that Mark was more than just a mistake, and it was I who thrust it upon him. I killed them."

"Mister Eric, there's no way you could have seen any of this coming," Riley said in a vain attempt to console Eric.

"It was a foreseeable possibility, just like the woman leaving in the day with Rolf. Rolf has always been a vicious little pagan, and I can't argue that the lives we have provided for his pack have made them grow soft. Amunds disappearance was more than enough evidence to suggest that it was time Rolf took on new vampiric leadership." Eric explained.

"What will we do now?" Riley asked.

"I can't ask you to stay, Riley. There's more than enough time for you to escape, and you owe me nothing."

"No, I wasn't born for this. I didn't want this, but I won't run from my only chance. The only chance to build a life for myself or to join something greater than myself, Eric. I won't go back to being used for my unnatural abilities."

"I do suppose this would be an excellent opportunity to work closely with someone as incredible as myself." Eric smiled. "You may stay, but you must keep yourself safe, young Riley. It would be unfair of me to hold you to the same standard as myself. I shan't make such a horrid mistake twice."

"So what's the plan?"

"My car is in the garage. We'll wait here and clear everything out before making our escape. We will regroup at the manor, and then I will take this city in vengeance." Eric said as he rolled his shoulders. He took a large drag from his hookah, exhaled, and downed the remainder of his glass before stepping into the hotel suit to face the door.

Eric slowly began unbuttoning his suit. He let out a deep sigh as he removed it. And held it out in his left hand. Riley took it from him and stepped back. Eric popped his neck, then stretched his back out. What had been an exasperated frown was slowly twisting into a wretched smile. Eric's fingers began to twitch, and he found himself bouncing on the balls of his feet. His flexed calf muscles could be seen beneath the fabric of his tailored dress pants. He took a deep breath and began to slowly exhale as his excited movement stopped. He could hear footsteps beyond the door, many of them. Riley began to tremble with both fear and excitement.

The door of the suite shattered open as a large disfigured vampire rushed through it. The vampire appeared to be a half transformed amalgamation of a man and bat. His muscles were bulging, pressing its veins to tear through the skin, but his form was inconsistent. Though this transformation gave him power, Eric could feel the agony of his forced movements. He was strong but slow, and Eric felt the responsibility to put him out of his misery.

The grotesque beast lunged for Eric, who quickly sidestepped its batlike claws. Eric had ducked beneath its arms as he stepped and quickly shot his hand just below the ribcage of the beast, piercing its unprotected torso. In a swift motion, he ripped the wretch's heart from its chest as he cast aside, looking in the direction of the next wave of assailants. Eric threw the heart away as he calmly strolled toward the exit. Two thralls with black veins crawling with their bodies charged at him. The first approached faster and futilely stabbed at him. Eric caught the thrall by his wrist and tore his arm off in a rapid jerk downwards. He then eyed the next, quickly stabbing the exposed bone from the arm of the first thrall into the through the bottom of the jaw of the second.

A vampiric figure emerged from the entrance, calmly advancing on Eric. The vampire was well-dressed and held two stakes in his hands. He pointed the stake in his hand at Eric and smiled.

"See if you're so scary when I'm the one who's dangerous?" He taunted.

Eric laughed as he viciously ripped the arm out of the thrall's throat, throwing blood into the vampire's eyes. In the moment that his vision was obfuscated the vampire could feel Eric's hand grip his right wrist. When he could see, Eric was on his outside flank, pushing his wrist in with his left hand. Eric's right hand, however, gripped the vampire's bottom jaw. Eric wasted no time ripped it from its hinges. The vampire tried its best to counter with a stab from one of its stakes, but Eric quickly used the jaw to parry it away, knocking the stake from the vampire's hand.

"Who was it who was dangerous?" Eric asked, smiling at his victim.

Eric then used the jaw to rip his opponent's throat out. Tainted blood splattered from the vampire's gaping neck. The force of the slash turned the vampire away, but the loss of blood dropped him to his knees. Eric followed up with a furious downward chop, feeling his nails slice down the back of the vampire before plunging his hand in and grabbing the creature's spine. His victim howled in horrific agony. Eric ripped his spine out from the bottom to the top, taking the vampire's head with it. The muscle tissues kept its shape and elasticity as Eric began to twirl it in his hand.

Eric began to whistle happily as he walked out of the front door of his hotel room, still twirling his new trophy. He looked down the hall toward the elevator and reveled in the faces of pure terror staring back at him. They were the grim faces of strays now realizing the horror they had unleashed upon themselves. Eric began to gleefully skip towards them, his face filled with a twisted smirk. He had decided to enjoy himself, temporarily shaking off the chains of his guilty conscience. He had been gifted the opportunity to seek immediate revenge in a secluded area where he could indulge himself in only the highest form of his state of being: violence.

He skipped four good bounds before exploding into a deadly sprint. The sudden burst of movement made his enemies recoil for only one second. This one second was all Eric needed to swing his toy at full force into the head of the first new vampire. The thunder from the upper half of the worthless creatures' skull shattering echoed across the hotel floor. The sound caused one of the other lesser vampires to heave and gag. The shattered vampire dropped to its knees as it tried to maintain consciousness, keeping its one unruptured eye on Eric in an attempt to save their friend. The third ungagging vampire charged at Eric's stake in hand. In a hellish and graceful motion, Eric continued the swing, which shattered the first, and followed through, spinning into an uppercut. This uppercut had manipulated the skull of his trophy to face its fangs upward, tearing the third vampire's eyes from their sockets, popping one like a water balloon and skewering the other. The wounded creature pawed at its eyes in a desperate attempt to find its sight before turning to crawl away, screaming in pain. The second vampire couldn't even maintain eye contact with Eric as her knees buckled, and she fell back, scooching to the wall, hoping she would be overlooked as she cried. The third continued to pathetically crawl away, turning its screams to weeping. The weeping changed to a sudden cough as Eric swung his trophy down, catching the weeping wretch between the shoulders with its fangs. In one painful yank, Eric pulled the creature back to him, flaying open its back, causing it to scream once again. Eric silenced this annoyance with a quick stomp through the vampire's head. There was a sudden crack of the skull, followed by a loud squishing as brain matter parted in a desperate attempt to avoid Eric's Oxford dress shoes, the vacated sockets providing a convenient avenue of escape.

The second vampire had curled herself in a fetal position, rocking against the wall and sobbing uncontrollably. Eric dropped his trophy and slowly walked in front of the wailing vampire. He slowly crouched down with his finger against his lips.

"Shhhhh. Now, now, little one." Eric said as she finally made eye contact with him. He gently stroked her hair to calm her. Tears were still streaming down her face. "Nothing so pathetic deserves these."

"What?" She asked in horror.

Eric stopped caressing her hair and slowly moved his hands, touching her cheeks. He then brought them closer together and into her mouth and her eyes widened. Eric's trigger fingers caught the backs of her top fangs, and his thumbs began pressing against the tops of them. It started as pressure, then gradually grew more painful. The vampire grabbed Eric's wrists and tried to pull them away, but they wouldn't budge. Eric's strength was overwhelming in comparison to her own. The pain was now excruciating, and she was helpless. She began to cry out and scream, violently struggling against Eric's slow and methodical actions, to no avail. Slowly, she could feel her fangs begin to shift inside of her gums, tearing at the roots. Eric began to slowly pull back his fingers until, finally, her fangs snapped out of her mouth. He began to cackle as the vampire grabbed her mouth and screamed into her hands.

"Shhh, see? All done. Now I need you to concentrate and listen very well. Do you understand?" He asked as he began to brush her hair with his hand. She nodded at him, shaking blood and tears from her face. "Good, good. Now, I'm afraid you have a few more friends down in the lobby waiting for me, and if I continue, my new associate will lose heart and leave me. So be a doll and convince them that, well, staying may not be in their best interest. If you can accomplish that, you can be my new refreshment fetcher, or you can simply keep running. The choice is yours, but if you run and I catch you, well, you've seen already, haven't you?"

She began nodding her head in agreement, and Eric released her. She ran to the elevator and took it down. Eric walked over to the remaining vampires, who slowly recombobulating. He kicked one to where it was closer to the other. He then knelt down and flayed their backs open.

"No, wait, silly, you've already crushed their skulls," Eric said as he shook his head. He then plunged his hands into the flayed backs and ripped the vampires' hearts out.

Riley stepped behind Eric. "And you made me think staying may have been the wrong decision. I'm thinking this was the right call."

"That gives me a great deal of comfort, Mr. Riley. I suppose we'll wait a few more moments before descending. I do hope our refreshment fetcher will be there waiting."

Riley and Eric began laughing. Eric began looking at his watch, and the two sat for a few minutes. Eric then began walking toward the elevator, and Riley followed suit. Eric hit the button, and the two waited a few minutes longer. When the door opened, the elevator was clear. The two stepped in, and Eric pushed for the lobby, and they began to descend. Eric stretched and leaned against the wall, propping his hands up on the elevator's rails. There was a quaint ding, and the doors slowly opened. The lobby was empty save for one sobbing little vampire. Eric laughed devilishly as he approached her. She sat on a couch just to the right of the front entrance.

Eric took his finger under her chin and lifted her head to look into his eyes. "Now, no one's waiting in the garage to accost me and my dear friend, are they?"

"No, sir, I'm the only one who stayed." She whimpered.

"That's a very good girl," Eric responded as he slowly stroked her hair. He then offered his hand to help her from her seat. "Suppose this means you'll be joining our little escapade."

"Yes, sir," she said behind her tears. She took his hand, and he brought her up in a cold embrace.

"Don't worry, my little fangless darling. You get to see how the better side handles things. Riley here has already been shown the way. Fetch me my refreshments and provide me with intel, and we'll get along just famously."

She nodded her head in response. Eric smiled, and they began walking toward the parking garage. It was barely lit and far too quiet. Eric continued to smile as he turned his eyes toward Riley.

"Riley, you joined me because you felt that you were betrayed and disrespected, didn't you?" He asked.

"Yes sir, look what they did to my face. Sure, I did it myself, but they taught me wrong on purpose."

"Do you suppose lies and betrayal are a common pattern of behavior among this stray household?"

Riley looked back at Eric puzzled, and as he began to open his mouth to question Eric, he could see a figure emerge from the shadows of one of the pillars bearing the weight of the parking garage. He tried to warn Eric, but his mouth was too slow, however, Eric could see it in his eyes as his smile changed to his hideous toothy grin. Without a moment of hesitation, he grabbed his new fangless friend by the nape of the neck and held her in front of the shadowy figure. She began screaming as the figure revealed a pump-action shotgun and began to unleash his volley.

The shot tore her left arm from her body, and she cried out in agony. As the arm flew from her, Eric caught it. As the second and third shots rang out, Eric shifted her, catching the second in her stomach and the third in her leg. As Eric was shifting miss fangless he was also pivoting himself, and as the third shot ripped her leg open, Eric threw her dismembered arm like a javelin into the shadowy fiend. As the tips of fangless' radius and ulna gouged out his eye the assassin tilted his head back as the bones continued through his eye into his brain. He was too discombobulated to fire his remaining rounds, and he was only conscious enough to see Eric toss his friend aside and leap at the assassin. Eric landed in front of the fiend and paused. The shadowy figure took the opportunity to raise his weapon. As he did so Eric stepped forward, grabbing the grip of the shotgun, jamming the pump back. The resounding click sent the assassin into despair as he made eye contact with the wretchedly grinning monster he had failed to slay.

Eric wrenched the gun from his hands, right to left, then swung it as a hammer into the arm still lodged in the fiend's eye socket. This would drive it through the remainder of its skull and out the back of its head. Eric then flipped the shotgun in his hand, catching it and quickly firing a round in each knee of his failure of an assassin. The first shot crippled the fiend, and the second severed the opposite leg in half. The shadow fell to its knee and nub, letting out muffled and confused cries and whimpers.

"The nerve of someone to knowingly put their comrade in mortal danger and then miss. I'm sorry, my good sir, I can neither find a use for you or even tolerate such foolish behavior. I would demand an apology for my dear fangless friend, but I'm simply too pressed for time, you see. I'm sure you'll understand." Eric explained. As he did so, he lifted the vampire's chin with the barrel of his new shotgun. He then poked the barrel into its neck, pushing him back, pointing it where the spine and skull met. The vampire let out a confused cry for mercy as Eric pulled the trigger. The force sent the creature's head only a few feet back, spinning two full revolutions before bouncing off the concrete of the parking garage.

Eric handed the shotgun to Riley and then walked over to their refreshment fetcher. She was forcing her mouth closed, but tears were streaming down her face. Eric could hear her muffled grunts of agony deep in her throat as she desperately tried to hide her weakness, fearing an outward display of suffering would lead to her immediate execution. Eric stood over her and watched for a few moments before lifting her up in his arms and carrying her toward the car.

"Worry not, my fangless friend. We have only the best packs in the trunk of my car. We will make sure you are well fed, wrapped up in a nice warm blanket, and propped up in the back to sleep it off. You'll get used to it, I promise." Eric assured her. He looked over to Riley as they neared his car. He held the girl in one arm and popped the trunk open with his free hand. He signaled over to Riley, who then walked past them and, pulled two packs out of the cooler and handed them to Eric. Riley then carefully put Eric's coat away and grabbed a weighted blanket from the trunk. Eric wrapped fangless into the blanket and carefully placed her into the back seat. He then hand-fed her the first seat. She got her remaining hand free from the wrap, and Eric handed her the second pack before walking over and getting into the driver's seat.

He carefully backed out of his parking spot then drove out of the garage. The road was clear. Even the streets were free of onlookers, the glow of the lamps beaming down onto empty pavement. Eric looked into his rearview, seeing that fangless was making an impressive recovery. He then looked over to Riley, who sat there, hyper-alert. Riley's eyes darted, looking at everything that moved within his vision. Eric had been surprisingly impressed by these strays. Riley was incredibly focused, and fangless was sturdier than expected. They weren't premium prospects by any means, but they would have their uses. Eric had turned his attention to anticipating the response with regards to his failure. He had warned against this exact scenario and was disregarded, but he still felt responsible. His young associates may have been the best chance for a peaceful return, but the chance was so low that it hardly warranted the risk involved. Now, they had failed, and the only remaining option was simply to recover their heir by any means.

Eric was also keenly aware that there was now a secondary objective to crush the coven of strays. They had done the unthinkable in challenging a vampiric household and had pushed further beyond by hunting their heiress. The wages for such egregious sins were surely death. They also couldn't risk interference once they had found Marcella. The strays had to be dealt with.

Eric couldn't help but feel proud of Marcella. A wretched and ill-mannered whelp had grown into quite the willful woman. If the circumstances hadn't yielded such danger, even Marcella's own father would feel a sense of pride in the young woman he raised. She had taken a great leap forward in her own path and broke Eric's heart to know it was his duty to divert her path from one of her own choosing, but she was an heiress. She was the blood of the Patriarch of their household and would have to acquiesce to the responsibilities that came with such a privilege.

Eric's head swirled with thoughts of the household's future. He felt a sense of anxiety taking account of their position within their region. Their blood farms had yielded them a comfortable lifestyle, but they hadn't fielded any true warriors in at least a decade. Eric thought they had grown soft and, in a way, agreed with Rolf's assertion. He understood, to a degree, why he would leave, but he could not suffer a traitor to live.

Riley could see Eric's eyes buzzing and pondering. "Man, if you've got the GPS programmed, why don't you let me drive while you get a sip and a wink?"

"I would appreciate that greatly Mr. Riley." Eric said as he pulled the car over. The two men switched seats and Eric took a sip from his favorite flavor and closed his eyes to relax.

Riley drove silently for two and a half hours. The GPS had informed him that his destination was up on his right. As he approached, Riley could see a tall privacy fence, one-quarter of its height stone, the rest wooden. He soon neared the drive, which led to a foreboding gate. As Riley turned into the drive, the gate began opening on its own. He pulled past the gate and drove for at least a mile before he had finally reached the manor. In the courtyard of the great house stood a singular figure. He was plainly dressed, with a nice gray polo and khaki chinos. His captain boots kicked rocks as he waited. As he saw Riley approaching in the car, he adjusted his herringbone scally. His nonchalant demeanor evaporated as Riley stepped out of the car.

"Are you strays truly so impertinent that you would invade my home with a single car?" He spoke with a frozen voice.

"Excuse me, sir?" Riley asked in confusion.

These were the only words he would be allowed to speak as his world would suddenly and violently shake. Riley could hear a horrible crumpling noise coupled with a fracturus bang before all around him became blurry. The horrible noise and sudden impact awoke Eric, who quickly exited the car.

Eric let out a deep sigh as he looked upon his associate and his master. The father, in his anger, had grabbed Riley by the face and slammed his head through the roof of the car, stopping halfway to avoid the twisting metal cutting his shirt. Riley attempted to raise his hands in surrender, but the horrific damage done to his brain only allowed him to slightly wave his hands. Fortunately, the father had seen Eric and remembered that he had recruited the assistance of a tainted stray. He released Riley from his steely grip and turned to look at Eric.

"Remind me, when the new boy regains cognisance, I will have to apologize. Are there further surprises, Mister Eric?" The father asked.

"I have also brought a new refreshment fetcher, recruited from the strays who sought to block my departure," Eric answered.

"Very well. We will wait until this one returns to us. Clean yourself up and meet us in the dining room." the father commanded.

"Yes, master." Eric bowed and made his way into the manor.

The father pulled Riley from the car before walking around and picking up fangless. He gently carried them to the dining room where they sat and waited for Eric. Eric made his way through the manor toward his room when an all too familiar voice shot through his ears.

"That's a lot of nerve to return after failing so spectacularly. Has the great Eric finally fallen far enough for Father to come to his senses?" a figure asked as he exited his room to face Eric.

"Dear Lucah, if your memory served you well enough, you would have known that I had projected that the mission would fail, but it was Father who insisted we do things his way. Therefore, I should ask if you are truly inept enough with your words to venture into saying that Father has failed so spectacularly?"

"If you wish to abide by such excuses." Lucah sneered.

"If you wish to believe you wouldn't have blindly followed orders like a good little lapdog, go ahead. In fact, I dare say you would have lacked the courage to speak your mind, but pondering further, I would boldly assume there would be no thoughts within it to speak of." Eric chuckled. "Return to your courtesans and leave matters to those capable."

Lucah thought of replies and remarks but simply rolled his eyes as he turned back into his room and slammed the door. Eric continued to his room, changed his clothes, and began making his way to the dining room. When he entered, the father sat at the head of the table smoking a Cohiba Riviera Robusto. Smoke puffed from his mouth like a freshly squeezed thirty-eight. He pierced Eric's eyes with his gaze. Eric stuttered a moment, and as he did so, the father grinned. Riley regained consciousness, and fangless had been awakened as she was carried to the dining room.

The father took a delighted drag from his cigar. "My my, tell me, Eric, does anything beat a well-made cigar? The encapsulating aroma, the entrancing flavor, can you really think of anything?"

"I suppose not, sir," Eric replied.

The father began bellowing with laughter. "You poor, silly, scared little boy!" The sudden explosion of the father's voice sent shivers down Eric's spine, and Eric's hands began to shake as he lost what remained of his nerve. "Do you not revel in the screams of your prey? Does your thirst not become insatiable as the smoke fills your lungs? As it floods your senses with memories of muskets and rifles roaring as humans tear each other asunder? Can you not recall the day you ascended? The first time you ever hunted the hunter? Surpassed the most dangerous game? Have you grown so fearful that you think something as a simple cigar could ever compare to the ecstasy of conquering houses? Of securing your legacy?"

"Sir, I…" Eric tried to speak.

"Silence!" The father roared as he stood from the table and kicked the twelve-foot slab of mahogany into Eric's chest, pinning him to the wall. "Do you think I have a place for a whipped dog? I would cut your tail off before my eyes would suffer the vision of it between your legs!"

"Then fetch your knife!" Eric screamed as he threw the table from his ribs. The father raised a single hand and stopped the table cold, his body not reverberating from the force. "You were told this would happen! That they were too young! Too rash and too foolish! Everything was not only predictable but predicted! By me! We had done things your way, and now we must do them the correct way! We will return your daughter and crush these stray dogs that dare to call themselves a house! I will fetch my men, rouse my hounds, and wage war! I am no dog!"

The father's smile stretched from ear to ear as he began to laugh heartily. "Welcome home, Eric." He then put the table back to its proper place and threw Eric an already punched Riviera and lighter. "Introduce me to your new friends. Then you may debrief me."

Eric stared for a few moments at the precisely punched hole in the cigar. Then he looked at the smiling father. "It would seem that getting a rise out of me certainly beats your well-made cigars."

"The day I can run over you, I will no longer have use for you." the father chuckled.

Eric chuckled in response, then lit his cigar. "This is Riley, and this is fangless. Riley, Fangless, this is Douglas Fitzgerald, sire and head of this vampiric house."

"I believe we've already had the pleasure of meeting, but for some reason, I can't quite recall," Riley said.

Douglas laughed aloud. "I like this one, Eric. If he proves himself, we may just keep him."

"He's done all I've asked thus far, I selfishly denied him the opportunity to prove himself tonight so that I could vent my frustrations," Eric explained.

"And what of the blanket burrito that appears as if she may wet herself?" Douglas asked.

"I've taken to calling her Fangless. She is a recent addition and my refreshment fetcher." Eric answered.

"Ah, a refreshment fetcher, moving up in the world, I see. Tell me, though, will you have her in a crop top and little skirt jumping up and down as you persecute our enemies?" Douglas smirked.

"Only our sire would have such flare." Eric smiled back.

"Well, I certainly didn't just walk into this position, so tell me, what caused your expedited retreat? I had thought things were going swimmingly until your dear friend Riley popped out of your car. I had gotten your text regarding your return, but I assumed you would have my daughter in tow."

"I'm sorry, Master Douglas, Amund, and Mark vanished, and Rolf betrayed us. My hotel was raided by the stray household, and I determined their force and influence to be sizeable enough to warrant our attention and request reinforcements." Eric explained.

"Why so glum, dear friend?" Douglas asked.

"I cost us so much making foolish mistakes. We lost two good men to my arrogance." Eric solemnly replied.

Douglas burst into laughter. "You are truly too good for our house."

"Explain, please?" Eric requested, puzzled.

"You are not some foolish, arrogant little man, Eric, you are simply a naive little vampiric boy." Douglas giggled.

"Excuse me?"

"Excused. Look, Eric, did you not say that Mark was too impatient, too rash, with a terrible temper? Were you not worried that Amund was too inexperienced? You were right in every regard, but you are too young to understand a very cruel and important concept."

"Which is?" Eric's concern grew.

"In order to be a great household, everything that does not meet such a standard must be culled. Do you think me so shortsighted that I could not have seen Rolf's betrayal? Nay! I gave him an excuse! To think his pack is growing soft in accordance to the ways of old, he has removed himself and afforded me the opportunity to install my own alpha in their pack. One who shares my vision for our Household's future. And Mark? What of him? A putrid little mistake that I took pity on. I should've culled him myself. After all, how did he repay me? Made a play for my daughter? Ran her away from us all? And do not think I ever failed to notice his nasty little temper with my darling baby. Do you think it was that nasty little temper that cost him his life? I certainly hope so!" Douglas calmed his growls as Riley and Fangless became visibly uncomfortable. "I regret the loss of Amund, but you must understand that some sacrifices become necessary."

"You'll have to give me time to digest this, Master Douglas." Eric pleaded.

"You'll have time in the car. I will be redeploying you with a troop of thralls, a few prospects and vampires, and Lucah as your second."

"Lucah? Are you certain? You know how he feels about myself and Marcella!"

"You're absolutely right." Douglas wore a hideous grin as he spoke. "I expect results, Eric. Now you have all the resources you need and more on standby. The stray's foolish act of war will warrant an annex of their territory, and you've already done well enough to find a dissenter. Use him and his knowledge and bring chaos down on them. Bring my daughter home no matter the cost, Eric. I had initially respected her flight, but there have been developments outside of my control, and she cannot be kept safe from a distance."

"Will you not be join us, Master?" Eric asked.

"I'm afraid that's not possible. I must pay my respects and travel to a newly awakened Lord who has returned to his house. We have ancient ties and allegiance to this Lord, and my absence would be unacceptable. Should the problem not be solved upon my return, I will take it to the field. Understood?"

"Yes, Master."

"Then rest today, and sally out tomorrow after dusk. I will be in the courtyard smoking for a time if you wish to join me."

"Yes, Master." Eric nodded.

EPILOGUE

Marcella had slept in this morning. When she awoke she was alone in her and Coal's bed, and upon looking at the clock, she realized it was ten a.m. She hurried and dressed herself and then made her way downstairs. The living room was empty and most of the cars were gone from their driveway. She then made her way out the back. When she walked onto the back patio, she could see a wisp of smoke coming from behind the chicken barn. When she arrived at the base of the hill, she could See Coal and Jim-Bob laughing with each other and at Amund, who was lying on the ground. Amund appeared to be dizzy and confused.

The three of them were next to a large metal beer keg atop a propane stove. A tall cylinder was fastened to the top of the keg, and it ended in a joint to a copper pipe. The pipe flowed down into a spiral, which led into a fifty-five-gallon drum that seemed to be filled with water and ice. The copper pipe stuck out of the side of the drum, and a clear liquid flowed from it into a jar. Coal stood next to it, smoking his cigar and carefully observing a thermometer fastened into the metal cylinder.

"He boys, what are you guys up to today?" Marcy asked them.

"Just doin a quick run from a mash we forgot about." Coal answered.

"And what's wrong with Amund?"

"Ain't no hick shit gone put me on my ass. Let me try!" Jim-Bob hollered in a mocking voice. "Those were his last words before he turned that jar up," Jim-Bob said as he pointed to a broken jar not far from Amund's hand.

Coal pulled a bottle of water from a cooler next to the still. He crouched over Amund. "Open up, bud. Gotta hydrate before you vegetate." He said as he began to pour water onto Amund's unopened mouth.

Amund opened his mouth and began swallowing as fast as he could until the bottle was out. "Preciate it."

Coal stood and walked over to Marcella. He grabbed her by her hips and pulled her to him, kissing her on the lips, then her forehead before looking into her beautiful orchid eyes. The gray storm clouds in his seemed to part as she gazed back at them.

"You sleep good, babygirl?" Coal asked.

"Yeah, too much. You should've woke me up, baby."

"Nah, you looked too cute to wake.

Amund began violently and loud coughing. "Damn, that shits nastier than this fuckin jar!"

"Don't you disrespect my liquor, boy!" Coal yelled in jest.

"Last jars nearbout done, Coal," Jim-Bob said.

"Cool, you guys want to cap that up, and we can all go eat?" Marcella asked.

"Sounds good, baby girl. We'll head that way in a bit."

"Awesome, I'll go ahead and fire up the oven. What's the plan for the day?"

"We just chilling today, aside from the regular chores and this here liquor, but we gotta go see MeMaw tomorrow.

Marcella was struck with a sudden sense of dread and anxiety. "Oh, Lord."

"Brothers, sisters, and mortals!" Eric called out to the courtyard. There stood Lucah, the vampires that Douglas had selected, a handful of prospects, and a sizable number of thralls. "We have been granted the opportunity to prove ourselves this night and the nights that may follow! Our heiress has been taken from us! Our own have been slain, and now we are charged with vengeance! Father Douglas has chosen you all! Our task has been made simple. We are a true vampiric house, and all we must do is drive the stray scum from the city, reclaim our precious princess, and lay claim in the name of Douglas Fitzgerald! This is a task where vampires become honored, prospects ascend, and thralls prove themselves worthy of our father's gaze! Now, sound off as I ask! Will you fail Father Douglas?"

"No lord Eric!" the thralls and prospects roared.

"Will you slay the stray dogs?"

"Yes, lord Eric!" Mortal and Vampire alike thundered in response.

"Will you prove yourselves worthy?"

"Yes, lord Eric!" the crowd bellowed.

"Are you made ready for war?"

"Yes, lord Eric!" the warriors cried.

"Then let the shadows recoil so that no false whelp may hide! Let the crevices cry out where the strays dare flee! And let the night's moon bleed and weep as the true and chosen to slay the worthless and fearful! Forward my brothers, sisters, and even my mortals!" Eric commanded as he waved his hand. As he waved, the crowd screamed with joy and excitement. Quickly, they all rushed to their vehicles, checking their rations and equipment and making sure to pile in with those they knew and trusted. Lucah was slow to move, smirking at Eric as he turned and began to stroll to his car.

"These are the nights where we all prove ourselves worthy or guilty, dear brother," Eric spoke softly as he began to smile.